Modern Chinese Literature from Taiwan

Running Mother AND OTHER STORIES

Modern Chinese Literature from Taiwan

Wang Chen-ho, *Rose, Rose, I Love You*

Cheng Ch'ing-wen, *Three-Legged Horse*

Chu T'ien-wen, *Notes of a Desolate Man*

Hsiao Li-hung, *A Thousand Moons on a Thousand Rivers*

Chang Ta-chun, *Wild Kids: Two Novels About Growing Up*

Michelle Yeh and N. G. D. Malmqvist, editors, *Frontier Taiwan: An Anthology of Modern Chinese Poetry*

Li Qiao, *Wintry Night*

Huang Chun-ming, *The Taste of Apples*

Chang Hsi-kuo, *The City Trilogy: Five Jade Disks, Defenders of the Dragon City, Tale of a Feather*

Li Yung-p'ing, *Retribution: The Jiling Chronicles*

Shih Shu-ching, *City of the Queen: A Novel of Colonial Hong Kong*

Wu Zhuoliu, *Orphan of Asia*

Ping Lu, *Love and Revolution: A Novel About Song Qingling and Sun Yat-sen*

Zhang Guixing, *My South Seas Sleeping Beauty: A Tale of Memory and Longing*

Chu T'ien-hsin, *The Old Capital: A Novel of Taipei*

Guo Songfen

Edited and with an introduction by JOHN BALCOM

Running Mother AND OTHER STORIES

COLUMBIA UNIVERSITY PRESS   NEW YORK

Columbia University Press wishes to express its appreciation for assistance given by the Chiang Ching-kuo Foundation for International Scholarly Exchange and Council for Cultural Affairs in the preparation of the translation and in the publication of this series.

Translated quotations from Lu Xun in "Snow Blind" are from *The Complete Stories of Lu Xun,* translated by Yang Xianyi and Gladys Yang (Bloomington: Indiana University Press, 1981).

Columbia University Press
Publishers Since 1893
New York   Chichester, West Sussex

Library of Congress Cataloging-in-Publication Data
Guo, Songfen, 1938–
[Short stories. English. Selections]
Running mother and other stories / Guo Songfen ; edited and with an introduction by John Balcom.
p.   cm. — (Modern Chinese literature from Taiwan)
ISBN 978-0-231-14734-7 (cloth : alk. paper) — ISBN 978-0-231-51930-4 (electronic)
I. Balcom, John. II. Title. III. Series.
PL2860.U56A6   2009
895.1'352—DC22
2008011613

Columbia University Press books are printed on permanent and durable acid-free paper.
This book was printed on paper with recycled content.
Printed in the United States of America
c 10 9 8 7 6 5 4 3 2 1

Contents

Foreword *Summer 1961*

STELLA LEE (李渝)

It was an ordinary as well as an extraordinary summer.

The warmth and the endless sunlight were ordinary. That the college entrance exam was finally over after the long preparation and anxiety made it extraordinary. I passed the exam and was admitted by the Foreign Languages and Literatures Department of National Taiwan University as a freshman.

The College of Arts building that housed the FLLD and its library was an old and graceful building in the colonial style of the Japanese occupation period. The walls inside were painted a cream color and the wainscoting blue. Offices lined one side of the hallway; on the other side windows let in the summer greenness of acacia trees.

No one was in sight as I walked in. The foyer was cool and quiet. As I ventured down the hall, the door labeled "The 3rd Research Room" opened and a young teaching assistant appeared at the threshold. His dark-rimmed eyeglasses gave him a very scholarly air. His face and figure were rather boyish.

Two strangers, we exchanged glances. It was incidental and uneventful. The hallway was long. The cicadas were singing insistently in the woods.

Memories fade, but Songfen's glance at our first encounter remains as fresh as ever.

He had an impassive look. A flicker of aloofness made it even discriminating. Yet at the same time it was observant and understanding, as if he had known you long and well. A certain confidence or assuredness in his eyes was able to hold you up unguarded—never had I seen a person look so intensely intellectual yet so composed.

A year later, when he began to teach the English poetry course, just as impressively Songfen showed his excellence in language. The classroom became a place to display the force of words, and each lecture was a brilliant manifestation of an earnest mind at work for the depth in language. Complex thoughts rendered in unique wording, highly refined imagery, and elegant sentences marked his style of teaching, and later his art of fiction.

Initially our relationship was the admiration of a student for a teacher. As time went on, we became friends, husband and wife, companions or comrades in the student movements, and to each other, readers and writers. Our relationship evolved and expanded until it was so encompassing that it eventually became an intimate bond in which the two identities were difficult to differentiate.

We spent most of our time after work reading and writing, yet our daily life in suburban New York was quite simple. In Songfen's study there were two windows, one facing the quiet street and the other the side yard. Songfen developed a liking for Asian maples when he began to work at the UN. So we planted a variety of them in our very sinicized yard. After a day's chores we would often lie down in a small bed by the window for a break. The conversation was always about writers and writing—*Madame Bovary* was our all-time favorite. Camus' *The Stranger* received a unanimous vote for the best modern novella. Faulkner's *The Sound and the Fury* was awesome, and so were Joyce's "A Piece of Cloud" and Hemingway's "Ten Indians" and "Big Two-Hearted River."

We read Lu Xun for his impeccable prose and his humanity, but it was perhaps Shen Cong-wen's gentle stories that carried more of the weight of life. And we would talk about the shifting daylight as it came filtering through the maple leaves, falling softly on us, about its changing hues as it changed angles.

The light eventually dimmed, and we would put the dialogue on hold until the following day, only to seek comfort in each other's arms, and let the day turn to night imperceptibly.

We still meet often in dreams. Once a friend kindly took me to her house when I was feeling very low. At night I dreamed I saw Songfen sitting outside on her front lawn, making sure I was all right. Another time we were walking on a trail in the woods. There were puddles of water left by the rain, and he held my hand as we skipped over them. And in still another dream he was lying on the couch and asking me where I was going. When I said to him, "Of course I'm not going anywhere," he was relieved and smiled boyishly.

And in a dream to come, we both will return to that cool and quiet hallway, half cream-colored, half blue, so long as if it will never end in all eternity, and we both will be transformed back into our youthful selves, meeting once again for the first time, looking into each other's eyes like gazing into crystal balls, and finding that we will in the future have shared the rest of our lives together.

Introduction Guo Songfen, Taiwan's "Lost" Modernist

JOHN BALCOM

Guo Songfen is associated with the remarkable group of writers who came out of the Foreign Languages and Literatures Department of National Taiwan University in the 1960s and became the key figures in Taiwan's modernist literary movement—writers such as Wang Wenxing, Bai Xianyong, Chen Ruoxi, Ouyang Zi, and Wang Zhenhe. Guo, however, never achieved the same sort of fame as the others for a number of reasons: first of all, he did not remain in the public eye as they did—he lived abroad in the United States from 1966 until his death in 2006, and all of his major works were written during that time; second, his output was sporadic and small—in fact, most of his important works did not appear until the 1980s. He was also a perfectionist who rarely published unless a story met his high standards.[1]

Guo Songfen was born in Taipei in 1938. The son of the painter Guo Xuehu, he grew up in an artistic household. His first published story appeared in 1958 while he was still a student at National Taiwan University. His second published work did not appear until 1970. After that, he published a number of articles, but no more fiction until 1983, when he published six stories in *Wenji*.

He graduated from National Taiwan University in 1961 and taught there in 1963 and 1965. At this time he met the writer Lee Yu, his future wife. In the mid-1960s, he was involved in theater and acted in at least one movie. In 1967 he began attending the University of California, Berkeley, where he obtained an M.A. in comparative literature in 1969. In 1971 he quit the Ph.D. program to participate in the Protect Tiaoyutai Movement, a series of consciousness-raising student movements that first erupted in the United States in January 1971. In essence, it was a protest against the U.S. State Department's decision (April 9, 1971) to return the Jianguo or Senkaku Islands, about 50 miles northeast of Jilong, to the jurisdiction of Japan in 1972. (Tiaoyutai is the largest in the group of eight islands.) The People's Republic was in perfect agreement with Taiwan regarding China's territorial claim on the islands.[2]

In 1974, along with Liu Daren, Yang Cheng, and others in the movement, Guo visited mainland China, where he met Zhou Enlai; after this, he was not allowed to return to Taiwan. As with many of the Taiwanese students involved in the movement, his record as a political activist was held against him. He was even labeled an agent for the "Communist bandits." Guo was hired by the United Nations in 1972 as a translator and reviser, and worked there the rest of his life. He began publishing again in 1983. Over the following few years, most of his major works appeared. Unfortunately, he suffered a stroke in 1997, from which recovery was difficult and slow. He died in New York in 2006.[3]

The modernist movement in Taiwan fiction was launched by a group of National Taiwan University students with their journal *Xiandai wenxue* (Modern literature), published from 1960 to 1973.[4] The magazine showcased the work of many talented young writers and also introduced the work of Western writers. The modernists in Taiwan sought to break new ground by challenging the conservative neotraditionalist mainstream of political orthodoxy and what many perceived to be a moribund tradition of realism. They did this by borrowing from the West, combining a humanistic liberalism with a modernist aesthetic. Artistic autonomy was the rule, as the young writers had no choice but to shun political engagement. Aesthetically, they were concerned with the primacy of language and form over theme and content.[5] As Sung-sheng Yvonne Chang points out,

> Concerns with national identity have played a much less significant role in writings of Taiwan's Modernists. Instead, the majority of the Modernists have been inordinately obsessed with "depth," as manifested in their preoccupation with psychological exploration, their fascination with the uncanny, and their general predilection for expressing the "truth" through symbolic methods.[6]

Guo Songfen, while embracing the tenets of modernism, was, as a Taiwanese member of the diaspora, also obsessed with identity. Indeed, it is the Taiwan experience that informs Guo's thematic concerns. The burden of history is palpable in his writings. He is one of the few modernist writers to deal with the traumas of postretrocession Taiwan, including the February 28th Incident, the White Terror, and political exile. Yet his approach is psychological and symbolic rather than documentary. The events of the day enter his narratives as secondary details; we are privy to the innermost thoughts of characters, often in minute detail, and the dilemmas they face as their ideals and aspirations clash with reality. But behind the thoughts and actions of Guo's characters stand history and tradition, like some malign forces against which all are powerless. Modernist writers from Taiwan have captured some of the dilemmas faced by the Taiwanese in the postwar period, especially the changes due to economic development and the mainland émigré experience, but no other author has captured the political fallout like Guo. His often barren, desolate style is as much a reflection of personal idiosyncrasy as it is an allegory of the historical situation in which he found himself trapped: his modernism is a "symptom" and a form of his troubled state of existence.

"Snow Blind" (1985) deals with several of Guo's principal themes of postcolonial or "neocolonial" identity and the diaspora. It is three stories in one, all interrelated and focusing on the same theme, and one of Guo's few stories told from the point of view of a male character. The protagonist is living in a small desert town in the United States where he teaches Chinese in a local second-rate police academy. He too lives a banal and less than satisfying existence. He has few friends save a Japanese co-worker who is slowly drinking himself to death, depressed by his life situation. He is not married; he once had an affair with a young woman from Taiwan, but lacked the will to continue the relationship despite the affection he felt for the woman.

In addition to recounting his own story, the narrator tells the story of his school principal, a man who, to some extent, was successful under the Japanese and later was able to make the transition under the Nationalist government. Upon retiring, the principal runs a tobacco kiosk and later retires to the seaside, where he does some fishing. He is henpecked by his wife, another strong female character. The principal's life is also haunted by an older brother who committed suicide and a past affair with a young woman. Yet, despite the principal's modest successes, the narrator finds the man's life, restricted to the small neighborhood where he grew up and later languishing in a small seaside town, too confining. From an early age he develops a strong desire to break free from his environment and travel the world.

One important link between the principal and the narrator is a book. When the narrator is a boy, he and his mother visit the principal and his wife in their seaside home. Seeing that the boy is somewhat bookish, the principal gives him a Chinese book, the only one he has in his house. Years later, when the narrator is living in the United States, he still possesses this book. It is a collection of stories by Lu Xun, which was published in Taiwan with the authorization of the Japanese colonial government. From his first reading to his reading it on the train home to carrying it with him to the States, the book has become an obsession of sorts. The narrator shares it with his friends, including his one girlfriend and his Japanese colleague; he is also teaching Lu Xun in his advanced Chinese class to a bunch of disinterested American students.

Lu Xun, arguably the greatest Chinese writer of the twentieth century, established the direction for much of modern Chinese fiction. He had originally gone to Japan to become a doctor; instead he became a writer who sought to heal the souls of his countrymen. As C. T. Hsia has written about the tradition he initiated: "What distinguishes this 'modern' phase of Chinese literature is rather its burden of moral contemplation: its obsessive concern with China as a nation afflicted with a spiritual disease and therefore unable to strengthen itself or change its set ways of inhumanity."[7]

The book carries a number of symbolic implications in Guo's story. It is a physical link between generations—we find out later that it had belonged to the principal's brother, a medical student who committed suicide because he was unable to face the world or change it. It is an inheritance of sorts, but an unspoken inheritance, and a negative talisman. We also learn through the narrator's drunken conversation with the Japanese instructor that he would not be able to teach Lu Xun at home in Taiwan. Lu Xun's works were, of course, proscribed by the KMT government. Likewise, the recent past and much of the occupation period were off limits—Japanese was banned; the use of Taiwanese was prohibited in school, government, and broadcast; and no one was allowed to confront recent events such as the February 28th Incident.

Lu Xun's work also stands as a diagnosis of a shared spiritual malaise. "The True Story of Ah Q" is Lu Xun's most famous short story. Its immense success with the Chinese public was mainly due to its recognition of the hero as the embodiment of a national illness.[8] The illness diagnosed by Lu Xun also haunted and afflicted the Taiwanese—the principal and his brother were both victims, and the narrator, who also at one time had aspired to act upon the world, likewise succumbs. Although he succeeds in leaving Taiwan, he ends up in a position that is even more dissatisfying than the principal's and is just as powerless to do anything. Through the inclusion of a number of passages from "The True Story of Ah Q," Guo in fact situates the Taiwan experience within the larger Chinese context. Guo, like Lu Xun, examines the illness but does not offer a cure.

One often-noted feature of many of Guo's stories is that they are written from the perspective of a female character. In all cases, the narrator has received a good education and is familiar to some extent with modern trends; however, she exists in a transitional phase between cultures and/or generations and is still subject to the traditional social conventions. Therefore, in Guo's stories, society and the male characters are often interpreted through a female subjectivity governed by tradition in a transitional period.[9]

The women, as influenced by tradition, place an emphasis on marriage and family. Yet in most cases, the marriages are unhappy and childless. Seen through this subjectivity, external events seldom receive much attention unless they somehow impinge directly upon the women's lives; therefore, such events are often registered in passing but without any analysis. In "Moon Seal," which was published in 1984, for example, Wenhui is vaguely aware of the February 28th Incident but doesn't give it much thought; most of her attention is focused on her ailing husband.

The dilemmas of the male characters are different. By contrast, they seek to engage the events of the day and try to change things. Normally they are motivated by idealism, but circumstances often prevent them from achieving success. The men ignore their wives, leaving them frustrated, but they themselves also end up frustrated by their own failures. The men fail to live up to their own hopes and expectations as well as those of their wives. It is not only that the male characters are weak (they are often portrayed as sickly or effeminate); they simply cannot overcome what appears to be a more powerful fate. Failure stems from a nexus of factors—the inability to adapt to cultural changes, like from Japanese rule to KMT rule or living abroad in a foreign country. In this regard, Guo's disillusioned pessimism is similar to that of Thomas Hardy in novels such as *The Mayor of Casterbridge, Tess of the D'Urbervilles,* and *Jude the Obscure.*

Guo's portrait of the male and female Taiwanese psyche renders the burden of history on the Taiwanese consciousness far more deeply and subtly than any documentary depiction of the events of the day ever could. The feminine perspective utilized by Guo is telling in that on an individual level it mirrors the Taiwanese perspective in the postwar period, which is to say that just as the feminine is marginalized in society, so the Taiwanese were marginalized and disenfranchised in postwar Taiwan society. Within the sociopolitical parameters established by the ruling elite of the KMT, the Taiwanese were considered second-rate citizens. The female perspective provides the perfect imaginative corollary to reality.

"Moon Seal" is a fairly representative work in that it contains many of the themes and features of Guo's writing. The story is set against the backdrop of the end of the Japanese occupation and the wartime period, moving into the postwar period of KMT rule, including the February 28th Incident and the White Terror. The style is unique in that it is written often in one-sentence paragraphs. This gives the impression of reading poetry, but also a focused cinematic quality.

Another story told from the female perspective is "Wailing Moon" (1984). Here Guo again takes up male-female relations. The story is written from the wife's perspective—in the form of an interior monologue—at and between visits to her dead husband in a funeral parlor. Through a series of flashbacks, the wife recounts their life together. It was a rather traditional, though childless marriage of thirty years. She finds that in all that time she never really liked her husband, but had developed an almost maternal affection for him by the end. The constant refrain in her mind as she looks back over their life together is that their marriage should have ended years earlier when her husband set off for Japan to study.

After her husband's sudden and accidental death, the wife is visited by a Japanese woman, accompanied by her son. They talk about her husband and the wife feels close to the woman but cannot place her—she thinks that perhaps they were classmates. She eventually learns that the woman knew her husband in Japan. As the woman departs with her son, it suddenly dawns on the wife that the boy is actually her husband's son. She finds it incomprehensible that her shy, quiet husband was not who she thought he was and that they had lived for so many years with such a secret. The triangular relationship becomes an allegory of Taiwan's postwar status.

"Running Mother" (1984) is another story about a difficult relationship. It is told from the perspective of a man talking to a psychiatrist friend about his relationship with his mother. From an early age, the man, who is now middle-aged and with children of his own, has been afraid that his mother would leave him. The narrator's account of his relationship with his mother begins during the Japanese period, when one day his father leaves to "make some money" and never returns. He was no doubt conscripted by the Japanese to serve in the South Pacific. The boy's mother, a well-educated and elegant young woman, has to learn to fend for herself and her son. Despite being capable and having received a modern education, she is still subject to traditional social conventions and rules. A few years after the war, the narrator's grandfather forces his mother to remarry against her wishes.

As a child, the male narrator is always afraid of being deserted by his mother; after he grows up, he goes abroad to study and rarely returns home. Living far away, he is not able to take care of his mother, for which he feels guilty. He is torn between fear and guilt. The man's troubled relationship with his mother is reflective, on a symbolic level, perhaps, of his relationship with Taiwan.

"Clover" (1986) is yet another story told from a woman's perspective. The protagonist is a student living in the United States, where she is working on a Ph.D. She meets a young Taiwanese man who is studying philosophy at a seminary in the States with whom she has an on-and-off relationship. They run into each other on occasion and they visit each other during vacations. She leads a fairly banal existence, teaching to make ends meet, and is in no hurry to finish her degree until the university threatens not to renew her teaching contract. Through her internal ruminations we learn that she has fled an unhappy childhood in Taiwan—her father is an alcoholic—and that the young man is a sickly idealist who doesn't seem to fit in his village. His goal in life is to be a pastor in Taiwan. Both are governed by their past and the limitations of the present; neither one seems to be able to overcome their psychological inertia and move forward with the relationship. Time goes by and the young man seems to vanish from her life. She is happy with her routines and only occasionally wonders about him. One day she receives a care package from her sister and notices his name in a newspaper—it seems he returned to Taiwan and was arrested for subversion.

The last story in this collection, "Brightly Shine the Stars Tonight" (1997), at first seems unlike anything else Guo ever wrote. The main character, a general, is supposedly based on Chen Yi (1883–1950), the Governor-General of Taiwan who was responsible for the February 28th Incident. In a later interview, Guo denied that the character was Chen

Yi. That a Taiwanese writer could actually write a story sympathetic to an archvillain of postwar Taiwan history or a similar character is no simple matter. Whether or not the general is based on Chen Yi is really unimportant. What is important—more than anything else, in fact—is that Guo grapples with the notions of representation and history, and with identity on a more abstract level. It is a multifaceted work that exposes the gap between history and how it is written or represented, between a person's notion of self and identity and how such things are interpreted by others, as well as the gaps in a person's understanding of himself.

The entire story takes place the day before the general is to be executed for unspecified crimes, but through the use of flashbacks, the historical perspective is broadened. In taking stock of his life that night, he has an epiphany, experiencing a moment of enlightenment. His meditations possess a dual focus. He spends a good deal of time reflecting on the past, recalling his student days abroad, his military career, and even a moment or two when he saw through the world's vanities. On this level, he expresses a good deal of world-weariness. He finds that the activities of the Nationalist Army have not benefited the people and have largely been responsible for plunging the nation into catastrophe, which ideally he would like to see ended. He comments to his wife on his weariness and how he would like to retire to his property to farm and study. His wife, in her letter, which stands as a sort of commentary on the story of the general's life as he recalls it, notes how all men seem to idealize domestic life, but in reality they spend their lives running here and there trying to change the world, and in most cases not for the better.

On another level, the general directs his attention inward, trying to determine his true identity, one that transcends his worldly identity as a general. In his quest he is accompanied by his companion, a mirror. He spends a good deal of time looking in the mirror, or beyond or through it. Behind his image, he sees another form taking shape. It continues to develop from the merest outline and forms a network of blood vessels. Yet the image is not stable and is often overpowered by reality. Eventually, the real and the ideal merge on the execution ground, giving rise to something else altogether. As the central character is executed, the identity in the mirror steps forth, a new identity born after his demise.

Despite the oddness and abstractness of some parts of the story, it includes many of the obsessions the reader encounters in Guo's other stories: a lack of understanding between the sexes, the malignancy of historical circumstance against which the individual is powerless, the burden of history, the apparent arbitrariness of fate—life is like a game of chess (an analogy frequently used by the general), the end of which cannot be foreseen.

Guo Songfen's work is unique in the canon of modernist writing from Taiwan: it exhibits a concern for a Taiwan identity coupled with a modernist aesthetic. His work possesses the psychological depth one associates with modernism, but it also grapples with the burden of recent history in ways rarely encountered in the movement. Guo's writing stands as an indictment of the human condition in general and of the Taiwan experience in particular.

NOTES

This brief introduction benefited from discussions with Yingtsih Balcom and David Wang.

1. David Der-Wei Wang, "Lengku yijingli de huozhong" (The seed of fire in a cruel, strange land), in Guo Songfen, *Benpao de muqin* (Running mother) (Taipei: Maitian chuban, 2002), 3.

2. Joseph S.M. Lau, "Obsession with Taiwan: The Fiction of Chang Hsi-kuo," in Jeannette L. Faurot, ed., *Chinese Fiction from Taiwan: Critical Perspectives* (Bloomington: Indiana University Press, 1980), 64.

3. See Wang, "Lengku yijingli de huozhong," 3–4, 8, and a telephone interview with Lee Yu by the author, April 15, 2007.

4. Leo Ou-fan Lee, "'Modernism' and 'Romanticism' in Taiwan Literature," in Jeannette L. Faurot, ed., *Chinese Fiction from Taiwan: Critical Perspectives* (Bloomington: Indiana University Press, 1980), 13.

5. Sung-sheng Yvonne Chang, *Modernism and the Nativist Resistance* (Durham: Duke University Press, 1993), 1–22.

6. Sung-sheng Yvonne Chang, *Literary Culture in Taiwan: Martial Law to Market Law* (New York: Columbia University Press, 2004), 12.

7. C. T. Hsia, *A History of Modern Chinese Fiction* (New Haven: Yale University Press, 1971), 533–534.

8. Ibid., 37.

9. On Guo's female characters see Xu Qinglan, "Liuwang de fuqin, benpao de muqin" (Exiled father, running mother), in Guo Songfen, *Benpao de muqin*, 277–301; and Marie Laureillard, "The Image of Women According to Guo Songfen," available in the Taiwan Studies Files on the School of Oriental and African Studies Web site (http://www.soas.ac.uk/taiwanstudiesfiles/EATS2005/panel21aureillardpaper.pdf).

Moon Seal

TRANSLATED BY **MICHELLE YEH**

1

When Tiemin was discharged from Unit 63 at the end of the war, he was carried home on a stretcher.

Wenhui's mother, as a result, had reservations about their wedding.

But Wenhui was hardly able to contain her happiness. Whenever Brother Min's name was mentioned, she could barely refrain from jumping up and down for joy.

Returning to Taipei from the countryside, where they had taken refuge during the air raids, she again donned the uniform of the Third Girls' High School. Gazing into the mirror, she was lost in reverie.

It wasn't until her mother called to her that she snapped out of it. She pulled herself away from the mirror and, carrying a basket on her arm, headed for the market.

She walked alone down the street, immersed in the visions she conjured up of married life to come.

The despondency she had known during the war was gone. Stirred by her daydreams, her steps quickened, leaving a draft behind her.

Every time Wenhui walked down the street, she cried out in disbelief. She hadn't expected Taipei to have been so badly bombed. The streets and houses that she and Tiemin had passed before the war were no longer there.

In March the last composite brigade sailed for the South Pacific. Many of the soldiers were Taiwanese; some were relatives and the brothers of classmates, a good many of whom she knew.

Despite Tiemin's illness, what could be more comforting than knowing that he would not be sent to the front owing to his chronic condition? After her long hard wait, sickly Brother Min was going to be by her side, and any pain would be transformed into happiness. As long as they had faith, it seemed they could start a happy life at any time.

As she walked down the bombed street, a stream of warmth flowed through her heart. She couldn't hide her joy.

The war had not ended. Seeing her state, her mother felt an inexplicable sadness.

The dawn sky paled amid the chattering of gray starlings. Then a ray of sunlight poured through the mosquito net.

She was like a patient who had regained consciousness. Nestled comfortably under the quilt, she opened her sleep-filled eyes.

During the last year of the war the news from the South Pacific steadily worsened. Wenhui often secretly prayed that Brother Min would stay safely in Taiwan.

Everyone said that Taiwan was the front line of Japanese defense, and all the high school students were reserves. Schools were turned into training camps, all of which were collectively known as Unit 63. The next step was probably to turn them into barracks for the reservists.

Wenhui was prepared to endure any pain as long as she could spend her life with Brother Min. If suffering meant that she would be more likely to have him, then she would welcome the worst pain.

One day she heard the adults say that a boy, who was a distant relative of hers, had escaped from the mental hospital at Songshan. The next day he was found dead on the railroad tracks to Keelong.

Everyone said that the mental hospitals were poorly run, and the patients were always running away. The hospitals were understaffed because graduates from the nursing schools refused to work in them.

"The patients beat up the nurses for no reason!"

"I'll go, I'll go!" she thought as she listened, unaware that she was speaking aloud. "Then I'll go!"

Before she could collect herself, the grown-ups burst into laughter.

In October the war finally came. Airplanes dove out of the sky one after another, nearly brushing the rooftops. Soon the B-29s appeared in the sky above Taipei. Scores of airplanes soared high among the clouds, rattling all the windows in the houses.

People said that high school students were going to be drafted. As soon as the order came, they would all become privates in the army.

Jeeps with their tops down and motorcycles were seen everywhere; even cavalry soldiers with sabers rode their horses on the streets.

After the first B-29 bombings, the women in the neighborhood were organized. They conducted fire drills every few days.

A Japanese lieutenant with a long saber arrived from the barracks. He sat in the sidecar of an army motorcycle, clutching his saber with his white-gloved hand. Before he dismounted, his face stiffened as if he were facing some deadly foe.

The lieutenant stood in front of the closed post office to address the women. Wenhui was among them, perspiring heavily behind her heavy gas mask. Her ears were ringing. She felt dizzy. She could no longer hear the lieutenant's impassioned speech.

Recently the expression "to break like jade" often appeared on the neighborhood bulletin board.

"Saipan broke like jade." "Guam broke like jade." "Iwo Jima . . ."

The time would come when the South Pacific islands would all break like pieces of jade.

She heard the lieutenant urge them to defend Taipei Bridge with their lives. She wondered if it too would break like jade when the time came.

It was said that the enemy was going to land at Balixiang.

After the new year, in the deep of the night by the sea, Wenhui sat up in her bed crying, shocked. Dazed, she sat there in a cold sweat. Then she heard her heart pounding.

Her mother, sleeping next to her, was woken up.

The old lady turned over and fell back asleep, mumbling "Silly girl!" as if talking in her sleep. "There are no air raids in the countryside."

"It's not a siren. It's just some bird," she told herself, half asleep.

After a while she could only hear the waves breaking on the shore. The sea was so vast and frightful, yet the night so peaceful.

She and her mother had just moved to the coastal town of Wuqi from Taipei.

But she hadn't really heard a bird. Was she having a nightmare?

As she lay down, she thought of Taipei so far away. She thought of Brother Min, who was going to be drafted, and wondered if he still coughed blood.

A month before she left Taipei, Brother Min skipped a day of school. They went to see the late-night show at the First Theater on Peace Street. After the show he stood facing the wind, with a hand on his frail chest, and started coughing incessantly. Then he spit blood.

His coughing that night sounded just like the crashing waves she had heard a moment ago. Wave after wave surged forward, unstoppable.

She had secretly saved the blood-stained handkerchief that Brother Min used.

She remembered that on their first date they also went to a late-night show at the First Theater. That night he left home with a fever and waited alone under the arcade across from the movie house. Seeing him from a distance, she ran all the way up.

The show had already started. As she ran up to him, the lights on the front of the theater went out. The place, which had been shining gloriously in silver a moment ago, was suddenly overcome by the darkness.

He stood by the *benjo* ditch and smiled at her from the dark roadside as he watched her run toward him. His smile nevertheless gave away his condition.

She asked, panting, "Aren't you feeling well?"

They went into the theater and sat in an empty corner. She held his burning hand, but she didn't know then that he was already ill.

In the dark she whispered, "Do you regret it?"

Her question referred to the fact that he had laid aside his writing to go to the movies with her.

He took out his handkerchief to cover his mouth and said, still coughing softly, "No."

The day Wenhui left Taipei, she stood with a bundle on the platform at the train station. She looked around but did not see Brother Min. He had promised to come, but he didn't. He was nowhere to be seen when the train began to move.

It must have been because the army wouldn't give him leave. She heard that they were going to work as engineering corpsmen at the Yilan Airport.

Returning to the barracks that day, he turned around and shouted into the distance to remind her: "Don't forget to write!"

She held the blood-stained handkerchief throughout her train ride. Those once crimson stains had faded; now, in the twilight shining through the window, they looked like fallen petals.

The whistling train ran south along the coast. Stop after stop the train was taking her farther and farther away from Taipei, from Brother Min.

The sunlight glancing off the sea shone on her tired face through the carriage window; she had not slept a wink the night before.

Brother Min was getting farther and farther away. He looked timid and shy in the sallow light on the gloomy street where they'd said goodbye in the rain.

"Tiemin is a shy boy." That was what her mother thought when she first laid eyes on him.

The first time Wenhui met him, he was sitting off by himself, trying to hide in the corner.

It was at Mr. Sara's place. She remembered that day: the living room was crowded with friends who worked on the magazine. The more animated the discussion, the further Tiemin seemed to withdraw. He scarcely said a word all evening.

Afterward she asked him why he hadn't said anything.

He only said that he had felt like spitting blood. "It was the first time I had a premonition about spitting blood."

"Why?"

All the way up Ali Mountain in the narrow-gauge train, he laughed happily, if not a little childishly.

"Listen, you can hear the sea," said someone on the train.

"From a mountain 6,000 feet above sea level?"

They all burst out laughing.

"Can it be that he was born with the legendary 'all-hearing ears'?"

"It's the rustling of the leaves."

When the train reached the top, the red cypresses were rustling.

On Ali Mountain, Tiemin dressed lightly and did his morning exercises outside the log cabin before sunrise, all by himself.

No one would believe that he was graduating from high school and going to a college-preparatory school. Nor could she believe that someone so young had written a play that sounded so mature.

One day Mr. Sara mentioned to Wenhui that a student at the Taipei First Boys' High School had sent him a one-act play.

"It's virtually a masterpiece." When he pronounced the word "masterpiece," his Japanese was particularly crisp.

After a while Mr. Sara suddenly sat up in his rattan chair.

"Well, would you like to meet the author of *The Capon?*" he asked in a jovial tone and smiled.

At that time she was editing some articles for *New Taiwan Literature* at Mr. Sara's place. The crimson twilight in the western sky outside the sliding *shoji* door shone on the manuscript pages spread all over the *tatami* around her.

When she heard his question, something flashed before her eyes. Yet she didn't budge and continued to work.

Haruhiko Sara was Wenhui's Japanese literature teacher at the Third Girls' High School. Her work had won much praise in his composition class. Later she was invited to his house to help edit the magazine.

"Why?" She looked up at his pale face. "Why did you have a premonition of spitting blood that day?"

With puzzlement written all over his face, Tiemin didn't know what to say. After a long pause he gave a vague reply: "Perhaps because I didn't enjoy talking about politics."

"But you didn't say a word."

That day Mr. Sara had talked the most.

"We'll see about the 'Empire's Southern Advance' policy this time."

The living room had been filled with animated talk, but it fell silent the minute he uttered these words. The atmosphere in the room became heavy. They all turned and looked at Mr. Sara.

After having spoken those words, Mr. Sara picked up his cup of English tea, held it close to his gray mustache, and gave a cynical smile as he sipped.

It was at times like this that everyone worried about Mr. Sara. How could he say such things in days like these?

At that very moment Wenhui noticed Tiemin's face darken as he sat in the corner.

One was always uneasy talking about politics when there were Japanese present. Was that why Tiemin had a premonition of spitting blood?

Mr. Sara didn't elaborate on his terse comment about the Japanese military, as if that were all he had to say.

After Mr. Sara returned from Ali Mountain with the magazine staff, he received a letter of dismissal from the Governor-General's office.

Summer was over, a new semester was about to begin. It was a matter of days before Mr. Sara was to leave Taiwan.

When school started, there was a new Japanese literature teacher. After class the students chatted among themselves. Mr. Sara was a dangerous element.

Wenhui had heard stories like this before. Every morning when she opened the newspaper, she was anxious to see if there was any news of his dismissal.

Two years earlier there had been a Japanese expert on Asian tropical warfare at the Department of Southern Strategic Study by the name of Seinosuke Kitamiya. He was suspected of sympathizing with the Taiwanese because he had helped a Taiwanese composer financially. The military ordered him to leave Taiwan and return to Japan. She remembered that a newspaper at the time had accused him of being a pseudo-liberal. However, no one expected that the day before he was to leave Taiwan, he would commit suicide in his residence.

Kitamiya had invited his composer friend to the house the night before he was to leave. The young composer arrived as invited. Upon reaching the place, he heard several broken notes from a Chinese lute. He knocked repeatedly, but no one came to the door. When he pushed the door open and entered the house, the music stopped.

The renowned author of *A Study of Tropical War Strategy* was sitting in the living room, fully dressed, cross-legged, with a Chinese lute in his hands. The moment the guest walked in, he slowly slumped forward and, without so much as a word, fell over on the mat, dead.

The man left behind a note of protest against the authorities.

When Wenhui came home from school, she found a hastily handwritten note from Mr. Sara inviting her and Tiemin for a last meeting. Holding the note in her hand, she felt ice cold all over. The dashing cursive script looked so unfamiliar.

She and Tiemin hurried toward downtown Taipei. But the moment they stepped inside the coffee shop where they were to meet him, they saw Mr. Sara sitting in a quiet corner, looking very much his usual self. As soon as he saw them, he smiled and waved.

He was wearing a white linen civil officer's uniform, starched and pressed, as if he had just come from some grand ceremony. The white uniform accentuated his salt-and-pepper hair.

Afterward she was puzzled by their final meeting. He had asked them to come, but in the coffee shop he was reticent. At sunset the old man kept smiling as he sipped his English tea. The noticeable silence, however, only gave away his agitation. Worried about Mr. Sara's situation, they didn't know what to say either.

Now that they were married, it suddenly dawned on Wenhui. At the farewell meeting Mr. Sara seemed to have something he wanted to say, but he ended up not saying it. Even at the last moment he still refrained from speaking his mind. Could it be that before he left Taiwan, he wanted to see them get married, but couldn't find the words to express his wish?

If only Mr. Sara knew that we are married, how happy he would be! she exclaimed in her heart, sitting in a Japanese-style house as a young bride.

In September Wenhui rushed back to Taipei from the coast. Seeing Tiemin again for the first time, seeing his pale face on the pillow, she wanted to give up her blood.

When the war approached Taipei, they each wore a blood-type A marker at their waist. When Mr. Sara saw that, he smiled knowingly. What a coincidence that they had the same blood type.

In private she made a deal with Brother Min: when the war came, whoever lost blood would receive blood from the other person. Having the same blood type gave her a marvelous vision of their future happiness.

When they were reunited after the war, he mustered all his strength on his sickbed and gasped with joy. Could it be that he too saw their happy life to come?

She remembered what her mother said: "Other girls can't wait to be brides. You can't wait to be a nurse."

Whenever she saw him perspiring in his sleep for no apparent reason, she recalled her mother's words. What did Mother mean by that? Wasn't she a bride now? Her whole being basked in the joy of being a newlywed.

She sat on the *tatami*. Every now and then she picked up the disinfected washcloth to wipe the sweat from his face, gently so as not to wake him. He had only just fallen asleep at a little past noon.

The December rain drizzled on the roof of their Japanese-style house. She looked out the window with delight.

Soon the eaves, which were in need of repair, begin to leak water, blocking out large chunks of the sky beyond the low walls.

Her mother told her that with a patient in the house it was a good idea to scrub the floor and the *tatami* every day to prevent the bacteria from spreading. Wenhui's hands were red and swollen from extended contact with the antiseptic solution.

She had never worked so hard. At the same time, she had never been so happy. As she shuffled across the newly scrubbed mats, she felt as happy as if she were gliding on ice.

In a letter from Unit 63 Brother Min had mentioned that tuberculosis patients were fond of ice. He often said that he yearned for the snowstorms in the north. "If I'm sent to the South Pacific, it'll be a punishment from heaven."

The train raced along the coast as she and her mother returned to Taipei from Wuqi.

She was fidgety and her mouth was dry throughout the journey. For the first time she experienced a burning sensation in her chest like what he must have felt.

When the train passed Banqiao, there was a scorched smell in the air. The passengers poked their heads out the windows to see what was going on. Someone said Taipei was still burning.

When the train neared the suburbs outside Taipei, houses could be seen silhouetted against the flaming western sky.

Everyone was anxious to see what Taipei looked like after the bombings. She didn't see anything. She could only hear the wheels rumbling beneath her feet.

Upon arriving, she ran straight to Brother Min's place.

As soon as autumn passed they were married. They did not have a big wedding. In fact, it was impossible to have one. Most of their relatives were still taking refuge in the countryside and could not be notified.

After the bombings, Dadaocheng looked bleak, even during the day.

Passing under the covered walkway, she felt as if she were walking in a huge air raid shelter. All the stores were boarded up. The sun shone brightly, but there were few people on the streets, just the distant echoes of a few *geta*, or wooden clogs.

Wenhui's mother went to a lot of trouble to get a friend to buy a few cans of food from prewar times.

The power lines were still down. After the sun set, darkness filled the house. Candles were lit on the night of their wedding for the one table of guests. The feeble candlelight flickered; the bride's face beamed with joy. But the groom could only hold up for the wedding banquet.

Tiemin collapsed the next day. Since then he had been bedridden in this small room of eight *tatami*.

Curious neighbors at Dadaocheng gossiped behind their backs, saying that the groom didn't even have time to love the bride before he fell ill.

Before the wedding someone had recommended this house surrounded by rice paddies in Gongguan to her mother. Though it was a little out of the way, the air was fresh and would be good for the patient.

Before they moved in, her mother brought her twice to look at the house. She loved it at first sight.

Wenhui was extremely excited as she envisioned herself leaving the dark old house and living a pastoral married life with Brother Min in a bright, airy place.

The house belonged to a Japanese officer. When Wenhui came with her mother, they found out that the owner was a lieutenant colonel in the cavalry. The news of his death had reached his family from the South Pacific just a few days before. He left behind no children. His wife was being sent to be part of an overseas Japanese group that would soon depart by ship for Japan from Keelong Harbor.

When they decided to take the house, the wife had just returned from a Shinto shrine. The newly widowed woman did not wear any makeup and looked lonely and forlorn. Her mourning attire consisted of a gray satin kimono with a pattern of winter chrysanthemums on the lapels.

When the widow heard her mother say that she, her daughter, was going to live there after she got married, she seemed touched. She relaxed visibly. At the door where she said good-bye to them, she bowed slowly in the early autumn wind wafting through the evergreens in the garden. Her ninety-degree bow made her seem more pliant than the reeds by the river. Lowering her face, she congratulated Wenhui warmly.

"Then let me congratulate you in advance on your wedding."

The breeze thawed the widow's frosty manner.

That day when they said good-bye in front of the coffee shop, Mr. Sara also bowed from the rickshaw. His impassive face, like the face on the advertisement for Rendan pills, softened in the breeze.

Blessings filled the eyes of the old man as he looked at them from the rickshaw.

In the late summer sunset, the cicadas had stopped chirping. The city streets were deserted. The rubber soles of the rickshaw puller could be heard falling on the wide asphalt road.

Wenhui watched as the rickshaw took Mr. Sara away. In the moving vehicle, he looked old in his white linen suit. Standing by the roadside with Tiemin, both warmed by the spreading twilight, she watched the rickshaw disappear at the end of the street.

Once, while drinking, Mr. Sara mentioned casually: "Tiemin is a little too obscure."

He was referring to the one-act play *The Capon,* recently published in *New Taiwan Literature.* The moment she heard that, she remembered Mr. Sara's comment about her: "It would be better if Wenhui could be more pessimistic."

Optimism was probably hereditary, she always thought. She was like her mother.

When her father passed away, everyone was worried about her mother, who had always been obedient to and dependent on her husband. But no one could have expected that after losing her husband her mother was able to fly toward the early summer sun by herself, like a cicada sloughing off its skin.

Following a neighbor's suggestion, her mother turned to Christianity. After the mourning period of forty-nine days was over, she started going to church. When her mother reemerged on the street with a Bible from the Seventh Day Adventists in her hand, home still made Wenhui feel warm inside.

Days went by, but Tiemin did not get any better.

Now, in the second year of her marriage, as her nursing responsibilities grew, Wenhui suddenly found that her optimistic disposition, along with her girlhood, had vanished without a trace, never to return.

2

In the quiet of the night she heard someone weeping. She was unaware that her nose was running.

"It's cold," she murmured.

The electricity in Taipei was shut off at seven due to the blackout. She had to do the dishes before the lights went out.

Night came earlier in the fall. As usual, a busy day came to an end after she cleaned the sink and lit a candle on the table. Then she could sit down and take a break in the kitchen.

But tonight she couldn't wait to get out of the house reeking of medicine. After she lit the candle, she turned around and went into the backyard.

Soon the chickens in the coops started clucking.

The last trace of twilight had faded. Stars were shining above in the silky sky.

She took a deep breath of fresh air.

Exhausted, she couldn't seem to shake off the aches and pains that numbed her. After a hard day's work—no, more than a day—fatigue never seemed to leave her.

At five o'clock the tune "Wake up, You Who Refuse to Be Slaves" was played on the radio as usual. Tiemin hadn't awakened from his nap, so she walked over to turn off the radio. It was time to cook supper.

She walked slowly past the cypresses.

She lowered her head to look at her shadow crisscrossed with the swaying bamboo shadows. It was at such moments that she could temporarily forget her husband's illness and lose herself in the pure, clean night air, dreaming about a normal life.

Suddenly she cried: "It's cold."

She heard herself weeping.

She quickly wiped away her tears with her hand. Taking a few steps forward, she passed the low walls. She refused to admit that she was crying.

Yet she could not deny the fact that her heart, which had been so strong and calm, had begun to waver recently.

Watching as Brother Min's health deteriorated, she felt helpless, and sometimes she panicked.

"What if . . . what if . . ."

Questions like these began to creep into her head. Sometimes when she looked back, she realized the fear had always been there, in the deepest recesses of her mind.

At such moments of helplessness, she imagined that someday she would buy Western medicine on the street.

Dr. Cai said that during the war he read in a Japanese medical journal that the West was on the verge of discovering a cure for tuberculosis.

After the war, however, he was totally cut off from scientific developments in the outside world.

"It's like being blind." The doctor sighed.

The X-ray showed that the affected area had spread; it looked like the silhouette of a jade tree growing along the bronchi of his lungs.

Dr. Cai told her that his suggestion of moving the patient somewhere to recuperate might not work now since once the blood vessels had been invaded an aneurysm could develop, and an emergency could occur at any time.

"If he coughs up a lot of blood, it will be inconvenient for him to be away from Taipei."

Late at night she was awakened by Brother Min's coughing, which had reduced him to breathlessness. With his head on the pillow, he produced a long hissing sound, as if silk thread were spinning from his chest and entangling the whole house.

Wenhui could no longer take care of their new nest by herself.

For a long time she only floated on the bedding without really sleeping. She was constantly prepared for a possible emergency.

"When the patient spits blood, there is a chance that he could die from suffocation if the blood enters the bronchi." The doctor reminded her to watch Tiemin all the time.

Sometimes, she couldn't believe that she was still on her feet and wondered where her strength came from.

Darkness was everywhere. She stood outside the low walls, wiping away her tears with the back of her hand.

A leaf fell from the breadfruit tree by the ditch to her feet. The sound of the large leaf scraping the ground startled her. Her heart began to pound.

Suddenly all the stars in the sky were reeling. Stars came pressing down on the bamboo grove in the night breeze. She nearly fainted.

When she opened her eyes, the sky had retreated, far, far away. Space had regained its immensity. She panicked and felt lost.

Nausea welled up. While she could still support herself, she hurriedly turned, grabbed two eggs from the chicken coop at random, and ran inside.

She recalled the months after their wedding. March, April, May . . . Every month was the same, every month empty.

It was as if her body had shed all its flesh and blood, and now stood empty like a deserted house.

Summer was gone, but grief weighed ever more heavily upon her powerless chest, and would not budge until she collapsed.

A ray of September morning light shone in through the wooden shutters. It had been like that for a long time.

In the morning she got up late. She stayed under the quilt, still feeling the chill from the back yard the previous night.

She allowed the slanting light to envelop her. In the quiet house she heard Tiemin breathing heavily in his sleep.

In front of the mirror she was taken aback. She could hardly believe she was looking at herself.

She should not have aged that much, but an invisible hand had her in its clutches and would not let go till she fell apart. How horrible! From the very beginning there had been a plot to interfere with their happiness.

The day before yesterday Brother Min had gotten out of bed. It was rare that he felt clearheaded and asked to sit in the sun.

She put a rattan chair on the porch. He picked up a book and strolled out from the shade into the warm autumn sun.

What a joyful day that was! But heaven played a trick on them.

After a short while in the sun he suddenly raised his head from the book and, with mouth tightly shut, gesticulated with his hands waving in the air.

She was shocked. When she talked to him, he just kept his lips closed.

Then blood flowed silently out of his mouth. She cried and hurried to fetch a towel.

Blood, so powerful and so hard to staunch. Before she returned with the towel, two streams of blood trickled from the corners of his mouth.

He covered his mouth with the towel. Soon blood seeped through, staining the white towel. The torrent surging from within could no longer be held back.

He could no longer hold it back. He got up and doubled over the sink. The blood poured out.

With his hands on the windowsill, he bent down and coughed uncontrollably until his face turned ashen.

A rare sunny day was spent busily cleaning up blood stains.

The following March Wenhui heard a broadcast on the radio as frightening as spitting blood. Alarmed, she quickly turned down the volume.

At night she moved the radio into the kitchen, where she continued to listen at a low volume.

There had been a riot in Taipei. She heard that there was fighting in the streets.

After all this time being locked up in the house doing nothing except caring for Brother Min, she was completely cut off from the outside world. She did not expect another war. Two months before, she had been suddenly able to buy only rationed "household rice." People were saying that sooner or later something was bound to happen.

She wondered how her mother at Dadaocheng was doing.

The next morning she had to buy some rice on the black market.

At midnight Tiemin's temperature rose again. In a trance, he mumbled something as if he were drilling on a parade ground.

During the last year of the war they said there were some Taiwanese in the planes that took off from the airfield at Linkou who volunteered to join the kamikaze corps. Some of the family members suffered from nightmares. People started telling ghost stories.

The radio said that fighting continued into the night at Dadaocheng. An executive committee was set up at Sun Yat-sen Hall by those who demanded proper handling of the riot. Kneeling beside the feverish Tiemin, she was in a turmoil.

In early April, tender reed shoots burgeoned by the river amid last year's dry stalks.

Not too long ago he was so happy, figuring the war would soon be over and everything would be fine again. When he told her amusing stories about Unit 63, they often broke into laughter. They had not expected another war.

When the radio was at its noisiest, the rash on Tiemin's body kept him awake all night. Turning and tossing under the quilt, he felt itchy all over. But he was kept in the dark as to what was happening outside.

"Turn on the light," he yelled in the middle of the night when the itching became unbearable.

She dared not turn the light on or tell him about the riot. She lifted the mosquito net and by the light of the moon gently wiped his body with a wet towel.

Lights came on at four in the morning in the distant fields. Then she relaxed.

When daylight came, she went out on a bicycle and knocked on the doors of the rice stores. Now a single bar of Heavenly Scent soap cost twenty dollars, even more expensive than rice.

The inflation made her panic, and the road ahead seemed so long.

For weeks it had been quiet around Gongguan. Hardly a pedestrian was seen on the street; it was like death.

By the time she heard the church bell again, she had also heard from her mother.

Her mother said, "Everything is fine now."

Soon the lame district chief came limping. He went from one house to house, informing folks of the order from the top that they turn in all Japanese swords.

"Doesn't matter if it's a military bayonet, dagger, saber, or ornamental sword. Everything must be turned in." The district chief emphasized: "This is an order."

Wenhui asked him: "Is the riot over?"

"It is, it is."

Awakened, Tiemin turned his head on the pillow and asked feebly who it was.

"It's nothing. He's just here to deliver more medicine," she fibbed.

In the early summer twilight, the day warmed up. Pea-sized drops of perspiration appeared on her face as she put the military swords left behind by the Japanese widow into the bath furnace one by one. When the blades turned red, she pulled them out of the furnace, took them outside, and beat on them with a hammer until the straight blades bent.

It was getting dark. At the foot of the wall she dug several deep holes and buried all the swords that she had destroyed.

She spent three days completing the task behind Tiemin's back.

She discussed it with her mother. Her mother also felt that it was best to burn and bury them. If she turned them over to the government, it might have aroused suspicion since there were so many of them.

While she was burning the swords, she felt like a thief.

At night her limbs were numb and her mouth was parched. She drank some wine to soothe herself.

Now that the swords were buried, she sat on the porch with her feet perched on the stone steps and a bowl of rice wine in her hand.

When the blades turned red in the furnace, they looked like a rainbow in the sky, bright with life. After being pounded on and splashed with cold water, they sent up a puff of white steam, wafting to the sky, like the spirits of dead children ascending to heaven.

The night concealed her crime. As the wine went down, she felt more at ease.

Since it fell upon her shoulders, she had no choice but to do it. There was no time for hesitation or fear. She had a patient to look after.

She had become a different person.

All the things left behind by the Japanese widow were destroyed except for a firefly cage. Even the lacquered tablets of gods were chopped up for kindling.

The night breeze blew. With burning cheeks, she welcomed it. At night the empty field was pleasant. The field beyond the low walls was peaceful and quiet before the summer insects came alive.

Soon the bugle could be heard from the faraway elementary school. It took her a while to realize that it was the lights-off call for the military police stationed at the school.

"Wenhui, Wenhui!"

One day when she was hoeing the vegetable patch in the backyard, she heard Tiemin calling impatiently. She put down the hoe and ran over to find there was nothing to be alarmed about.

The fever had subsided. He was awake and very alert under the quilt. He wanted her to lie down beside him and look at the water stains on the ceiling with him.

Once they were pointed out, she noticed the white moldy stains for the first time.

He said that after looking at them for days, he'd finally connected all the stains into a story.

Now as she lay beside him, glad that winter was over, she was thinking of airing the bedding in the sun to get ride of the smell of medicine.

Two days earlier, she had washed his hair; she could still smell the tea fragrance on the pillow.

He said that after the wash he didn't feel like himself. He was light on his feet, hardly able to stand still. His nose was clear again; now he could smell the pork and olive stew in the air.

After telling the story on the ceiling, he said something else that escaped her.

Did he say that life was a trip for nothing or that it shouldn't be a trip for nothing? She interpreted it as a patient's pessimistic thoughts and paid it no mind.

He also said that for some reason after his temperature came down he kept dreaming about Seinosuke Kitamiya, the Japanese who'd committed suicide before the war.

"Well, it is worth it to die content, to end with a satisfying life, even if one dies young." At night he said such a silly thing.

On hearing it, she couldn't help holding his head to her bosom and comforting him: "You are almost well now. Why are you still daydreaming like this?"

Just a few days before, Dr. Cai had come. The moment he walked into the vestibule, she saw for the first time a smile on his face.

The doctor told her right away that judging from Tiemin's condition, his illness was stabilizing. The jade-tree silhouette on the lungs had not spread.

"Wonderful news!" She rejoiced in her heart. It would be a miracle not to have to have an operation.

Seated on the *tatami*, the doctor smiled as he talked to the patient sitting up slowly from under the quilt:

"Look, spring is here. Try hopping, Cricket!"

Yet Tiemin's illness did not stabilize right away. After his high fever broke, he had violent mood swings. One day he suddenly raised his head from the book in his hand. She saw a pale, frightened face. Afraid that he was about to cough blood again, her heart leaped. At night he pulled her to his side with a feverish hand and mumbled on and on.

Dr. Cai told her that the physical condition was easy to cure. What was harder to cure was "here," said the doctor as he pointed to his own head.

After the initial diagnosis, the doctor had recommended that Tiemin quit smoking, which he did immediately. But the doctor also advised against reading during recuperation, which Tiemin had not been able to obey.

Before Mr. Sara had left Taiwan, Tiemin had come back from his house with two huge bundles of books. Pointing at the books by Arishima, Mushanokōji, and others, Mr. Sara told Tiemin that even though the military tried to win over these leading writers of the White Birch School, they were actually very resentful. Mr. Sara also pointed to two or three English magazines, saying:

"There aren't any good articles in them. But since English has become an enemy language, we'd better be careful."

The noon sun filtered at an angle through the bamboo. Wenhui helped Tiemin to the porch and had him sit in a rattan chair. With a light blanket over his lap, he read quietly in the sun.

A few days earlier he had finished *Destiny of the Third Invisible Man*. Excited, he could not stop talking about it all night in bed. The next morning when he got up he felt weak in the legs, as if he had suffered heatstroke.

Now he had the play *Hurray for Humankind* in his hand.

Dr. Cai advised Tiemin to read less. But hadn't they taken an instant liking to each other because they were both avid readers?

Since the doctor had found out that Tiemin was the author of *The Capon*, they had developed a relationship far beyond that of doctor and patient.

As his doctor, he wanted Tiemin to put the books away; but as a lover of literature, he often got Tiemin going on the topic. Once Tiemin improved, the doctor talked loquaciously and forgot that not too long ago the patient in front of him was afflicted with stage two tuberculosis.

Yet Wenhui knew that much of the gloom in the house was swept away by Dr. Cai's presence. When the doctor was there, she was temporarily relieved of the responsibility of taking care of the patient and able to hand him over to the doctor. She could walk in the yard, away from the heavy smell of the antiseptic solution that permeated the house.

Dr. Cai was tall. Since he was not heavy, his head looked large. When he came to visit, he always wore an old Western suit from the prewar era that was too tight.

In the middle of the conversation he combed his long, thick hair with one hand. His salt-and-pepper hair was wavy and hung down over his ears. His brows were knit in a frown, revealing a contemplative bent. With a cigarette between his fingers, he sometimes turned his head sideways and a bashful smile appeared, something unexpected from such a big man. She loved seeing his childlike smile. After taking care of the patient for so long, the doctor had become part of her family.

She recalled how during those days when Tiemin was seriously ill, the doctor had often discussed what to do with her confidentially.

Gradually her father's image faded. Unwittingly Wenhui had found a reliable source of warmth and strength in the doctor.

The doctor himself often said half-jokingly that he should be considered a child of the Meiji Restoration.

"Even though I was born Chinese."

He recalled that when he went to Germany from Japan he was so moved by the popular Wilsonism that he neglected his medical studies.

"I almost gave up medicine to pursue politics, to take part in the National Self-Determination Movement."

In private Tiemin often said, "Dr. Cai is no ordinary doctor."

He was a man of thought. With the sharp eye of a pathologist, he diagnosed the illnesses in life.

"He is a perceptive social critic."

Day by day Tiemin was getting better. The doctor arrived and after he put down his stethoscope, there was more and more time for conversation that went beyond medicine. The doctor and the patient often had such a lovely time talking that they failed to notice the night falling.

Realizing it was late, the doctor would close his black bag. As he put his shoes on in the vestibule, he was still talking about such topics as Tolstoyism.

The doctor brought a stack of old magazines. Again, the two men sat on the porch, high-spirited, and pored over those old, slightly musty issues.

Dr. Cai pointed at the set of *New Village*, which he'd asked someone to buy from Mr. Sara. Speaking of the old gentleman, the doctor became sad. It was unfortunate that he hadn't had the opportunity to meet him before he was made to leave Taiwan.

"He may be considered the last liberal dismissed by the Governor-General of Taiwan during the war." Such was Dr. Cai's comment on Mr. Sara.

The doctor heard from various sources that Mr. Sara led a miserable life after returning to Japan, all alone in Hokkaido countryside, trying to live a simple life of farming and reading, after the model of Tolstoy.

With a cup of tea in hand, the doctor and the patient sat facing each other and carried on a conversation on the porch in spring. Their topic shifted from Mr. Sara to the White Birch School, from humanitarianism to the last years of Tolstoy's life.

At the mention of Tolstoy the doctor livened up.

"Even at the ripe old age of eighty-two he was still intrigued by the enigmas of life. A melancholy man, he eventually left home and died in a remote train station during a terrible winter. The epitome of a restless soul!"

When speaking of life beyond the human body and pathology, the doctor turned into an unbridled horse. He was vivacious, a magical light gleaming in his eyes. His whole body swayed from one moment of intensity to another, from one dream to another.

"He deserves the word 'great'."

With a half-smoked cigarette between his fingers, Tiemin was inspired by the doctor's words, as his mind drifted far, far away.

On such occasions, the doctor always made an exception and allowed the patient to smoke one cigarette.

Craning his neck, Tiemin was quiet. He was waiting for the doctor to continue. But suddenly he heard the train. In the north he dreamed of, the train came roaring nearer.

The doctor resumed his speaking.

But Tiemin no longer heard him. He felt feverish and a little faint, as if he was sick again.

Before his eyes, the boundless Russian plain in winter spread before him. The leaden sky from which snow was about to fall pressed down on the desolate plain as the train rumbled by.

The train stopped at a small village. An old man who had left his wife and children because he rejected ownership had chosen this deserted train station to be his final destination. At the moment of death his heart was still beating wildly and would not stop for any reason.

In the old magazines stacked between the two men, there was an article entitled "The Station at Astapovo."

The last bit of life galloped toward the Russian plain, left an enigmatic message at the train station, and then passed away.

The doctor still remembered how the tiny railroad station in the deserted Russian village once occupied the mind of an overseas Chinese student. Now he was smiling, for he seemed to see the seed of fire that Tolstoy sowed before he died in the northern country rekindled and burning bright in the bosom of a young patient thirty years later.

"Oh . . ." the doctor was thrilled. He was about to go on. But when he raised his head he saw Tiemin's flushed face and heard him stammering as if choking back his tears.

"That's great!" He echoed the doctor's earlier remark.

The moment he said it, Tiemin thought it abrupt and childish. He coughed gently and tried to alter his tone, making it more balanced. But his mouth did not obey him, and still he said: "That's great!"

"An old fighter battling himself," concurred the doctor, sensing his embarrassment.

The midday spring sun shone, warming the two men as they sat cross-legged under the eaves. The doctor started talking about his practice. After he read *War and Peace* he underwent a radical transformation.

"That was . . ."

He was about to say "truth." Tiemin lifted his head and stared at the doctor's face, waiting eagerly.

The doctor asked Tiemin if he remembered the scene from *War and Peace* where Pierre is captured on the battlefield and is sentenced to death.

At the trial the eyes of the French judge and the Russian captive meet inadvertently, which gives birth to a spark of humanity, causing the judge to change his mind and be more lenient. Pierre's life is spared.

"Yes, well . . . ?" Tiemin was still waiting for the answer.

"Later when I started practicing medicine, I often bore in mind the spark of humanity that Tolstoy described and I found myself disturbed for no apparent reason." The doctor was lost in thought: "I simply could not treat the patients from a purely professional point of view. That bothered me a great deal."

"Do you often see that look in the eyes of your patients?" Flushed in the face, Tiemin sought an answer.

"No." The moment he said it, he sensed tension in the air. So he adopted a more tentative tone and continued: "Perhaps I should say, it's rare."

"Mm."

Both fell silent.

"The look of humanity . . ." the doctor resumed, as if talking to himself.

"As for the light in the patient's eyes, it's easy to understand." He took a sip of tea. "I have met roughly two kinds. One is greed, the other is despair."

He paused again. "Actually, I shouldn't say this in front of you, but I know you won't mind. After all, we are discussing an issue. I never demand to see anything in a patient's eyes. Rather it's that I have doubts about Tolstoy since I cannot see patients from a humanitarian perspective. The more I force myself to do so, the more doubt I have about the scene of the judge and the captive. Perhaps it only exists in fiction. In the real world you can't find that look of humanity. When I think this way, I feel resentful toward Tolstoy and toward myself for not carrying the light. You see, how can a doctor who's angry with himself treat patients?"

The sunlight in the back yard harbingered early summer as it shone on the fields behind the low walls. Green rice stalks drooped in the wind. Tiemin took a deep breath of the fresh air.

Wenhui came out and said, "Lunch is ready. Would you like to have it outside?"

In this way the doctor and the patient often put aside the topic of tuberculosis and let their conversation drift.

Strangely, Tiemin actually improved as the days passed in conversation. As if distracted by something remote, the patient forgot all about his illness.

At night he no longer had a temperature. During the day when he went outside to stand under the eaves, she could see the glow on his face from the vegetable patch where she was working.

Now when she went out with a basket in the early morning, she secretly stooped to catch a glimpse of herself in the mirror. Back from the market, she worked briskly in the kitchen. Life was moving into the sun and becoming quite dazzling.

"There." She ran from the kitchen and lifted a handful of thick white bamboo shoots for him to see. "These are the first wild bamboo shoots since the war."

He read the note Wenhui left on the pillow: "I've gone shopping. Have something to show you in the kitchen."

On the table Tiemin saw only a big soup bowl. When he moved closer, he saw a bunch of newly hatched swellfish. Seeing the human shadow, the tiny fish darted about in the porcelain bowl. Some leaped out of the water and got stuck on the milky white sides of the bowl, their pale stomachs shimmering with a lilac sheen in the sunlight.

Then it dawned on him. Just now while he was sleeping, he heard a delicate metallic sound in the house. It was these tiny fish bumping against the bowl.

A few days before, while lying in bed, he'd caught sight of Wenhui's reflection in the mirror from behind; he was amazed that his wife was as beautiful as those women on the calendars.

"In the ditch outside the wall a whole bunch of swellfish hatched."

Wenhui spoke facing the mirror, without realizing that he was looking at her. Nowadays when she was not home, he lay in bed imagining how she waded into the ditch with bare feet and her skirt tucked up to catch the tiny fish.

What did she look like this time last year? The question popped into his head. For a while he could not picture her.

Time went on. He seemed to be awake for the first time after years of sleep. Dark clouds hung low in the afternoon. He smelled the freshly scrubbed mats. Lying there, he felt like he was floating on water. Thunder and lightning struck. Alone in the empty house, he tried to imagine her body.

Recently, especially when Wenhui was not home, he was often stirred by thoughts of her. He had longed for spring. Now that it was here, somehow he always felt drowsy and not fully awake.

"Spring is especially bad for the patient. You must be extra careful," Dr. Cai warned.

Is it spring drowsiness? Wenhui wondered. At dusk the rain stopped. The yard was flooded; the newly sprouted mustard greens stood in muddy water.

"Let's go fishing one of these days," he shouted. The house was quiet, but Wenhui couldn't hear him. She was moving the wet firewood from outside the kitchen.

Tiemin walked into the kitchen and repeated himself loudly.

"Let's go fishing one of these days."

"Sure." She was busy with her hands and replied tersely.

Now she was working harder than ever.

First of all, new life burgeoned in the vegetable patch. The morning frost melted along the eaves as the sun rose. The plot that she'd mulched yesterday still looked glossy and rich. There she stood, hoe in her strong hands, her head tilted up, gazing at the open azure sky. When she gardened, the same rhythm moved her that moved her in the house; it was driven by the will to live a certain kind of life—peaceful, stable, and filled with hope.

After supper, before it got dark, she went out to the vegetable patch again. Standing on the porch, Tiemin couldn't stand it anymore, so he suggested that he do the digging.

But when they stood shoulder to shoulder in the garden patch, she blushed. All of a sudden she could no longer recognize her own voice.

How long had it been since they last stood side by side?

Since they got married, they had seldom talked about anything other than his illness. Now they were standing together again, talking about their vegetable garden.

The orange glow of sunset illumined her coy face.

Summer had arrived.

Throughout the summer they rode the bicycle through the town along the running stream, with the wind kissing their faces in the morning fog. Throughout the summer they often got up early in the morning to go fishing at Emerald Lake.

The sunlight shining on the broken seashells in the windbreak dazzled her eyes.

She stood barefooted on the warm pebbles, holding a parasol to protect her face from the sun.

She watched him wading into the swift current. When he cast the fishing line with a sharp flick, she felt as if her girlhood had returned. Time had traveled full circle and brought them back to their student days.

The other day her mother had come and told her that a relative had returned from the South Pacific, where he said Taiwanese soldiers had been eaten. Standing by the water and looking at his body, she suddenly felt aroused.

A breeze came. She held her straw hat on with one hand.

He waded toward her with bare feet; the big straw hat looked heavy on his newly healthy face.

The tip of the fishing pole bounced in the air with every stride he took. Perspiration dampened his shirt; the smell of his wet leather belt wafted on the wind.

She recalled the way he'd looked as a private. The warm summer sun filled the riverbank. She took the basket from him.

She could feel the fish jumping in the basket she held in her hands. She was still thinking of those Taiwanese soldiers.

3

Tiemin was awakened by Wenhui's footsteps. Turning on his pillow, he saw her tiptoeing toward him with a bowl in her hand.

"What's that?"

"A peddler came by; I bought a bowl of tea oil."

The daylight in the backyard pierced his sleepy eyes. She looked as if she were holding a bowl of sunshine.

March, the month of the bride.

At noon she'd heard a rattling outside, from up the alley. She ran out and opened the gate.

She saw a peddler selling cosmetics. The peddler, carrying a myriad of things, came swaying with a small leather rattle in his hand.

What? Peddlers come to country villages now?

Delighted, she ran inside the house. When she returned, she had a bowl in her hand.

Tiemin looked out the window by the sink while brushing his teeth.

She was combing her just-washed hair in the yard in the sunny afternoon.

As he brushed his teeth, he gazed at her, entranced, through the windowpane, unaware that foam was running from his mouth and down his forearm.

The faucet in the kitchen was left on, waiting for water in the evening. Before water came out, the faucet made a hollow, squeaking sound.

The next day he could still smell the tea oil in the house.

Now she sat on a cushion on the porch outside the open sliding door. She was mending a pair of riding breeches for him. The needle and thread emerged from the fabric and slowly she pulled them up. The thread was long; she lifted her arm all the way to her ear. The fine hair by her ear took on a brownish tint in the sunlight.

In the sunny backyard of early spring, there was still some dust in the air left from beating the bedding in the morning. It was gray everywhere, but it smelled fresh.

The sun was setting. The field beyond the low walls grew quiet. After his recovery, he enjoyed watching her from afar. Each time a new look flashed before him and made him wonder secretly. The person he had seen during his illness seemed completely different.

Now her quiet was touched with sadness. Her newly washed hair, soft and full, wave after wave, casually told a story. He approached her from behind and held her in his arms.

He was still bashful. After his illness he was even more bashful.

The embrace was somewhat forced. He had mustered all his courage to do it.

It was impossible to have no physical impulse. But at the first touch of her skin, another urge immediately replaced desire. The action did not come naturally.

The silent space was like a tablet of a god erected before him. He knew that words of deeply felt gratitude could not possibly come from his lips.

The week before, while he was shaving, he'd seen a patch of bluish stubble on his chin in the small square mirror.

He had an epiphany regarding the silent field outside the house.

He told himself that he would never get sick again.

Wenhui still had the needle and thread in her hand, yet she sensed a newborn strength in his chin clumsily caressing her cheek.

Now with their faces close together, they didn't have a word to say.

Now and then the sound of carp blowing bubbles in the basin could be heard in the kitchen. Tiemin had caught them in the pond on the hill behind the house. She had been feeding them with leftover rice.

When the sun set in the west, they heard the oxen lowing in the distance. It was time for them to go home.

Lately, the only thing on her mind was when to visit her mother. The idea had been with her for some time. Now that the silence at night no longer frightened her and she no longer felt lonely.

After his recovery, quiet afternoons evoked the memory of the whistling train racing away.

Before she graduated from high school, Taipei had been thrown into war. Her mother took her to the seaside of Wuqi at Second Auntie's suggestion.

In her hometown, she was always awakened inside the mosquito net by the chirping cicadas in the summer grove.

After passing under the bamboo poles on which the laundry was hung and going through the pine grove, she would find herself face to face with the sea.

Every morning after breakfast, when the sea was still calm, she ran to the beach.

At noon the sea breeze brought the smell of oysters.

At dusk she became depressed as she leaned against the phoenix tree by the sea and thought of Taipei.

The train stopped at the mouth of the tunnel; the air was heavy with moisture. When she and her mother stepped on the wet platform with bundles in their hands, she could not have known that this place was to become the home that she would miss so badly.

Past the granite ravine, the train entered the tunnel slowly; the sunlight amid the pines in the grove became her first memory of home.

At the train station back home, there was only an old station master who also sold tickets. When the train drew near, he would put on a red-trimmed cap and come out of the station with a kerosene lamp.

The old station master stood at one end of the platform, the red trim of his cap contrasting with his short gray hair as he swung the lamp back and forth to guide the train into the station in the sea fog.

The windows at the station were pasted over with cotton paper strips in beautiful patterns to absorb any shock in the event of a bombing. But the war never came to this place.

In winter fishermen waited on the platform with their baskets full of fish for the northbound train. Always looking relaxed, they chitchatted as they squatted on the platform, white puffs of breath coming out of their mouths.

At night she lay in bed with her mother. Her ear pressed to the pillow, she could not hear the train. Her mother had long since fallen asleep while she still stared at the wall with wide-open eyes, imagining the train taking her back to Brother Min.

By the time the war ended, they had lived in the country for a little over six months. But she could never forget the coast where Third Auntie lived.

Now in her mind the train was still rumbling through the pine grove along the coastline. The whistle in the canyon sometimes rang in her dreams too.

She did not mention any of this to Tiemin; she hadn't had time to tell him.

She could only hold it within her, like a woman who had just become pregnant, full of joy but not willing to share the news yet.

In her memory, home was so far away; she realized that she had matured into a woman.

Now she could wave good-bye to her girlhood with joy. Though life was not without worries, her efforts had been rewarded and had given her courage and confidence. Life made her come to terms with her home, which she did without any hesitation.

She was proud of herself, of her home too. She couldn't remember when she'd become the head of a household.

She was like the train engine rushing ahead, leading life forward.

Yes, the once gravely ill Tiemin needed someone to guide him back to a normal life, she thought.

Every day she guided him in bathing, getting dressed, taking a walk on the hill behind the house, and shopping. Someday she would guide him back to her hometown, like the day before yesterday when she'd taken him to the public bathhouse.

That day she held his hand throughout the trip as if he were a little brother.

There was a water shortage in August. The rationing of tap water had been made even tighter. For days they didn't have water for a bath. By the time water came, she had become quite impatient, so she suggested that they go to a public bathhouse.

But the minute he stepped inside the place, he was baffled because the old doorman asked them if they preferred the public bath or a private bath.

Tiemin fell mute, standing there in a stupor. She answered from behind: "Private bath."

The room was filled with steam, a milky white steam.

There weren't many people even in the public bath, and because it was still early. Behind the wooden partition the splashing sounds were sporadic. The water splashed sharply on the cement floor.

Tiemin felt dizzy as he listened to the splashing. Looking at the numbers on the doors, she helped him find their private bath.

There was no electricity during the day, so the light bulb above the partition between the two private pools was not turned on. The only light in the cramped space came from a tiny window above. She started running the warm water in the bath. Water drops leaped about amid streaks of slanting sunlight.

He took off his clothes, his teeth chattering even though it was August. Before getting into the bath, he rinsed off with a small bucket of water and lathered himself up with soap, because he was afraid he still carried the germs of his illness.

Seeing him squatting on the wooden bench, his body curled up in a ball like a skinny duck, Wenhui said from the bath: "Why don't you come in? It'd be terrible if you caught a cold."

In the small room that had begun to steam up, her voice sounded far away, like an echo in a canyon.

He remained squatting there. Through the steamy white mist he gazed at her in the bath.

The ripples spread in concentric circles as the water poured out of the faucet. They wrinkled her fair skin. The sunlight streamed in at an angle, making her look dazzling.

With no clothes on, she, who was so graceful and capable of running around all day without any rest, looked beautifully fragile.

He pictured how in the winter she folded up the bedding for him, or took it out of the closet and then put it back. She lifted the folded quilt, which resembled a little mountain, with all her strength until it blocked her face.

In spring she lifted the bedding again, and took it out to the backyard to air on a bamboo pole.

The water was still running. Steam filled the room; in the bath, she was concealed by the misty vapor.

He smelled the scent from the wood soaked in soapy water.

All of a sudden he felt her gaze upon him.

The air in the room was lit up instantly. He became frightened as if he had just awakened. His beating heart rendered him too weak to lift the bucket of water.

Her gaze touched him through the steamy mist.

He evaded her eyes. In the birch wood floor under his feet he could see the wood grain curved and made conspicuous by the hot water. It had a glossy sheen.

With both elbows on the rim of the bath, she seemed on the verge of being poured out of it.

"Are you still not coming in?"

Her voice reached the other side of the canyon. He shivered.

He was shaking. He raised the bucket to his shoulder, but it slipped and bounced against the bench. The sound of wood bumping wood was dull, but it made him feel secure.

Still squatting on the bench, he did not pick up the bucket. For a moment he was stunned.

Then, maintaining his bathing posture, he moved closer to her.

From the edge of the pool, he embraced her. Holding her weight, he felt weak in the knees. His chest was burning as if he were getting sick again. Embraced tightly in her arms, he felt like coughing.

Was his blood surging up again? he wondered.

The next moment a dark stone in his chest split open from top to bottom.

He held her with greater warmth. He was entirely submerged in the pleasure of the water.

His face was still turned away from hers. His lips were closed tightly, for fear lest the germs would fly out of his mouth.

Seeing all this, she understood.

Seeing his clumsy, childlike movement after his illness, she held him tightly.

At last, as if choked by the steam, she stammered as she embraced him: "I'm so glad the war is over."

The sky was so blue, without so much as a wisp of cloud to be seen.

With both feet swollen from the hot water, Tiemin staggered like a drunk. He couldn't even put his *geta* back on. Walking on the cobbled road home, she had to carry the bucket with one hand and help him along with the other as if she were helping a little brother.

At night Wenhui made him drink some wine.

At dinnertime the twilight lingered over the rice paddies.

He was tipsy after only a few sips. Supporting his head with a hand, lying on the *tatami*, he watched the sun set behind the low walls.

The trees started swaying in the evening breeze. Soon the shadows danced on the *tatami*.

Now it was completely dark. The power went out as usual.

She lit a candle. As she watched him lying there on the *tatami* by the table, she drank alone.

It was a habit that she had acquired after he became seriously ill. It was in the second year of their marriage that she started drinking alone at night.

At first, when disinfecting the utensils in the house, she would inhale the alcohol in the air and feel the fatigue melt away. After a while it became a way of lifting her spirits.

At night, after he had gone to sleep and before closing the wooden shutters, she enjoyed sitting on the porch for a break. She would rest her sore feet on the cement steps, listening to the frogs croaking in the field as she drank alone.

The first time she saw him coughing up blood by the sink, she almost passed out. Later she washed away that horrible image with wine.

Remembering all that as the night closed in on her, she felt lonely and scared. Sometimes she almost went crazy. There was nothing left and nothing to hold onto. The sky after Retrocession, the clouds, the streets, and her mother—all left her one by one in her midnight intoxication.

Until finally, only she was left. She couldn't even hold onto her husband; he was leaving her to die at any time.

She fell asleep with a heavy head from the wine. She thought about nothing, she couldn't think. Everything was temporarily put off until tomorrow. She enjoyed being tipsy and letting that cloud float before her eyes. Things looked brighter that way.

Just like now. Tiemin was lying on the *tatami* in front of her as if he were floating on water. By candlelight his face was so handsome, like that of a high school student. Her mother used to say that he looked so young.

"He's like your little brother."

He turned around and got up, then came back to the table.

Suddenly she recalled the time when he was wearing the uniform of the Taipei First Boys' High School.

Tiemin was the one who was drunk. He couldn't hold his drink at all. He was still dizzy from the few sips he had just had.

He sat up abruptly. The moment he picked up the chopsticks, he was dazed. His chopsticks froze in midair; a light flashed before him. The candle flame on the table flickered; his heart leaped up.

He's drunk, she said to herself.

He shivered and hiccupped.

From the other side of the table he stared at his wife and found her a stranger. It was as if the woman sitting across from him were someone else. The flame of the white candle flickered in the night breeze, casting light all over her.

In the middle of her blouse was a row of tiny mother-of-pearl buttons. The silvery buttons gleamed in the candlelight. The familiar calico dress looked exotic tonight. It moved up and down with each breath she took, which reminded him of the pond of water lilies on the other side of the hill behind the house.

The buds in the pond reached straight up toward the sky, supporting a fullness on the brink of bursting.

His gaze made her sober.

When the two lay down inside the mosquito net, she was wide awake just like during the day.

Time had reversed itself in him. He had to start all over; he was too much of a child. This morning in the bathhouse when he raised the bucket with both hands, two rows of ribs protruded; the sight almost made her cry.

His illness had almost destroyed him. Even his body looked like that of an immature adolescent.

Thinking this way, she held him as her tears fell unseen.

He felt the jade bracelet on her wrist, felt its coolness.

At the wedding banquet the dim candlelight had made the bracelet look dark green. He put it on her wrist in front of the relatives.

That day Wenhui's mother intentionally put a bar of scented soap that she had bought before the war into a celluloid box. When the groom put the bracelet on the bride's wrist, she stood up to rub some soap on the back of her daughter's hand.

Her mother made her hand slippery before she handed it to the groom.

Yet the bracelet was too small. Even with her mother's help, it still would not slide on.

The bride was doing her best to hold her fingers tightly together, but the bracelet got stuck on her knuckles and was hurting her.

With the relatives watching, he was embarrassed. His hand no longer listened to his command; he had to push the bracelet down.

The bride didn't cry out. Ever so graceful, she stretched out her hand for the groom and welcomed the bracelet that was halfway down.

At that moment, how grateful he was to her!

Refined and understanding, she extended her hand and happily accepted his gift. The jade bracelet had an old-fashioned design, which didn't fit the young bride. Yet it was the only token of matrimony that he could afford after the war.

He still remembered that night at the banquet; by the time he finally succeeded in getting the bracelet on over her wrist, he was all sweaty.

For a while after they got married, she would lift her hand to admire the jade bracelet that had become part of her body.

Now he lay inside the mosquito net, his body on fire. Still a bit drunk, he was lost in his memories as he caressed the bracelet.

Soon the bracelet was warm; only she was cool. When he clung to her, it felt as if he were lying in a pool of water.

Lying there, she too mused, but her thoughts were drifting elsewhere. She uttered a cry for no reason, as if awakened from a dream.

At once silence fell; everything had come to a halt.

The alley had fallen asleep at midnight. When one listened closely, there was nothing but dead silence.

She startled herself when she cried out: "No, it can't be!" She found him on top of her.

When she regained consciousness, the dark bedroom looked bright as if lit.

She moved out from under him and, turning toward him, said, "Let's wait a little longer." She held him lovingly. "You must get well first."

Concern spilled out of the tiny space inside the net. Her heart was full like the sea, enveloping not only him but herself as well. When she embraced him, she heard the wind in the pines in her hometown.

The sun set at the other end of the sea. The wind from the sea always soughed through the pine grove. When it subsided at night, the cicadas started chirping.

Then the lonely heart of a young woman made many wishes as grand as the sea under the darkening sky.

When she told him he had to get well first, she was also speaking for herself.

She was stalling. She was aware of this all the time, but she was willing to accept it.

During those days and nights when he was ill, what grieved her was her helplessness, about the futility of time passing.

How could she, who had become a wife, not wish to build a healthy, normal life, to freely expand her horizons? But the resolution to survive destruction was firmly made in those days of caring for him. It had become her will, a part of her body.

Now as she lay inside the mosquito net, she wanted to tell him a million things. Yet she knew there was an unspoken understanding between them. It was the quietest moment, a moment that did not require a single word.

Just like now, her heart was calm like the sea in the morning light in her hometown.

For a while she wondered if the first step of guiding him along the road of convalescence would be to take him to Wuqi to see her hometown.

After the devastating illness, he was listless, and perhaps she needed to lead him to run toward the sea together, to let the strong sea wind wake him up from his stupor.

4

They did not go to Wuqi. They went instead to Dr. Cai's house.

But Wenhui felt like they were going to the sea when she led Tiemin out the door. The rickshaw ran swiftly on the rainy street; its oilcloth curtain emitted a pungent odor that made them cough. They swayed along throughout the ride. The December rain hit the canvas top like beads of oil leaping in a frying pan.

It was his first outing after his illness. Furthermore, it was a rainy day. Tiemin looked nervous and mortified, and opened the curtain frequently to peek out.

Outside, the wind cut like a knife, trying to get in. His hand, though it had long lain in hers, was still cold and sweaty.

"So there are no more human-powered rickshaws anymore?"

"They are long gone," she said. "While you were sick, they switched to motorized ones."

"I can't believe there are no more to be found!"

After a while he ran out of things to say. In the rain he reminisced about the wonderful old rickshaws. He sighed as he remembered them.

"I became ill a long time ago."

The darkening rain outside the curtain came in gusts; raindrops fell densely on the canvas. The power lines on the street sagged as if they were about to break.

The night before the winter solstice Dr. Cai had sent them an invitation to view his flowers. He said that friends from the mainland had given him an old potted plum tree. Though not yet in bloom, it already filled the air with a subtle fragrance.

"You are invited to have dinner at my home. I'd like to introduce you to some friends from the mainland. It's also a celebration for Tiemin's recovery."

When winter arrived, she could not go fishing and didn't know what to do. As she read the doctor's note, a smile blossomed on her face despite the bitter, incessant rain.

The rickshaw entered the downtown area. Flashing neon lights rendered the giant colorful movie posters visible in the misty rain. *Arabian Nights, Robin Hood, Feud of Blood.* . . . Swords and arrows flashed on the buildings. It was the first time Tiemin had gone out since the war. Hiding behind the curtain, he was tongue-tied as if he were entering another world.

Her mother said that roasted chestnuts were again available on the streets.

When they passed by the Great World Theater, she told the driver to make a detour and bought a bag in front of the theater. It was still warm.

"I hear chestnuts come all the way from Tianjin."

She opened the bag made of newspaper. The aroma of caramel from prewar times scented the air. The rickshaw jolted along as they peeled the chestnuts in the dark. Wasn't it like this when she went to the movies with him during her high school days?

Looking back, it felt like another lifetime. She did not expect him to be so sick. During his illness she was always busy and did not feel time passing. Now that he had survived, those days of the past were bundled up like a stack of old books, but she had long since forgotten whence they came.

Tiemin's spirits were revived after returning from Dr. Cai's party.

More than that, he was like a new man.

Throughout the winter they spent a lot of time at Dr. Cai's place. At first they went together. Later, when Tiemin could go out alone, she stayed home and let him go by himself. Every time he came home, there was so much to talk about. His chest was filled with words to overflowing. Seeing him like that, she was secretly pleased. Sitting quietly, she listened to his nonstop talking. Once in a while she interjected: "You are turning into a public speaker!"

Loquacious, he talked about the mainland. He talked about the Golden Sand River, the Northwest, the Tarim River . . . Qaidam Basin, Taklimakan Desert, Qinghai, Lhasa, Turfan. . . .

Strange names spilled from his lips, unfamiliar, exotic, lovely names. When she heard them, she conjured up a beautiful picture that only existed in dreams.

"Wow!"

The first time she saw the Manchurian gown, delicately trimmed and bright-colored, at Dr. Cai's house, she couldn't help exclaiming in her heart. *Isn't this an image from a dream?*

The fire was burning bright, dried mullet eggs were being roasted, the aroma of Pacific herring filled the living room.

They sat with new acquaintances around the fire.

It was getting late. Everyone was drinking and high-spirited. The initial awkwardness was gone; now they were talking freely on every imaginable topic. But none of the conversation found its way into Wenhui's ears.

She was captivated by the beautiful Manchurian gown. Against the charcoal fire, the dark velvet shimmered. It was the first time that the Taiwan-born Wenhui had seen this style of clothing.

A young woman whom she called Sister Yang was wearing the gown. Dr. Cai had just introduced them.

Since she entered the room, Wenhui had not taken her eyes off of beautiful Sister Yang.

She enjoyed watching her sitting casually and listening to her voice. When she moved, her gown revealed a dove-colored lining. The rain outside was coming down harder, falling noisily on the roof. Inside the house Sister Yang's voice was relaxed and carefree, making the sound of rain retreat into the distance.

In the living room only her voice was heard. Wenhui felt happy, like walking barefooted into Emerald Lake. Her heart opened.

The more she listened, the more she was amazed. She had never met a woman who could speak so eloquently. Everyone was listening attentively.

Sister Yang looked in her direction many times, expressing affection. She also changed her seat to sit by Wenhui. The two women chatted.

On her way home Wenhui was glad that she had found an older sister. It was the first time that she had met so many strangers. But, thanks to Sister Yang, she quickly overcame her awkwardness.

"We are all Chinese!"

Those were the words Tiemin had learned at Dr. Cai's gatherings. At home he told her what his friends had said.

When winter passed and spring came around, the sunny sky could be seen beyond the bamboo grove. Sister Yang's Manchurian gown still flashed before Wenhui's eyes, still glittered. *Yes, the gown is Chinese too!* she said to herself.

Flipping through magazines, Wenhui sometimes saw boas of purple wool or silver fox, numerous types of trim as well as sequined collars for Manchurian gowns. In the chilly twilight the beautiful pictures reminded her even more of that warm, ancient land.

As a child she'd seen pictures of her grandparents dressed in lavishly trimmed Manchurian gowns in the family albums. But what age did they belong to?

The December rain was drizzling. Sometimes the conversation in the living room paused; water dripped from the tiled eaves. Dr. Cai's home was a spacious yet simple Japanese-style house. When Wenhui had first entered the house through the shuttered doors that led to the clinic on the other side, she was surprised to see the brightly lit living room. She did not expect the room behind the partition to be so spacious. When one entered the alley, the sign DR. CAI'S CLINIC loomed large on the roof, making the house look much smaller.

Dr. Cai was fond of flowers. Returning from the clinic every day, he worked in his garden. That day Dr. Cai wore a Chinese scholar's gown, not his usual Western attire. He looked handsome and gentle. The long dark-brown gown contrasted sharply with the gray hair at his temples, looking like two wisps of cloud. When he walked, the bottom of his gown leaped up like waves on a rocky shore.

She had not experienced Dr. Cai's hospitality before. He was so energetic, as if wanting to convince people that playing host was his real specialty. He led the guests under the eaves that jutted into the garden, pointing here and there, never losing patience as he talked about his favorite flowers and plants. A fruit tree with thin-skinned fruit on branches growing skyward stood amid the greenery by the wall. He said that the tree had almost cost him his life. It was a green persimmon, which yielded an abundance of fruit every year. But if the plucked fruit were put into a rice jug, no matter how long it was kept there, it would not ripen. Green persimmons were astringent and tasted awful. He wondered if he should . . .

When it came to plants, the doctor could not stop talking once he started, just the same as with Tolstoyism. He was enthusiastic and wholly attentive. As he went on, his voice became hoarse.

"This year the Siberian cold front came early," the doctor's letter said. "Dried mullet eggs are already on the market. My friends from Shanghai have long heard about dried mullet eggs but have never tasted them."

Tonight the doctor wanted to treat his guests to the island specialty. The sound and aroma of dried mullet eggs roasting on the grill filled the room. Holding cups of wine, they talked about the war on the mainland. They also talked about the recent February 28th Incident, the imposition of martial law in Taiwan, and the Three People's Principles, among other subjects. Soon the topic of conversation shifted to current news: illegal deforestation. Whatever subject came to mind, they discussed it with gusto. The high spirits in the living room overcame the drizzling rain outside. Wenhui got up from the *tatami*; the charcoal fire was too warm.

She left Tiemin and the others who were sitting in a circle. With a warm glow of contentment, she got up to go out for some air. Outside the sliding door the rain had subsided. She was welcomed by an unexpected, delicate fragrance.

She walked up to the plum in the *tokoma*.

There was a bright light above the niche, like a full moon shining on a valley. The moonlight caressed the demure pot. The niche was a world unto itself; though it was adjacent to the living room, it was detached from the clamor within.

The first time she had seen the plant, she'd only thought it was beautiful. Now that she saw it again, she appreciated it more. Earlier one of the friends from Shanghai was saying that this was a rare species. The branches were aged and bony, gnarled and dry. But there were numerous buds on them, each waiting to open. When one got closer, one could smell the exquisite perfume.

"It's sending forth fragrance already."

The connoisseur said that it boasted the best blooms.

"With this kind of flower, it is best before it opens completely. When it's in full bloom, it's not as interesting."

She didn't realize that people from the mainland knew so much about flowers. In comparison, she was ignorant like some hick provincial.

The first time she saw the plum flower, she felt that it could relate to humans. As if trying to please the viewer, it displayed a rich array of blossoms, the red petals in sharp relief against the white wall.

Yet, though the blossoms were abundant, on closer inspection they were shy. It was reserved in its own way.

"In the midst of mist and cloud lies the essence. Such is the wonder of the red plum."

Now that she had learned more about it, she appreciated it more. It was fitting that it came from that delicate land.

Facing the flower, Wenhui thought of Mr. Sara for no reason.

The old man lived alone in Hokkaido. It must be shrouded in snow, all the trees dead.

A few years back, at a gathering for the magazine staff, Wenhui had found out that Mr. Sara was also a connoisseur of dried mullet eggs. He had learned to prepare them the Taiwanese way: first you poked the slices many times with a needle, then dipped them in wine. When they were on the grill, one mustn't forget to put slices of scallion on them. He said that the scallion added a pungent flavor, which always reminded him of the unbending mainland temperament. It had an earthier flavor than Japanese mustard.

That time at Mr. Sara's place, dried mullet eggs were being roasted over the fire too. It was also a rainy winter night; in the midst of the sound of rain they were also talking about politics.

At that time Taipei was celebrating the seventh anniversary of the Taiwan Colonization Society as announced by the Governor-General's Office.

"Even at the Taipei Imperial University there appear red . . ."

It was first brought up by Mr. Sara.

"Who would expect it to exist at the core of the military, in the South Pacific Historical Research Institute? Ha, ha!"

Wenhui did not care for dried mullet eggs; perhaps she had lost the taste for them back then. When they were talking about how the Japanese military police were after the underground red elements, she had a fishy taste in her mouth, making her nauseated. She rushed to the lavatory.

The following year when the Kushiro current arrived, she did not forget to ask her Third Aunt to send her some premium-quality dried mullet eggs for Mr. Sara. Yet before they arrived, he had been dismissed and left Taiwan.

A few months ago, she had received a long letter from Mr. Sara through indirect channels. It was a late blessing. The old man heard about their marriage only recently.

"I regret that I was unable to attend your wedding," said the letter.

When Mr. Sara mentioned the White Birch School, which cooperated with the Japanese military, he was full of reproach, describing those writers as "advocating Tolstoyism in words, yet in deeds betraying Mr. Tolstoy."

The letter also said that Mushanokoji had been declared a war criminal and stripped of his civil title; he had also resigned from the House of Peers.

Finally, the old man calmly mentioned that his son had died in Manchuria in the last month of the war.

"As a citizen too weak to protest, I feel my son's death may perhaps alleviate the pain of guilt. . . . But when I think of my son whose life ended so early, amid the drifting snow in a barren land, despondency arises in this dying old man."

As Wenhui sat there musing before the fragrant flowers, she decided that one of these days she would try to send the old man some dried mullet eggs.

"Chinese women!"

When she got back to the fireplace and saw Sister Yang again, she recalled Mr. Sara's comment about Chinese women: "They always carry the grace of the continent as they walk elegantly in a crowd."

Sister Yang was sitting by the fire, talking casually about the days of being a student refugee. The fire illuminated her slightly intoxicated face, beautiful as a summer's day.

Wenhui seemed to witness the catastrophe on the mainland unfold before her very eyes.

It spread from northern to central China, from central China to the southwest, then all over the land south of the Yangtze River.

Bandits, locusts, Japanese soldiers. . . . Famine, drought, civil war. The beautiful land had been ravaged.

The more she listened, the more shocked she was. She could not imagine that such a hard life could produce someone like Sister Yang.

"The Chinese people are the children of rivers. They live by the river, run along the river, even when they die they want to die by the river."

Sister Yang seemed to choke on something.

Silence filled the living room.

"That land . . . belongs to us all."

These words made everyone reflect.

The next moment it was silence again.

Sister Yang turned her gaze toward Wenhui, which made her uneasy. "Wenhui, do you think the land belongs to us?" Sister Yang asked gently, changing her tone.

"It's yours, it's mine too. It's ours."

The air was stuffy and filled with smoke. Wenhui was stunned. When her eyes met Sister Yang's, she looked away as if burned.

She had never thought that way. The mainland was a beautiful land in her dreams. She had never thought about whose it was....

Yes, it is ours; it belongs to the Chinese people. But in what way is it ours? She had never thought about it. Now that Sister Yang asked her, she was confused. Indeed, it was an issue, she thought.

In the smoke and heady aroma filling the living room, she felt ashamed of her ignorance. Before the older woman, she was reduced to a schoolgirl, unable to speak before her teacher.

Sister Yang smiled knowingly and changed the topic. The living room became lively again. She was grateful to Sister Yang for coming to her rescue in time.

Graceful, mature, beautiful, and understanding, Sister Yang was the perfect woman for her at this moment.

Wenhui did not drink any wine that evening, yet on her way home she was drunk, intoxicated by Sister Yang.

Several months later, when Sister Yang unexpectedly showed up at her house, Wenhui was intoxicated once again.

The glass door at the vestibule slid open; the summer breeze wafted in from the yard. There she stood, alone at the entrance. She smiled with her head tilted to one side. The noon sun filled the alley.

When Wenhui answered the door, Sister Yang opened her mouth slightly and greeted her silently as if greeting an old friend.

She did not expect Sister Yang to come by herself.

She had not yet recovered from her awkwardness when Sister Yang apparently read her mind from the doorway. She appeared relaxed, as if a splendid landscape painting scroll were slowly unfolding before Wenhui's eyes.

It was Sister Yang who was welcoming Wenhui.

Facing the graceful woman, Wenhui was momentarily stunned. It was as if her hands and feet were bound.

Today Sister Yang was wearing a faded blue blouse. Coming in from the sunlight, she brought a lulling lake into the vestibule.

Wenhui was airing Tiemin's old books in the backyard. One by one she was laying them out in the corridor. The damp, moldy smell still lingered in the air.

Sister Yang stood there in the vestibule. When asked to come in, she said:

"I don't have time today. I'll drop by some other time."

When she spoke, she looked so at ease. Wenhui, who had grown up accustomed to Japanese women, momentarily felt that they looked so pitiful, as though they were walking in thin clothes on a chilly autumn evening.

That day at Dr. Cai's place she had been dazzled by Sister Yang's Manchurian gown. She'd heard her say that it was an old garment she had dug out of her trunk.

"The pattern is outdated. But I have to wear it in cold weather. I have no choice."

Leaving the doctor's house at midnight, Sister Yang put on a silver silk scarf at the door. She said that no one would see it in the dark; otherwise she would become a laughingstock. "This stuff is out of fashion. But when you are a refugee, you put on anything you have as long as it keeps you warm."

For Wenhui, though it was out of fashion and out of season, it looked so appropriate, so free, and so handsome on Sister Yang.

They stood in front of Dr. Cai's house saying good-bye. The rain had stopped. It was chilly. A gust of wind snatched away Sister Yang's silk scarf; she almost failed to catch it, which made everyone laugh with delight. In the dark the scarf resembled a white egret soaring high above the fields.

She didn't have the scarf on today. Her slender neck was exposed above her low collar; Wenhui felt close to her.

"Can I borrow Tiemin for a while?"

In the vestibule Sister Yang was still standing there gracefully. Tilting her head, she asked half-jokingly.

The question embarrassed Wenhui.

The white, dazzling sunlight flashed before her eyes in innumerable tiny sparks.

She watched Tiemin and Sister Yang leave together till they disappeared into the fir trees at the mouth of the alley.

She felt disappointed. She was so ignorant and shallow. Compared with Sister Yang, she was just a little country housewife.

So as to hang out with their new friends, Tiemin practiced speaking Mandarin with the radio every morning. Taiwan had been returned to China; the Japanese era was over. She too would have to learn all over again.

"I have to make up for those empty days when I was sick," he often said. She also had to catch up. Wasn't Sister Yang a good role model? She could learn too.

Now when he came home, he looked absentminded and had few words to say to her. He was listless, brooding.

One day he suddenly said, "I can't go on this way any longer." Meaning that he didn't want go on idling his days away doing nothing.

"Let's lease the shop on the street. What do you say? We can run a book rental store." The idea must have been on his mind for some time. Now that he said it, his mind must have been made up.

At night he was busy reading Chinese books. To practice his writing he also took notes in Chinese. Though he had only spent a short time with their mainland friends, he had already made a great deal of progress in Mandarin.

"Soon I'll be able to write in Chinese."

Sometimes he came home with a steel stencil board, on which he wrote at night.

Wenhui lay inside the mosquito net. At midnight she could still hear the scratching of the stencil pen on the board. *Saasaasaa* . . . it never stopped. The promise of happiness flew by in her sleep. The sound of the stencil pen was like a lullaby coming from the study and lingering inside the net.

It was late at night. She could hear crickets chirping in the kitchen. Life had finally settled down.

Thanks to those good friends to whom Dr. Cai had introduced them, the book rental store was opened. Their life would no longer be lonely. Their friends started coming to their place. Besides Sister Yang, others came too. They became fast friends at first sight. They played chess and talked. After a while they were invited to stay for dinner.

All of a sudden, the lonely country life was transformed into a life of glamour. Happiness, so much of it, came so fast, like waves on the sea, she could hardly catch her breath.

After a while, their friends became busy. Everyone seemed to have endless amounts of work to do. When they came, they no longer stayed long. On the contrary, Tiemin spent more and more time away from home with them.

On a long summer afternoon she sat alone in the backyard for some air. It occurred to her that she didn't really know those friends as well as she thought.

Now when they dropped by, they left with Tiemin even before finishing a cup of tea.

She still went to Dr. Cai's house once in a while, but when they talked they got so serious, and she could not understand them. Before she knew it, she was left out. She could not even put in a single word. Once she got so fed up with everything that she left Tiemin to visit her mother. They didn't even ask her to stay. Dr. Cai saw her to the door with just a perfunctory gesture.

The next morning Tiemin got dressed and poked his head in the kitchen and said, "I have some business to take care of. I'm going out." He turned around and left as soon as he had spoken.

The house was empty and quiet.

She was distraught. She squatted by the ditch outside the kitchen, plucking the feathers of a duck with tweezers, thinking that the sweet rice mixed with duck blood was almost done, that he could have it after he finished his Mandarin lesson on the radio.

Yesterday, her mother had given her a duck she had raised and told her to save the blood for Tiemin.

Who could have known that he would get so worked up? When she went back into the house after washing her hands, he was long gone.

There were stacks of used books purchased recently, waiting to be catalogued.

At night he was back, but his heart was not. When she asked him questions, he was absentminded and didn't seem to hear her. Before falling asleep, he lay alone inside the mosquito net, smoking, staring at the ceiling with wide-open eyes.

"If they use explosives again, sooner or later the gold carp in Emerald Lake will be gone." Suddenly he protested, without any explanation. She wondered where he had heard about that.

Sometimes he stood outside the low walls by himself, looking at the twilight sky. Then he turned around and looked depressed. Coming under the eaves, he complained, "The egrets on the hill behind the house will disappear too."

"How can that be?"

"How can that *not* be?"

It was as if he was angry with someone: "If they keep on hunting without restraint . . ."

Dr. Cai was right after all. Since his recovery Tiemin had turned into a hopping cricket. His mind bounced here and there, not standing still for a moment. When she asked him who "they" was, he turned silent. She was worried about his health again.

Now he went out early and came back late almost every day. The store became her responsibility.

When she was not at the store, she was at home alone.

She had nothing to do except look at the sky over the low walls. She remembered an evening several months before and felt like it was ages ago. That day a flock of egrets flew over their house.

They happened to be standing under the eaves and saw the white birds returning to their nests.

"They look like a squadron of fighter planes."

The first day Taipei was bombed by fighter planes, she was at the hilltop zoo with Tiemin. The siren went off. She was astounded, seeing the pedestrians fleeing in all directions and the buses taking cover under the palm trees. Everything fell silent. They stood mortified in front of the glass window of the specimen hall. The lions, tigers, and baboons had all been electrocuted and made into specimens. A while back they had heard that with the imminent war, all the wild animals in the zoo would be electrocuted so that they would not escape after the bombing and hurt people. At the time she didn't really believe it. But it was true that the animals were all preserved as specimens.

They heard a flapping sound overhead; it was the birds flying by, over Xindian Stream on their way back to the hill. The stream flowed slowly toward the setting sun, coming to a halt at the windbreak and disappearing among dense evergreens. Before dark, egret cries came from the grove on the hill behind their house.

"Time to lay eggs," Tiemin said.

After the crying stopped, silence was restored in the paddies in early summer. Soon they could see baby egrets taking flight from the grove.

After dinner they used to walk along the low walls, around the palm trees, into the delicate twilight air till they reached the field by the stream.

Except for a few oxen lowing in the distance, it was quiet in the twilight field. They stood in the open field watching the sun set in silence. Their hearts were transparent; there was no need for words.

Not long ago, she'd gladly seen him out the door.

Before he turned onto the main street, he would stop at the mouth of the alley and, turning, raise his arm, skinny like the egret's leg, and wave at her.

He meant good-bye.

After his recovery, she lived more seriously. At the produce stand in the market she bent down to select vegetables. She was so serious that she cried for no reason other than for life itself.

In winter, warm blood coursed through her body. She carried a bucket into the yard and sloshed water into the chicken coop, which she then swept out with a bamboo broom. The dirty water, mud, specks of charcoal, lint, the water dripping under the eaves, and splashed oil from the frying pan all fell on her. But the pity, worry, and anxiety of the old days had been transformed into a passion. Evenings she stood under the eaves as the wind soughed among the tree branches and leaves.

She wanted to welcome the coming days and nights even more heartily.

The hope of early summer tiptoed on the *tatami*. Tiemin still enjoyed admiring her from behind, just as when he was sick. Without turning around she felt the weight of his gaze on her back.

When she felt uneasy, she stood up and hurried into the kitchen, leaving her brisk footsteps behind. That she could act in such a way startled even herself. If there was something in the kitchen, such as a bowl of hot innards soup, she would carry it out carefully.

Now he was not home much. So she raised a brood of chicks to while away the time. She also started crying during the day.

Spring arrived. The moment she cried she ran into the yard. When she came back in, she had an armful of wildflowers that had grown by the ditch.

She put the flowers in a silver vase, looking at them from this angle and that.

It was windy after the rain. The firewood under the eaves was damp and could not be kindled no matter how much she fanned it. The suffocating smoke brought tears to her eyes.

Since Tiemin was not home, it was pointless to cook dinner. There was no fire in the stove. The rice pot on the stove was wet and cold. Frustrated, she could no longer hold back her tears and let them fall as they pleased. She had a good cry in the heavy smoke.

Not so long ago she'd seen happiness. Now in an instant it had vanished, like the smoke, gone.

Happiness was written all over his face when he came home. The setting sun at the mouth of the alley gave his face a healthy glow.

Every day now he was in a hurry. He left early in the morning and came home late, ignoring her completely.

With him away, she was alone in the empty house. She felt tired; all her hopes were gone.

He had a trunk of books locked up by the desk. He told her not to touch it. Alone at home, her curiosity was aroused.

What was locked inside? He wouldn't even tell her.

There was a space in her husband's heart where even she was not allowed in. Displeased, she felt wronged.

During his illness, she had been familiar even with the dirt behind his ears. Now a secret stood between them. She remembered the time when he had a rash: the February 28th Incident was raging outside; inside her husband was struggling between life and death. Her dreams were in pieces. One night as she watched his pale, sickly body, she became so grief-stricken that she forgot to wash his rash and just allowed her teardrops to fall on his naked body one after another.

She knew every one of his bones, every inch of his skin. Even now, with her eyes closed, she could find the two vermilion birthmarks on his groin. Yet at the mention of the locked trunk, his long, unruly hair stood up.

In time the area that she could not verbalize expanded. She even felt that in the blink of an eye they had become strangers.

Back in their school days, they'd been to see the circus from Tokyo. After the show it was already dark. A shower brought the two who had not known each other long together under an umbrella. Raindrops were falling pitter-patter on her satin umbrella.

They could not find anything to say for a while, and just listened to the rain on the umbrella. They were like the umbrella, tense in the shower, unable to say a word.

But the sun came out. Under the apricot umbrella they looked into each other's hearts and smiled.

The locked chest was like the dark cloud hovering over her girlhood. But when the night came and she felt his warmth under the quilt, the painful suspicion dissolved and she forgot all about it.

Sometimes she blamed her own narrow-mindedness and held him with even more affection. Now that her husband was busy all day long, at night he fell asleep the minute he crawled inside the mosquito net.

Late at night his snoring lingered. She remembered the time when they rode the narrow-gauge train, listening to the wind in the red cypresses on Mount Ali. The feeling of satisfaction returned in the darkness. The caresses from the past came alive before her eyes. A comforting sweetness permeated her whole body.

By and by she realized that perhaps life was meant to be lonely.

Nowadays she often spent her time quietly in the empty house.

When she was bored, she turned her eyes to the corner where the bedding was laid out and recalled those days and nights when he was bedridden.

He was a little bird she had hatched. She raised him day by day; then suddenly he was fully grown and flew away, never to return.

Daydreaming this way, she laughed at herself in the midst of her misery. When it began to get dark, she turned on all the lights in the house.

During the day she opened all the sliding doors to let the sun in. It made her feel a little more settled.

She sat down and looked absentmindedly at the palm trees and thought of the lady who had owned the house previously.

Before the news of her husband's death reached her, the widow of the Japanese cavalry lieutenant colonel showed much hospitality by taking Wenhui and her mother on a tour of the house. Her slender figure skipped briskly about the stepping-stones in the yard.

Now Wenhui understood why the Japanese called those irregular-shaped stepping-stones "flying stones."

The moon was shining on the flying stones with a deep blue glow. The stones were arranged neatly one by one, all the way to the gate. She seemed to see the widow's white socks skipping from one stone to the next, slowly into the dark.

The first time she saw the paddies was on a summer evening. She almost jumped with joy. A pastoral married life had unfolded before her eyes.

When she focused on the dense Chinese fan palms, they looked as they had when she'd first seen them, glistening dark green, standing in the twilight amid the sound of buzzing cicadas.

The moon rose behind the barracks in the distance.

The halo of the moon slowly widened, shining on the vegetables that had grown stout.

With the nightly bugle call, loneliness surrounded the field, the house, and her, sitting in the house alone, day after day.

She had fallen in love with the bugle call from the barracks.

Even during the day, its magnanimous notes drifted across the clear sky sounding lonely and sad.

Maybe life is meant to be lonely, she reminded herself.

5

Shortly after the Dragon Boat Festival, her mother brought a basket of sacrificial food from Dadaocheng.

Wenhui could not eat any. For a while now she had had no appetite. The thought of food made her nauseated.

"Are you pregnant?" her mother asked, smiling.

For days on end she sat in a daze before the mirror, which she kept covered with a piece of cloth. She bit her lips tightly as she stared blankly. How little her mother understood her!

When she woke up at night, she wanted to have a good cry. In the late autumn night she felt so cold that she couldn't sleep. Neither would she get up to put on some clothes or add a quilt. She just let herself lie there in the cold. The next day she felt numb like a stone.

To care for Brother Min all her life was what she had wanted all along. She did not forget that wish once she made it. Yet the fact that they still led a life of celibacy made her begin to have doubts.

A while back she was concerned that he had not fully recovered. It seemed that he was well now, but he spent all his time outside. Sometimes he came home in the middle of the night.

After she'd nursed him back to health, he was abandoning her.

Is that what it was? Was it that simple?

The carp they caught in the pond on the hill behind the house were still in the basin. They were her only companions these days.

She had been feeding them with leftovers for a year. Once in a while she fished them out and noticed that they were three fingers wide.

Last summer on the dinner table there were always deep-fried minnows. Tiemin liked the bitter taste of fish gall bladder. He could swallow a whole fish in one bite.

Even those days after his recovery when they went fishing in Emerald Lake had become a beautiful memory, never to come again.

Her mother had strongly opposed the idea of their going fishing. "He's not well yet. He shouldn't get wet."

Her mother was worried that he'd catch cold. He loved mung bean pastry. Dr. Cai said that he could have as much as he desired. But her mother said that mung beans were cooling by nature, and were especially bad for tuberculosis patients.

With bare feet and trousers rolled up high, Tiemin stepped into the cold lake. For a second she was worried that fishing would be bad for him.

But summer passed by peacefully. They had so much fun that often they didn't want to get out of the water.

After they had fished for a while, she learned how to find minnows on the riverbed before the sun reached its zenith.

When the sunlight was refracted through the water, the shadows of the fish were visible on the riverbed. The quivering brown shadows indicated that the fish were perfectly still in the water and could be seen ahead of their shadows, their backs a glistening green. When disturbed, they darted swiftly through the water, not to be seen again.

As she stood on the bank, she could see his toes clutching the pebbles like suction disks.

The current below the surface was swift. When he waded with bare feet, his skinny body was almost swept away. He took a few steps back, shaking a little.

At a distance the silver bellies of the fish flashed above the pebbles in the current.

He cast his fishing line from over his shoulder with a swish. The pole arched like a rainbow, the fishing line hurled in a straight line through the air.

She couldn't take it anymore. She waded into the water barefooted with her parasol. A cold shiver crept up from the soles of her feet.

He was walking ever closer to the center of the current.

Following him, she was getting closer too. White foam swirled around her legs and would not let go.

Suddenly she found herself immersed in water. She felt dizzy as if she were being pulled down by the current. White foam, like a white bridal gown afloat on the water, was all around her.

At noon they sat in the shade on the riverbank and ate the lunch she had prepared. The white rice in the lunch box took on a bluish tint because of the surrounding bracken.

After lunch they climbed to the hilltop and looked around. When the weather was nice, they could see all the way to Taipei.

The sun was setting. Schools of minnows jumped out of the water in the shade to catch insects in the air. This was the best time for Tiemin to fish.

By the time the water turned cold, she had a basket full of gleaming fish.

Warmed by the sun during the day, they seemed to carry the day's sunshine on their backs when they rode the bicycle home in the evening.

He walked barefooted as he pushed the bicycle.

They passed the small town between the railroad tracks from the lake. When they reached the end of the paved road, he put her on the bicycle before he jumped on.

By that time they could see chimney smoke in the country sky.

The wind caressed their faces, the way it did when they rode out in the morning. Happiness touched their bicycle. Just as in the morning, they entered the world of trees and shadows along the railroad tracks and traveled through the grove.

Once they went home late. It was not completely dark yet; they could still see the path. But the moon was already above the treetops.

The bike moved slowly through the grove. In the gentle breeze they were not in a hurry.

When the wheels jolted over a stone, his beard stubble pricked her face like rough bracken fronds.

On the evening road she felt a wave surge uncontrollably through her body. For the first time, she yearned for a child.

She was sitting on the crossbar of the bike, against his chest that had gradually grown stronger.

In the moonlight her thoughts drifted. An idea she had at the age of seventeen suddenly came back to her. She imagined having a child in her body, like a flower growing.

Her dress was lifted by the breeze and brushed against the pedals. She smelled the lakeside grass; it was the Korean raspberry on her skirt. Sister Yang said that her child was still on the mainland, not with her. Speaking of her child, Sister Yang looked as soft as moonlight. A crystalline brook flowed from her eyes. It made Wenhui envious.

Wenhui shivered on the bike.

Yes, a childless woman sooner or later would hide in a dark corner, oppressed by an unknown emptiness. Her soul would shrivel, and cold winter would be locked in the marrow of her bones.

She imagined what Tiemin would be like when they had a child.

The next day when the bamboo brushed against the metal on the eaves, the image of a child crossed her mind again.

For no reason, the thought made the field behind the house unusually bright, as if a layer of color had been added. *If I have a child . . .*

She decided to take a good look at Sister Yang next time to see if her beauty had anything to do with having had a child.

When Sister Yang came to her house later that day, Wenhui stared at her. Of course she couldn't see anything.

When Sister Yang showed up at the door, it was pouring outside. Yet she still looked as beautiful and sunny as always, making one forget the dismal weather.

"Wenhui, I need to borrow Tiemin this afternoon."

There was a touch of anxiety in her voice. Then she added, "Is that okay?"

She seemed to be waiting for Wenhui's reply, but not really waiting. Her voice was friendly and sincere.

Raindrops fell on Sister Yang's chestnut-colored oiled-paper umbrella. A gust of wind blew; the rain beat more urgently, thrumming against the umbrella.

There she stood by the door, as if the storm had nothing to do with her. The face under the umbrella was still smiling, but her mind seemed elsewhere.

Wenhui could not figure it out. It was she who became worried.

Again, she watched her husband leave with Sister Yang. This time they walked together under the umbrella as they slowly disappeared in the wind and rain.

She heard their footsteps on the pebbled road, then they faded away.

Now it was quiet. There was only the sound of rain.

She closed the door. The silent house smelled of paulownia oil from the oiled-paper umbrella.

Strong and heavy, the scent lingered in the vestibule.

"Soon you'll understand."

From time to time, lying inside the mosquito net, she asked him what he was busy doing. Tiemin lit a cigarette and, taking a thoughtful puff, replied to her.

A long silence settled between them.

Once Dr. Cai told he,: "Sooner or later you'll find out. But for the time being, just concentrate on nursing him back to health and making him stronger."

"We have entrusted Tiemin's health to you," Dr. Cai joked, but there was a hint of seriousness. "Look, Tiemin is no longer yours alone."

She listened to everything the doctor said. She had committed every word of his to heart. Just like that winter night last year, the first time she went to Dr. Cai's house, sitting by the fireplace listening to the rain dripping from the eaves outside the window. The sound had stayed with her ever since.

The scent of paulownia oil that Sister Yang had left spread to all the corners of the house. Wherever she went, it followed. The thick, heavy scent wafted into the kitchen and the bedroom. It also lingered around her dressing table.

That afternoon, after Tiemin left, she sat at home uneasily.

The rain was getting heavier. Wenhui used a pail to catch the water leaking from the ceiling. Pitter-patter, the rain hit the roof incessantly. Her mind was total confusion.

All of a sudden, the trim for the Manchurian gown, collars, hems, boas of purple wool, silver fox, gleamed before her eyes, making her giddy.

On top of it all was the enchanting face of Sister Yang against the background of the low charcoal fire last year.

After Tiemin left with Sister Yang, Wenhui found an umbrella in the closet and rushed out.

She was not going to the book rental store, as he had told her to do. She ran in the rain. She ran all the way to the district police station.

When she came home, she felt as if a burden had been lifted. Then she calmed down. As usual, she quietly went about doing the things she was supposed to do.

At night she slid open the linen closet door and took out the pile of bedding. She spread it out on the *tatami* before she hung the mosquito net. The next day she folded it up and put it back in the closet.

She did these daily chores quietly. There was no sign of absent-mindedness.

Silence had settled between them unnoticed.

Someone from the district police station came and took Tiemin away. It happened shortly after they got up.

Like the day before, she watched him walk out of the vestibule and slowly disappear among the fir trees at the mouth of the alley. Only this time, walking beside him was not the dazzling figure wrapped in a Manchurian gown; instead there were two big men, one on each side of skinny Tiemin.

The rain had stopped.

It was a sunny day, but there was a chill in the air from the previous day. It was still autumn.

Wenhui gradually began to feel lost.

For days he did not come back. The nuts had fallen from the trees. Hearing this inside the mosquito net, she felt as if the earth were quaking, causing the house to tremble. Alone, she was frightened.

When spring arrived, Tiemin had come up with the idea of cultivating a vegetable garden. But after digging for a while, he did not feel well.

She remembered the newly turned spring soil, dark and silky, glistening in patches in the sun.

"The soil is really fertile," Tiemin said.

Now the moist soil had dried in the wind. Patches of turned soil were left there by the wall, and looked like small graves for the Japanese swords she had buried after the February 28th Incident.

The firefly cage also lay abandoned by the wall.

The first summer after Tiemin's recovery, they ran into the field to catch fireflies after dinner. Later they were told that to keep them alive they had to take the cage out at night to let it soak in the dew.

She could not remember when it was taken out and never brought back in. It was left by the wall.

"Are you Mr. Lin?" the man had asked when he came the other day.

"Uh . . ." Tiemin looked confused.

"Please come with us." The man spoke with a forced smile.

Tiemin was alarmed. "Uh, let me put something on."

"That won't be necessary. You're fine the way you are." The man from the district police station spoke as he approached Tiemin.

Before Wenhui, who was in the kitchen, had a chance to bring out the tea, the two men had taken Tiemin away.

They were gone.

White steam was still rising from the teacups.

The pebbled road made the same crunching sound.

When Wenhui came back to herself, silence had been restored both inside and outside the house.

Now Wenhui was really alone. During the day the house looked empty. She was jittery. When she stepped outside, all she saw was the empty field.

She panicked, feeling as if she had lost touch with the outside world, the way it was during the February 28th Incident. Was something happening again? she wondered. She turned on the radio hurriedly.

The radio programs were the same as usual. Nothing was wrong.

Wenhui could no longer live by herself. She asked her mother to come and stay with her. With another person in the house, she felt a little calmer.

She took out Tiemin's shirt to sew the buttons back on.

Before he'd fallen ill, Tiemin had disliked the metal buttons on his shirt, saying they were too shiny. So she had removed them. Later she was so occupied with his illness that she never found the time to sew on the new buttons. Now, as she sewed, she hoped he would come back soon.

After he got better, one day he stood on a chair to wind the clock on the wall that hadn't run for days. She still remembered the delight she'd felt then as she looked up at his back.

"So long as you are healthy, there's no greater joy than doing the things you like to do," she told Tiemin in the rickshaw the first time they went to Dr. Cai's house. Then her only hope was for him to get well soon.

Each morning her mother knelt in front of the east window in the living room with her Bible, praying that her son-in-law would come back safely soon.

Who could have foreseen that only two weeks after his arrest Tiemin would be executed at Machangding?

The police station sent someone to notify them to pick up the body. Otherwise the body would be used for medical dissection.

Something was stuck in Wenhui's throat. She was shocked by that unexpected turn of events. Yet she couldn't bring herself to believe that they actually had executed Tiemin.

She'd only gone to the police station to report a trunk of books that he was hiding. That was all.

That day the men from the police station made a mess in the house and at the book rental store. They also took the locked trunk away with them.

That was all.

The talk about his execution was probably a scare tactic.

But when Wenhui went to Machangding with her mother, she had to believe it.

Now she sat alone in a daze in the house all day long.

"How could it be? How could it be?"

It had been days since Tiemin's execution. Still she could not figure out why it had happened.

At Machangding the sun was shining warmly on the Xindian Stream.

"It's a good day to work," Tiemin would have said.

"Wasn't this where Brother Min and I saw the circus before the war?"

When she and her mother rushed to the execution ground, the sight of the open field by the river suddenly brought back memories.

Her mother also said, "Wasn't this the horse racing track during the Japanese Occupation?

"How could it be . . ."

Some of the families at the execution ground were dressed in funeral attire. They stood behind the ropes cordoning off the execution ground, burning incense. Many incense sticks were planted in the sandy earth. Some people were burning paper money for the dead.

The wind lifted the white strips of cloth attached to the ropes and dispersed the blue incense smoke. Before the war, the same wind had blown on her and Brother Min's faces as they ate cotton candy and watched the circus.

The ashes of the paper money rose up from the ground. There was a scorched smell in the air, scratching her throat and making it itchy. She started coughing.

A truck drove up.

The people waiting behind the ropes pushed forward; a hubbub broke out.

They jostled up to the ropes, trying to find their family members through the tears in their eyes.

Among the jostling heads, she suddenly spotted Brother Min.

He was standing still on the truck. It was him all right.

Yet from so far away she lost him in an instant. Wenhui couldn't even get a good look at him. She only saw his wild, long, full hair blown by the wind.

Then he was gone.

Brother Min! She wanted to call him. But she did not. She only called timidly in her heart.

The sun climbed up slowly, drying her tears and parching her lips and throat.

Then Wenhui caught sight of Sister Yang. She hadn't expected to see her on the truck.

She seemed a stranger, as if Wenhui had not seen her in a long time. She wondered why she was there.

A gust of wind carried away Sister Yang's silver silk scarf, like a white egret flying from the field.

Next to Sister Yang, Wenhui saw Dr. Cai and their friends. They were all on the truck.

"There's Tiemin!" Her mother burst out crying.

But no matter how much Wenhui craned her neck, she could not catch another glimpse of him.

In the blink of an eye, they all disappeared.

One by one they were taken off the truck.

"Wenhui!"

Lying in bed at night, she seemed to hear Tiemin calling loudly to her. The voice was far away, but he seemed near.

In a flash she saw him walking beside her, in the living room, on the porch, in the garden.

The call, like the gunshot that day, echoed in the distant ravine.

She sat up with a start from her sleep, her nightgown sliding off her shoulders. There was a buzz in her ears.

How many times had she told him with tears in her eyes, "Let's wait till you are a little stronger."

Now in her midnight grogginess she could only expose her body with self-abandon to the chilly night air.

When she'd fallen in love with Tiemin at seventeen, she'd been so innocent. Later when she took a bath with him during his convalescence, she noticed her swelling breasts. In amazement she noticed her body grown fuller in the dressing mirror.

During his illness he would wake up from a bad dream, mumbling something in Japanese as if he were still in Unit 63. She would hold his head to her bosom. He was all bones then; his long hair felt like rice straw after the harvest, pricking her fingers when she touched it.

On the way home from the execution ground, she only saw his head bobbling up and down in the rented barrow attached to the bicycle. His hair, still long like rice straw, stuck out of the mat in which he was wrapped. During the February 28th Incident she dared not turn the lights on at night, so she had to wash his body in the moonlight to alleviate the itching from the bedsores. He was itchy all over and could not wear anything.

In the moonlight, pale and thin, he squirmed because of the itching. The two vermilion birthmarks on his groin were lost amid the rash on his body. The first time she saw them, she was so fascinated that she had to touch them. Brother Min told her that when he was a small child his grandmother had told him that these were seals left by the Mother Goddess.

She cried out all of a sudden. Picking up a sash inside the mosquito net in the middle of the night, she tried to strangle herself.

The next day when she woke up, everything was the same. Nothing had changed, nothing had happened. The house was still empty, the field outside still quiet.

She remembered that for a time Brother Min ate raw shrimp because her mother told them that eating live shrimp could cure tuberculosis. When she asked him if it worked, he said, "Everything is the same. Nothing has changed." Once he caught a shrimp as big as his thumb among the pebbles in Emerald Lake. Standing there in the water, he swallowed it whole in a hurry, which amused her to no end.

After they got married and moved into their house, she liked to sit by the bed and, while waiting for him to fall asleep, enjoy the view beyond the low walls.

Now the verdant ridges of the distant hill were visible amid the dispersing fog. Ribbons of morning haze in the ravine drifted over the gentle ridges and faded into the sky.

The newly appointed chief at the police station came to their house. With his head tilted to one side, he loomed large in the vestibule, making the eaves look so low.

The police chief could not speak Taiwanese and didn't know the custom of taking off one's shoes in the vestibule. He stepped onto the *tatami* with his shoes on.

"Righteousness above family ties. That's remarkable, truly remarkable...." From the moment he entered, he kept enunciating those words. After he sat down in the living room and was served tea by Wenhui's mother, he was still repeating them.

The old lady, who greeted the visitor, did not understand Mandarin. She was intimidated by the black uniform and the shiny insignia on his epaulets. Having served tea, she didn't know what to do next.

The police chief stood; his heavy footsteps made the wooden floor creak underneath the mats.

As soon as he stood up, the old lady stood up too.

From the back of the house Wenhui heard her mother shuffling around.

"What are you reading?" he asked in a consoling tone of voice.

After a while he was heard saying: "Good, good, the Bible, very good. Religion provides solace for the soul." His voice was approving and encouraging.

The next moment was silence. The house was silent for a while.

"Is the lady well? Is she well?" The police chief lowered his voice, then went on. "The lady is a remarkable woman, to do what she did. Truly remarkable."

After another moment of silence, he got up and took his leave. The heavy footsteps made the floor creak again, from the living room all the way to the vestibule.

Before leaving, he instructed Wenhui's mother at the door: "The lady should take care of herself. She needs rest, a good rest."

After the police chief left, the district chief arrived. He limped in.

"I'm the district chief."

Fearing lest her mother not recognize him, he introduced himself the moment he entered the house.

As soon as he sat down in the living room, Wenhui heard him asking her mother, "How is the lady, your daughter, doing?" His voice was so low it was barely audible.

After a while she heard him speaking again. "A box of prohibited books was found . . . they were all red." His voice assumed a mysterious tone.

"Well, the red books were secondary. They were just books after all, no big deal. The worst thing was . . . in the church . . ."

The district chief paused, then explained to her mother: "It was the small church across the street after you leave the alley."

He lowered his voice as if he feared being implicated even now. "In the attic of the church they had even set up a transmission station."

"They were really something," said the district chief.

He stopped whispering; his voice now carried a note of righteousness. "That was a big mistake, too serious to be condoned."

He hesitated, then added: "This kind of behavior should be punished by the law, punished by the law."

The solemn tone thickened the air. Hearing his words, the old lady couldn't help sobbing.

"It's a good thing that the lady knows right from wrong," said the district chief, changing his tone again.

"In Mandarin it's called 'righteousness above family ties,' which is very difficult. The lady is truly great. The average person could not . . ."

There was only her mother's feeble sobbing in the living room, on and off like a strand of silk thread on the edge of breaking but still being spun.

The district chief took a sip of tea and continued: "There were seven of them in total . . . just like—" he stopped himself to be merciful to a survivor.

They had heard it from others: "It's like a bunch of crabs strung together. When you pull the string, none can get away."

Summer was gone. There were no more chirping summer insects; even the crickets in the kitchen were silent.

The haze shrouding the hill had lifted. Green shadows delineated the graceful contours of the hill.

At noon the autumn sun after the rain felt invigorating and peaceful.

The wind rose. Wenhui could smell the bedding that her mother had taken out to air in the sun. It still smelled moldy from the closet.

She relied on her mother for everything. These days Wenhui was in a constant daze, and left everything to the old lady.

Yesterday she'd seen her mother asleep by the stove, saliva running from the corner of her mouth. The Bible that she carried around with her all the time lay at her feet.

But she still couldn't figure it out.

She sat facing the silent hill and field.

The stream was growing shallower. In the sun the reeds on the banks displayed tiny ears of grain with red specks.

Before her eyes a tree rose in the distance; the sea glimmered with countless sparkles.

It was the phoenix tree on the beach at Wuqi.

During those days of taking refuge in the country, she would walk around the tree every day, alone and lonely.

The summer before the end of the war, the phoenix tree suddenly burst into a sea of flames. Even Third Auntie came doddering on her small feet, supported by a cane, to marvel at the tree. All the folks living around the beach said that the tree had never blossomed so gloriously.

Third Auntie smiled, opened her toothless mouth, and said with a sigh, "It's about time we saw the light."

The sky above the sea, like the jade bracelet Wenhui held tightly in her hand, was a luminous translucent green.

The sea on the windless afternoon was as peaceful as the hill and the field around Xindian Stream before her.

"Brother Min!" she cried for reasons unknown even to herself.

Then she said, dumbfounded, "If I had conceived your child . . ."

The next moment she felt utterly ashamed for her inexplicable notion.

Wailing Moon

TRANSLATED BY **YINGTSIH BALCOM**

1

Why? Why? Why? ...

So she murmured whenever she saw the moon hanging before the window.

At midnight, she rose and got dressed; then she walked, following the moonlight, to the funeral parlor.

She had made the call abruptly and asked to see her husband's face before he was made up. But the mortician already had done the makeup on the departed.

"Ma'am, this..."

Her request to come to the mourning hall to keep her dead husband company at midnight seemed to create difficulties for the manager of the funeral parlor. But no one could stop her—without the slightest hesitation, she ran directly to her late husband.

Before going to bed, her husband always moved the plants away from the window for fear of breathing in too much carbon dioxide.

Then they lay in bed together and, with no potted plants blocking the view, they watched as the open southern window framed the slowly rising moon, much the way a pond in the dark of night encircled a large white water lily.

Many years before, she had read a letter printed in a special newspaper column from a youth who wrote to ask the columnist: why do all the plants in the world bloom during the day? Does any species of flower open only through attraction to the moonlight? For instance, when the night was quiet and no one was around in a remote valley, would a flower, unable to resist the call of the moonlight, spread the petals it would normally open only during the day, revealing in advance the secret folded within its bud?

The childish letter had made her smile. Although already a middle-aged woman, she suddenly developed a passion for that youth.

Unexpectedly, the columnist provided the youth with an affirmative answer in her column the next day. She told him that there was a flowering plant called the Beauty Under the Moon, or broad-leafed epiphyte, that bloomed at night.

Heading toward the funeral parlor, she walked down the deserted, shadowy street. She listened to the echo of her heels as they clicked on the concrete; the moonlight made her think of the youth who wrote that letter.

Did the night-blooming flower have some connection with the moonlight? Did it mean that the flower mistook moonlight for sunlight? she suddenly wondered.

So she let her thoughts run on the dark street, when after a fit of trembling, she sneezed.

The flower was easily deceived too.

She quickened her pace. The moon, bloated before the coming typhoon, looked despondent as clouds scuttled over it. A smell of mold suddenly assailed her. It was a smell she knew from her own house. For years, her husband had grown flowers outside the window; the flowerpots always emitted the same odor. Whenever she cleaned she had to clean his fingernail clippings out of the damp corner. He told her when he was little, his mother used to cut his fingernails in front of the window. Thinking of his mother, he would light a stick of incense for her in the evening and insert it in one of the flowerpots.

She had been assailed by the same perfumed flowery scent at the inn in Keelong. In the early morning, she had to open the window and hurriedly poked her head out and breathed in the foggy air to alleviate her suffering nose. But her husband said it was strange, he hadn't smelled anything all night.

Their marriage should have ended at that harbor years ago. . . .

It was an old Japanese-style inn with a deep and quiet garden in front. The small pebble path curved like an open umbrella and led to a luxuriant vestibule.

She cried out silently the first time she saw his dead face in makeup. He looked more lively and amiable than in life, something she had not expected. A faint smile remained on his lips.

The manager of the funeral parlor tactfully expressed his pride, saying they had the most skilled makeup artists in Asia.

Each time she visited her husband as he lay in his coffin, his expression seemed to spontaneously welcome her.

Moon-white chrysanthemums were thickly packed together and mounted to form the words "As if he were still with us," hanging high above his spirit tablet on the memorial altar. Even in death, he seemed clothed in the same orphan's loneliness he wore in life.

They stood together under the eaves of the inn where they were staying and he told her his memories about the starry light above his mother's grave.

Wearing a sackcloth scarf tied with a straw rope, he'd become an orphan when he was eight years old.

The adults had had to make haste to bury his mother before the proper date picked by a geomancer, because they could not postpone the burial into the seasonal period known as the Grain in Ear. They hurriedly chose another day, and his mother was buried just before dark. Amid a chaos of cogon grass, he lifted his head and looked at the stars with eyes swollen from weeping.

The inn was located midway up the mountain, from where they had a view of the rain-soaked harbor. The moonlight fell across a long stretch of shabby old Taiwan-made roof tiles. Rising and falling side by side, the low roofs seemed to carry the night along like waves rushing to the sea. His mother's death reminded him of the brilliant summer sun in late afternoon.

For several years after his mother died, he would get up every night and go to the courtyard, where he would cry alone.

As soon as dusk arrived, not a soul was seen on the depressing street. The sad sound of the tempura seller's brass bell could be heard far off in the distance. He would go to the soy sauce factory and sit by a muddy pool, looking at the red sun floating on the yellowish water. When the workday was done, the factory workers usually soaked their feet in the pool to wash them before going home. The big chimney of the factory stood against the vast night sky. The sunset looked like his mother's face, and he almost drowned himself in the pool.

How old was he then? He hadn't yet graduated from middle school! Unable to bear the loneliness on rainy days, he ran outside, and cried as he walked. He ran to the public cemetery just to clasp his mother's gravestone.

He lost weight and his face was thin ever after. In one old photo taken when he was a teenager, his eyes expressed a timid loneliness. It was the same even after he became a professor. All his life, since he was small, he'd said he wanted to be a vegetarian. On rainy days when the thunder roared, he would think of his mother. He said he almost gave up the idea of getting married.

It was in the inn, the night before he went abroad for advanced study, that he first told her about his past. The two of them were approaching middle age. He was still quiet, dull, and shy. He would flush before opening his mouth to chat.

She sat quietly next to him, observed his remains: his eyelashes, his eyebrows, the bridge of his nose, and his lips. . . .

When he came back from studying abroad, he returned with the same luggage he had taken; the only addition was a book of Japanese Ikiyo-e prints in his leather bag.

When she had nothing else to do, she liked to flip through the book. Each print depicted a Japanese woman—all with the exact same expression, showing no emotion, no happiness, anger, or sadness, and all in the exact same plain colors. One day it suddenly struck her that all those dull, stereotypical faces actually were imbued with ten thousand kinds of flirtatious expressions.

Sitting silently, face to face with her departed husband, the more she looked at him, the more his face, even then, seemed to change endlessly in unfathomable ways. She was filled with thoughts and feelings that had never troubled her when he was alive. Sitting next to him, she was disturbed, like the harbor buffeted by waves driven by high winds.

It was almost time to board the ship when he turned on the faucet and found himself, attired in his suit, drenched from head to toe by spraying water. He turned around and looked at her with an expression that seemed to say, "What am I to do?"

He lost his mother, that's why he was so very clumsy, she thought in her heart.

"My ears are the ears of an orphan." Not long after they were married, he had reproved her because she disliked his dirty ears.

She was worried about the makeup on his face, which now seemed excessive to her. To make matters worse, he had suffered from trigeminal neuralgia when he was alive. She wondered if the cosmetics would press painfully upon his nerves. She bent over the coffin, a look of concern on her face.

One afternoon in early summer, her husband was watering his flowers with the tea from the night before. His face suddenly started to twitch, and the teapot he was holding fell to the floor in front of the window and broke to pieces. He buried his face in his hands, crying involuntarily. It was the first time she'd heard a man cry, and it made her whole body feel soft and weak.

He first began to suffer from trigeminal neuralgia after returning from advanced study abroad. His temples began to turn white, so unlike the day he'd boarded ship in the harbor, when he'd had a head of glossy black hair.

At night, she softly massaged his cheeks with a hot towel. When he suffered an attack of neuralgia, she usually had to get up, even late at night, to massage him till daybreak. As the daylight whitened the window, her husband would quietly fall asleep again. In a half-waking state, she bent over him, softly massaging him.

She suddenly raised her hand. Shocked, she stopped her hand in midair.

Did she want to massage him? But the face in the coffin was so calm. . . .

"Ma'am, this . . ."

The manager kept addressing her as "Ma'am," which disgusted her, so she ignored him. A typhoon was coming and the air was very sultry. The manager was hovering around her all the time. He was so anxious that a cold sweat kept breaking out on his forehead.

How many days had it been since he was laid in the coffin? The coffin had to be closed and taken to the graveyard, or else . . .

Some time ago he had bragged about the funeral parlor's air conditioner.

"But, Ma'am, the air conditioning in the mourning hall is used only for short periods of time."

The manager now felt the difficulty of his position.

"Delaying day after day like this . . . I'm afraid it won't stop the weather outside."

She remained quiet, sitting demurely and calmly by her departed husband. It looked as if she intended to sit there day after day, and had no plans to leave.

In the coffin, her husband looked lively and amiable, didn't he? His faint smile seemed to tell her that he was starting his journey in peace. She was certain that her husband wanted her to sit there and bid him a quiet farewell.

In his third year of study abroad, she sat by the window alone at home, just like now, on a long and sunny summer afternoon. The shadows moved slowly across the courtyard. She thought of the days when he was home to help her collect the cool clothes hanging on bamboo poles outside. During the endless rainy days of winter, he would place the big bamboo basket by the oven fire, helping her to dry the damp clothes.

Her friends from the Sisterhood Association said that her husband was a little effeminate, but a good man.

Really?

The ship's engine started. A piercing old steam whistle was heard in the foggy harbor after the rain. Lashed by the waves, the ship disappeared along with her husband as she turned away.

Their marriage should have ended at that harbor years ago....

Standing alone on the shore, she saw her husband off for his advanced studies abroad, for what was actually the beginning of the happiest days of his life.

Leaving Keelong, she noticed that the roadside mailbox was still wet with overnight rain. The small sky-blue train, discolored and burned by diesel oil, sped on like a swift steed in early autumn. When she arrived home in Taipei, she glanced at the mirror and discovered that her cheeks were flushed. Soon thereafter she discovered that for the first time in her life she was putting on weight. Life at home went on much the same, except that one of them was absent. Occasionally she felt lonely because she had no child. At night, lying alone in bed, she always wondered if there was something rustling in the courtyard. The wind? Listening more closely, it sounded like someone was weeping there, as if her husband had returned to his early youth and sat on a bench alone, crying for his mother.

As winter came, she buried her head at his desk, writing him a letter, something that could take a good many days. She told him that on the way home alone from the harbor, she'd heard a *suona* being played as she saw a newly wedded couple in a traditional wedding ceremony.

"A woman can never be careless when it comes to emotions," said her aunt frequently and abruptly, as if defending herself, her niece, or all women in the world, for that matter. Sympathizing with her for being at home alone, her aunt often managed to find time to visit her.

When he returned home, nothing had changed—he carried the same old luggage and the same old black umbrella.

And then there was the embarrassment when he brought the first potted flower home from the market. She found it hard to imagine him falling in love with flowers as he aged. He had no hobbies in life, and perhaps that was why he was so difficult to fathom after he passed away.

He always took the bus, and, rain or shine, he always took his old black umbrella to and from the law school where he taught. Otherwise, morning and evening, he was ensconced at his desk in a dim corner at home to work on that magnum opus that he had begun at an early age, but that he never finished.

Until one day he came down with an illness.

Lying in the hospital bed, he looked at the flowering magnolia tree outside his window every day. The fragrance of the white flowers was identical to that on the day his mother was buried. Every morning and evening he heard a rusty bicycle creaking by under the magnolia tree. His ward was on the second floor. He couldn't see the rider, only heard the creaking sound of the wheels, but from the sound he knew the rider was an honest man. He couldn't say why, but the creaking of the bicycle reawakened in him a beautiful and ardent wish. He told her in a husky, phlegmy voice that after recovery, he wanted to cultivate some flowers.

His body had shown signs of decay a long time ago.

He and the postmaster three streets away from their house renewed their social contact. Both of them had been students in the departments of literature and political science at the Imperial University in Taipei, and they considered themselves old classmates. Everybody called the postmaster "director." Actually he just managed a tiny post office that was housed in a converted one-story house at the mouth of the alley.

He was full of zest and often talked to her husband about a face that showed up in the window of the toilet next door. The small window was dim, and seen through the bars of his own window, it looked very far away, but the face was so real. From his office, he could see a corner of the garden next to the toilet. Nothing in his life could make him prouder than such a garden.

"I work in that corner of the garden every day."

Being the director of a post office, he usually was not very busy, so whenever he wanted to, he stood up and leaned forward to enjoy the garden through the iron bars on the window. The neighbor also tilted his head to gaze out from the small barred window in the toilet to enjoy his flowers.

After a long while, their eyes occasionally met through the flower stems as high as cogon grass, and they grinned at each other and greeted each other with embarrassment.

They had never talked. The only thing they did was grin and greet each other in silence. But the mute face unexpectedly appeared in his dream.

"Although we never spoke with each other in all our lives, we could be considered old friends."

The director of the post office attended to his job with great interest because of the neighboring garden. Carrying the lunchbox his wife had prepared, he rode his old and shabby bicycle against the river wind blowing from the floodgate, and pedaled with all his might to get to the post office.

Her husband started to bring home one pot of flowers after another from the market. He was suddenly like a child—the moment he entered the door, he took on the evasive manner of a child as he fished out his small flowers.

He would hurriedly explain with a timid expression that they were on sale and cost only a few dollars.

He handed over his whole monthly salary to her at the end of every month, except for his tiny allowance. He also told her to see a doctor, but she wasn't sick.

The flowerpots soon filled the southern window of their house. How old was he at that time? Probably close to fifty.

The stealthy expression on his face when he brought flowers home was very familiar to her.

"How many years ago was that?" he suddenly asked. Before they were wedded, at the time of their first date when they walked silently along the floodgate.

"Yes, it was before the war."

It was at the glass factory in Xinzhu. The whole chemistry class of his middle school, led by their Japanese teacher, had taken the train to visit the glass factory.

The workers of the factory blew into long tubes, at the other end of which was a ball of fire that would become a glass vase when it cooled down.

The whole class circled around watching while she leisurely walked past the high-temperature oven.

Her silhouette in pigtails was framed against the shabby old window. Outside the sea birds swooped down from the sky and alighted on the piles of trash, where they started squawking and fighting over food on the mounds of waste.

On the day they met each other before becoming engaged, they were surprised when their eyes met. They seemed to be acquainted with each other.

"Why were you there?" he asked under the floodgate.

"Well," she said, smiling, "that was my father's glass factory."

Three days after their wedding, her younger brother made a special trip to her new home, a bundle of fresh flowers in hand, to invite the newlyweds to visit her parents.

But the bride's bouquet hadn't withered yet. So she put the flowers her younger brother brought together with those of the bride's bouquet on the southern window.

Returning from her parents' place, and before she could close her umbrella, she saw the lightning flash through the window. She screamed and grasped her soaking body with both arms as her umbrella fell to the ground.

The bride's face suddenly turned pale. It was his first chance to embrace and kiss her the way he had been longing to do. The thunder and lightning outside helped them to achieve their fantasies.

Several years later, he had fallen in love with that southern window. Coming back from studying abroad, he bought pot after pot of flowers, filling the racks in front of the window.

The first time his trigeminal neuralgia broke out was when he was standing in front of the window. His suddenly fell forward, knocking over several flowerpots.

"Do you remember the day we came back from your parents' house, the loud thunder?" he asked her when they lay huddled together under the quilt in bed.

"You mean . . ."

"Three days after I married you."

When had he asked this question? Before he went abroad? Or after he returned?

She sat quietly before the coffin trying very hard to think back, but she could no longer recall.

However, did it have something to do with the thunder through that southern window? Perhaps not. . . . She always felt guilty about her infertility. However, she still remembered the thunder and lightning that night and how it shocked her to the depths of her womb.

She had first become aware of having a womb when she was in grade school.

At first they were all playing hopscotch in the alley and then they started climbing up the floodgate.

"If I'm lying, may my head be covered with scabs," said someone on the floodgate. The sky darkened.

Another kid who was standing at the bottom of the floodgate asked anxiously, "Did you really see it?"

"Hurry up, come on up," said the kid on top of the floodgate. "If I'm lying, may my head be covered with scabs."

"You really see it?"

The girls stopped their play and ran over. They all climbed up on the floodgate by first stepping up on a trash can.

It turned out to be the full moon.

The moon that day could be said to be playing tricks. It was as big as a brass gong, hanging low on the other side of the river. Someone said it was yellow and looked like the shit of a kid who shit his pants out of fear.

The big gong of a moon seemed to have just risen from the bottom of the river to suddenly appear right before their eyes. It was so big and so round, completely unreal.

Standing on the floodgate, you could almost reach out and catch the moon. No, it was the moon that came to catch you.

She couldn't help but tremble, tremble all the way to the depths of her womb.

She tossed and turned at night. After watching the moon, she was thirsty and felt faint pains in her belly as if there was a pebble there. She thought of how her mother had scolded her older brother, who was born in the year of the tiger, for having watched the cat give birth. The mother cat ended up eating all her kittens. The following day her older brother suffered sunstroke.

She got up alone at midnight and went out to get a drink of water in the courtyard. Removing the cover from the well, she was shocked to the depths of her womb to see the big gong of a moon sink to the bottom of the well.

Her aunt advised her that her health would benefit from going south to soak in the hot springs.

That was several years after she got married. Her aunt said that the water could stabilize a fetus and that many infertile women got pregnant after a trip to the hot springs village.

She usually believed what other people told her, all but her aunt. She didn't like to listen to her. It was said that her aunt had planned to swallow up all the family's ancestral property.

Her aunt called out her childhood name, grabbed her excitedly, and, as if to wake her up, said loudly, "But you must trust your gut instinct."

Without saying a word, she left the courtyard of the temple on her own. She and her mother had to wait till that night for the old man to return and explain the bamboo divination slip that her mother had chosen. The old man, his Adam's apple rising and falling, read the divination slip aloud twice under the lamp.

"A fetus, I am afraid, is easily frightened," he said, his mouth full of phlegm. "It's best not to go walking at night."

She didn't say a word, but left the dark courtyard of the temple first.

Did she have selenophobia, fear of the moon? That was her suspicion. The cats on the tile roofs cried like babies. For years she took the incense pills from the Temple of the Lady Who Registers Births, the goddess who arranges births.

Then her neighbor had a baby boy. It cried at night, making it impossible for her to sleep. She got up and went to sit in the courtyard until daybreak. During the rest of the night, only the moon kept her company as it passed over the courtyard.

Every day she walked home along the brick wall of the kindergarten at the mouth of the alley to the market. She saw the kids inside the walls clamor to rush out the red door when school was over.

Several years later, at the doorway to her house, she could hear the neighbor's son, who was now old enough to learn to play the piano.

And all was the same as before for her. Every day she and her husband were silent. They sat at the table and ate in silence. The same old black umbrella hung on the wall.

Her neighbor's son was growing wilder all the time; the only thing he thought about was running outside to play. Through the wall she could hear his mother lock him up and beat him with a rattan rod, scolding him, "Your butt hasn't touched the piano bench all day."

She didn't spare the rod to spoil her son, and was finally able to beat all interest in music out of him. But later, when her son wanted to take the college entrance examination in music to pursue his interests, she forbade him.

"Music is just for killing time, not to feed your belly," the woman said to her as they chatted at the door.

Now the son's face was pimple-scarred and he was pale, thin, and puny. During the day, he absentmindedly walked along the brick wall of the kindergarten like a wandering spirit. Seen from a distance in the late afternoon, he seemed crushed under his book bag. As he approached, he looked evasive and timid and would lower his head and hasten his pace. But at night when he played the piano, his music induced a soul to sleeplessness.

One time the music he played alarmed her and made her nervous. The following day she went to ask him with swollen eyes what he had been playing the previous night. "The 'Moonlight Sonata,'" he answered impatiently, blinking. He then walked away, his footsteps crunching on the gravel path.

Very early in the morning, she was awakened by a clamor at the mouth of the alley. There were a lot of people outside.

"An abandoned baby," she heard someone say outside. That woke her up. Somebody had left a baby at the doorway of the orphanage by the kindergarten just before daybreak. There was a sum of money inside a red envelope that accompanied the baby.

She talked about the matter with her husband at the dinner table. His mouth stuffed with vegetable fern, he was unwilling to lift his head from his rice bowl. Middle-aged and threatened with high blood pressure, he referred to green vegetables as tender chicken.

They had no children, and had nothing to say all day long. Why not adopt one? The idea arose occasionally. Lost in thought, he watched the pigeons next door carrying grass in their beaks with which to build a nest in the eaves in which to lay eggs. After a moment of absentmindedness, he spit in the courtyard and went in.

Then there was the day she discovered that children disgusted her.

Nothing frightened her more than for her friends to suddenly begin talking about their kids in her presence, wondering if the impish ones would ever grow up.

"Soon he will be as tall as his father."

"He is smart and obedient, and will be a judge like his father one day. . . ." Those listening rejoiced in hearing such things.

Their words, like the thunder and lightning outside the window, would make her face turn pale, so she avoided her old classmates. She made excuses so as not to attend the sisterhood meeting once a month.

However, they had no children to distract them. Actually a wonderful affection developed between them once their finances improved. Their hearts settled and burned slowly with the gentle heat of late yearning as they reached middle age. After her husband returned from studying abroad, a spontaneous scorching heat appeared in their life, and the emptiness disappeared. What they understood was that they fully intended to walk hand in hand together into old age.

The first time this consideration arose was on a summer afternoon when they took a pedicab to see an orchid show at the Land Bank. Her husband leaned over to attentively examine a cymbidium orchid. She wondered why he alone so loved the small, dully colored flowers in the corner. At the same time she happened to notice that her husband had taken on the stiffness of an old man. But seeing the beloved flower, he acted as if he were seeing his own child, and was completely wrapped up in the excitement. She trembled with fear, and didn't know if she was sad or happy.

The hall of the bank building soared overhead; the amber-colored marble walls rose straight to support the arched ceiling, making a person feel insignificant when they looked up.

"Why not buy it since you like it so much?" She faintly felt something akin to maternal love. Then suddenly she grew impatient and felt like picking up the pot of flowers her husband so loved as if it were her own child to take it home. The spacious hall of the bank with few people was filled with gloominess, while her whole body burned with enthusiasm.

Life then was as happy as carrying a pot of beloved flowers home. There was no shortage of warmth and affection.

The year war broke out, her husband was the right age to go abroad for advanced study, but because he didn't go in time, he only worked as a lecturer in the law school. For more than ten years, he felt like a damp and stale corner of their house, and he would slump. They ate in silence without exchanging a word, as if they had already said everything. How many years did that last?

Life was stranded, and it looked as though it would be that way for the rest of their lives.

They were rescued by a scholarship. Her husband could go to Japan for his doctorate in law. Their life started changing and happiness arrived the day she went to see him off at the harbor. Pushing open the window of the room where they stayed, she saw the Taiwan-made tiles still wet from the rain, shining with moonlight that descended like a milky white river.

Leaving by ship the next day, he suddenly had a whim to go shopping. In the night market, he paid attention to every kind of bug flying around him. Before parting he pitied everything; even the bugs under the lamp received his tender consideration.

Looking down from the inn, she saw the square yellow skylights on every roof of every house in the basin around the harbor. So excited and unable to sleep, he told her about his childhood.

In his first letter from Japan, he told her that he followed the advice she had given him before they parted. He washed his underwear every day without fail. She had told him that wearing fresh underwear would make him feel good at the start of each new day.

Their life was renewed. They said a lot in their letters. When he was unable to express himself in Chinese, he would revert to Japanese, which he had learned since elementary school and in which he was highly proficient. And in order to write back to him in Chinese, she went and bought a Chinese dictionary, which she always kept near at hand.

Looking back now, she recalled that he never actually wrote about his life abroad save for irrelevant things. Only once did he mention a young Japanese professor, who, because he was so impressed with the new marriage law after the revolution in China, invited him to move into his apartment so that he could practice his Chinese every day. Whether he later moved in or not was unclear, because he never mentioned it again.

"Men cannot be expected to look after themselves," said her aunt.

The year after her husband left, her aunt came to visit her and hinted that she would be willing to pay for her to go to Japan to stay with her husband for a short while. She politely turned her aunt down. She thought her aunt, after swallowing up all the ancestral property, was trying to buy her over to her side.

After receiving his degree and coming home, he was very happy for a while. He would open his mouth and start criticizing this and that about the Japanese to the director of the post office. The Japanese songs heard everywhere on the streets of Taipei were, he said, actually the sad sighs of a concubine.

"They are the moans of a forsaken wife," he said in a deep, gruff voice.

She sat as a guard at his bier thinking of his elegant demeanor after he returned home, which had only increased her curiosity about his solitary life in Japan. How did he live?

And their marriage should have ended at the harbor years ago. . . .

The mourning hall was quiet all night; she was disturbed by no one. Past events came back to her without end as she recalled the happy times they shared.

It was just the thought of those three years . . .

The thread of life was decisively severed. The happiness they had built together was broken and couldn't be put back together. She just couldn't imagine those three years without good reason.

Thinking of this, she felt her husband in the coffin was a stranger, distant and cold. Had they talked about everything?

Yes, if only he could open his mouth, and say something, even a word, about those three years. . . . But the mourning hall was dead silent.

Why? Why? Why?

Suddenly upset, she leaned toward her husband with both hands tightly gripping the edge of the coffin.

The day finally broke. The first rays of the morning sun shone into the small hall through the four windows. She was exhausted, as if waking from a dream, but she felt that sitting with the dead, the night had passed very quickly, without a trace. Once again, feeling that it was all irrelevant, she stood up beside her husband.

In a somewhat confused state of mind, she felt she ought to go home and sleep.

Both the manager and the assistant manager stood by the window upstairs. The assistant manager told the manager that although the lady looked gentle and dignified, she actually was tortured by some anxiety. She had constantly gripped the edge of the coffin, leaving countless fingerprints.

Some time before, the manager, escorted by the assistant manager, had stood beside the coffin and brushed some dry loose paint from the edge. The densely packed, crescent moon-shaped fingerprints, like groups of newly hatched silkworms, covered the wood.

"Oh, how sad she is!"

They stood by the window and quietly watched her walk out of the funeral parlor.

She was dressed in a black *qipao* over which she had thrown a purple sweater. Her slim and graceful silhouette departed through the gate into the vast and serene morning sun rays. In a moment, she disappeared silently like a wisp of smoke down the sidewalk.

She already had vanished.

Under the wall in the front yard of the funeral parlor, a large clump of scarlet sage woke up in the morning sun. The brightness could not expel the unfathomable emptiness left behind by the lady.

On such a fine morning, the two of them stood by the upstairs window for a long time without uttering a word.

2

A visitor suddenly had appeared several days before.

At the time, she was wondering why she hadn't heard the piano sonata from next door.

The boy next door practiced the sonata every day in preparation for the entrance exam to study music at the Normal University. He repeated the same piece every day from morning till night. Now that he had stopped, space expanded and the room seemed more disturbing than usual. She felt more flustered at home than at the funeral parlor.

She hadn't seen the boy next door for a while. The last time she had run into him, he hastily avoided her. His face was still pale, and she wondered what sort of unmentionable disease he had contracted.

She shut herself up at home and spent her waking hours daydreaming. It was hard to kill the daylight hours and so hard to sleep at night. She spent the whole day absentmindedly at home.

There was a sudden spate of visitors, which cheered her up. She felt she was returning to the world of human beings again. Looking at herself in the mirror, she saw a face swollen from staying up late.

A middle-aged woman sat quietly waiting in her living room.

Upon seeing her, the woman slowly stood up and gave her a deep bow. Without any conventional greeting, she seemed to know that she was the widow who had just lost her husband. She conveyed her condolences through a silent bow.

A boy who sat close to the woman stood up too. He was very shy, almost hidden behind the woman.

When she bowed, the woman put one hand on the boy's shoulder as if in a gesture to greet the hostess for him.

After they were seated, she discovered that her plainly dressed visitor was quite pretty. But her looks betrayed grief. Upon a second look she appeared much older.

When had she made her acquaintance? She couldn't remember.

The visitor was completely unknown to her, and her fluent Japanese came as an especial surprise.

She wracked her brains trying to remember her from among her high school classmates during the Japanese occupation.

A classmate? She didn't look like a classmate or even one of the younger girls at school with whom she had become acquainted.

Her Japanese, which she hadn't used for a long time, though rusty, was still passable. It was only the complicated honorifics that she wasn't able to manage with the facility of her youth. The more she wondered about her visitor, the worse her Japanese became. She ended up stammering all the time, unable to utter a complete sentence.

She was embarrassed, but her visitor kept rising slightly from her seat and apologizing for coming without notifying her in advance. After apologizing, the visitor was suddenly silent, and, lowering her eyes, sat there quietly.

A long silence ensued.

The woman's sudden visit seemed to have been made with the purpose of sharing her loneliness during the mourning period.

She became more confused, and got up to turn on the air conditioner. Returning to her seat, she was just as confused. The noisy hum of the air conditioner helped to dispel the awkward atmosphere.

"Oh, it's a scorcher."

The woman, hearing this, felt the same, and said that it was hotter and even more humid in Japan at this time.

"When I left Tokyo, the weather forecast said a typhoon was on the way."

"Oh, it's the same here—it's usually very hot just before a typhoon."

"Is that so?"

The woman removed her hand from the boy's shoulder and solemnly folded her hands on her lap. Gentle and quiet, she was like a cymbidium orchid.

The silence hung again in the living room.

After a while, the woman murmured, her voice muffled as if she were talking to herself. As she listened more intently, it finally dawned on her that the woman was expressing her condolences to the departed.

Once again she was assailed with doubt.

The woman seemed to be an acquaintance; otherwise, why would she be so concerned about the funeral?

They sat face to face. Scrutinizing her, she seemed to notice a look of familiarity, which made it even more difficult for her to open her mouth. It would be funny if they actually were acquainted, and continued to act like strangers by exchanging formal pleasantries.

However . . .

The iced tea on the table had remained untouched. She tried to start a conversation by offering them some tea.

The woman was an excessively caring mother. Handing the tea to her child, she said softly, "You must be very thirsty?"

The excessive show of concern made the boy very uncomfortable.

The woman told her that this was the first time her son had taken a long trip, and she was afraid that he might suffer heatstroke. She felt more at ease since she had first brusquely entered and sat down in the living room that afternoon. She lifted her head slightly and glanced around the living room.

"You have a spacious house." She sounded a little envious.

She was still busily searching her mind, hoping to remember something that could rescue her from this deadlocked situation. She thought and thought, but still couldn't place the woman.

She was becoming anxious. As the cool air from the air conditioner slowly circulated, she actually sweated.

"This time your husband was . . ."

Her visitor finally broke the silence, the tone of her voice still expressing her condolences. But it was evident that she had forced herself to speak with some difficulty after hesitating for a time.

The words were no sooner out of her mouth than she felt she had been too rude. She changed her tone and said, "It must have just happened. . . ."

"Just a few days ago."

"It must have been devastating."

"And unexpected," she replied, directing the conversation back to her husband. "He had been writing diligently every day in hopes of publishing the book he had been working on for so many years."

"Oh, that is regrettable."

Saying this, the visitor sank into silence again. After a long pause, the woman spoke again, but seemed to be talking to herself.

"Then your husband really has ... passed away. ..."

She felt her visitor resembled one of the expressionless faces in the *Floating World*.

Dusk fell, and the darkness slowly crept into the living room.

The two unacquainted women slowly developed a thread of conversation. In the deceased, they found a topic that both thought absorbing.

The living room was permeated by a sad and enervating atmosphere.

"Your husband had been working hard; perhaps that is what caused..."

The conversation continued.

"Perhaps ... he died from ... overwork?"

"No," she continued, her voice soft and serene. "It was an accident."

"Oh!" Shocked, the visitor hurriedly unfolded her hands and latched onto the boy's shoulders.

Silence filled the living room.

"It was a motorcycle."

"How terrible."

She told her in full detail how her husband had been hit by the motorcycle and died immediately in the street.

She was a little surprised to find herself narrating her husband's death without the least hesitation. Her voice betrayed no grief; on the contrary, she hastily and in all earnestness narrated what had happened. She explained how her husband, after a day of writing at his desk, threw on his coat as usual to go out for a walk, and how he had overdone it and felt faint when he stood up from his desk, and finally how he had been hit from behind by a young motorcyclist during rush hour.

The motorcycle had skidded onto the sidewalk. ...

"It is so hard to imagine."

The woman sighed and was speechless, choked by the tragedy.

The sleepy boy nearby suddenly woke up, his eyes wide open. His fine eyebrows arched like crescent moons, he murmured something, then lowered his head and didn't lift it again.

The hum of the air conditioner once again filled the living room.

Hostess and guest sat quietly facing each other.

It was time to cook dinner. At the mouth of the alley someone chopped kindling. A little farther off, the brass bell of the pickle seller could be heard.

"In Japan . . . I was fortunate to receive help from your husband. . . ."

The visitor spoke again. Her voice possessed a quiet longing.

"I knew clearly that my sudden visit was improper . . . but I couldn't think of anything else to do."

" . . ."

"I thought and thought, and decided to come here in person. To pay my respects to the deceased, at the same time to . . ."

" . . ."

"So I took the first plane I could get."

" . . ."

"Alas, it's just so hard to imagine, your husband actually . . ."

As the woman talked, her voice suddenly trembled and dissolved into inarticulate mournful sounds.

"Actually died . . . at a time when he was accomplishing something," she said in a voice redolent with pity.

The visitor suddenly realized that it was improper to cry before the widow. She managed to control herself and regain her calm.

She couldn't believe that her husband had helped others when he went abroad to study. She soon felt as if they were talking about two different people.

Her husband was a quiet, introverted, and clumsy sort of man. What made him suddenly turn into a person who helped others? What kind of person was he? She helplessly sank into reverie.

A new and charming side of the man suddenly appeared before her. Her heart filled with admiration, she casually said, "It has been more than ten years since he came back from Japan."

"Time passes with unimaginable speed."

"A while back, owing to the fact that he lacked some Japanese reference books, he often mentioned that there was someone in Japan who could buy them for him."

"Did he?" the visitor answered vaguely.

"As a matter of fact, he had reached the age to accomplish something," she continued, picking up on her guest's earlier thread of conversation. "He was busy writing into the dead of night. There was a time I was worried about his old stomach trouble flaring up. It's lucky it never recurred. His health was pretty good."

She felt a little funny saying all this. It was as if she were talking to a bosom friend about her husband, when in fact, she was facing a complete stranger and had no idea where she was from.

"I remember that when your husband lived in my brother's apartment, he often suffered from stomach trouble."

"Oh..."

The visitor mentioned that her brother had worked hard on his Chinese in order to study Chinese postrevolution marriage law. He had asked her husband to move in because of the good chance it afforded him to study Chinese.

"It was convenient for my brother to ask his advice."

Yes, she remembered that. In his second year abroad her husband wrote a letter to tell her about the invitation, but never mentioned that he actually moved in. In three years of correspondence, his address never changed. She always wrote to him at the graduate school.

As if she suddenly saw a clear sky, the maze of doubts troubling her heart fell away, and she felt light.

"In that case, it was my deceased husband who benefited from your friendship."

"That's not so, my brother was the one who benefited from your husband." The visitor was anxious to explain. "My brother was worried, so he urged me to come here to pay my respects in person."

The sun rays shortened gradually, and the room darkened. The two of them conversed with a mutual understanding. In the end, they regretted not having met earlier. They had so much to talk about with regard to the deceased.

She talked about an incident that had occurred while he was still alive.

"Though it was an accident, there was something coincidental about it. Perhaps his death was fated. . . . His dead mother came for him."

"This . . ."

"A few days before the accident, when the twilight glowed in the house, a green frog unexpectedly appeared quietly on the southern window where the flowerpots are placed."

"It was . . ."

"It was when he was sitting by the window taking a rest that he found the frog. . . . It was strange that a creature like that came to the house. He gave a cry, and I ran from the kitchen to see what it was. There was a frog, absolutely still, save for its white throat that expanded and contracted, clinging to the glass with its four suctioned feet. 'Mom' was the only word my husband uttered. He was calling his mother, whom he lost when he was little. . . . I thought about it after the accident, and assumed that his mother had come to take him. He often thought about her, and always said he grew up in her shadow. . . . He never forgot to burn a stick of incense in front of the window for his mother in heaven."

3

With the fall of night, the hustle and bustle of the street faded. She was restless at home, but a calm sobriety would return as the moon slowly rose before her window. Then she would get dressed and walk, following the moonlight, to the funeral parlor.

"Why? Why? Why?" she murmured as she walked down the deserted street.

The lights were turned off in the mourning hall in order to maintain a low temperature, explained the manager of the funeral parlor, apologizing for the inconvenience. Making an exception, he turned on the lights in the corner where her husband's corpse had been placed. A chair had been placed nearby for her, so that she could see her husband's face under a dim blue lamp.

However, the manager was nervous. He had agreed on the telephone to her visit with the assumption that it would be for one night, and not a second, third, and fourth night, and on and on without end.

"Ma'am, this . . ." He paced back and forth outside the mourning hall.

The streets were utter chaos before nine o'clock. The typhoon had just blown through; electrical lines were down, and the ground was littered with fallen branches, tiles, and signs. Her taxi was stuck behind a truck. The taxi driver kept honking at the truck, but the driver seemed deaf, weaving and taking his time with no intention of yielding. The swaying truck carried racks of bird cages. The driver seemed to fear that driving too fast, he might lose the cages. Provoked by the honking horn, the caged canaries raised a melodic din from their swaying cages.

At the gate of the funeral parlor she got out of the taxi only to be met by the manager, who blocked her from entering.

"Ma'am, I'm afraid . . . Nothing can be preserved in this type of hot September weather. The dearly departed still looks good, but we can't wait any longer to close the coffin. . . . Ma'am."

She slightly pursed her thin lips.

Her soft and decisive footsteps faded as she disappeared down the hallway. A waft of air blew behind her, carrying a smell that upset the manager, making him crane his neck.

She was in a disturbed frame of mind that morning. She went home earlier than usual, but didn't sleep well. After she got up she decided to return again during the day.

"It would be best not to delay any longer," said the old director of the post office as well.

Since the incident occurred, the director had taken leave every day from the post office in order to help her handle the funeral. He told her to control her grief, especially during this time. He told her to take extra care and be sure to lock her door, because thieves often seized such opportunities to strike.

The first day the body was moved to the funeral parlor, the director thought the altar was cold and cheerless and suggested it would be best to have tricolored offerings. His death had been so sudden that she only had time to improvise by placing his treasured manuscript on the altar.

"It's really too bad that he didn't complete it," said the director tearfully.

He burned the first stick of incense before the remains of his old classmate without uttering a single word. After a while, something suddenly occurred to him. He approached her and whispered, "He loved orchids when he was alive...."

Before the old director finished speaking, he made a decision. Mounting his rusty bicycle, he leaned forward and pedaled with all his might against the strong wind of the rising typhoon. He rode all the way to Shilin. But he failed to purchase a cymbidium orchid of the type his old classmate so loved.

"Perhaps this western orchid will..."

His eyes still wet from riding in the wind, he respectfully offered the orchid. With great excitement, he pointed out that in addition to the offering of fruit, the altar also contained her husband's beloved manuscript and an orchid.

"It's more lively now," said the old director, smiling.

The night before, when she'd been there until midnight, she discovered that there were rats in the funeral parlor. She heard them scurrying over the cold flagstones. It was the same sound made by fabric against the floor when she sewed at night.

"Don't bother with the sewing tonight," he said to her haltingly in the inn at Keelong, as a token show of how he cared for her before they parted. He was looking at her from behind. The grayish sea was reflected, a shimmering light, in the mirror.

As he stood on deck, his serge shirt billowed tautly in the sea wind like a sail. He had gone to Keelong to set off for Japan for advanced study.

He'd missed the train when he graduated from high school, so whenever he saw the train station he would get nervous. Since then he could never rest easy until he was in his seat on the train. Taking the train was a big event in his life.

But in order to save money, he took a freighter to Japan for his advanced study. He had to take the train from his home in Taipei to Keelong, and from the Keelong train station he would have to carry his luggage to the wharf. When he thought of all the trouble, his lips turned dry and his face turned pale, because he figured he would never be able to make it in time.

He discussed the matter with her and they decided to set off one day early from home. They stayed the night at a cheap inn in Keelong. The following day he was able to make it to the wharf calmly and at ease.

However, their marriage should have ended at the harbor years ago. . . .

The inn was located midway up the mountain, which pleased him immensely. Opening the window, he could see into the distance. His face red, he stammered that if they could one day live at the harbor—renting a flat or something like that—they could watch the ships set out to sea in the morning and return to the harbor in the evening.

Shortly after they met, he said they could rent an apartment. At that time he even got cold feet about living too close to her home. Every time he walked her home, he would stop at the mouth of the alley. Though the weather was still warm, he would stand there and tremble. They didn't see each other for a whole month, and it seemed like a long time. One summer night, she was in her room on the second floor after taking a bath when she heard the crunching of pebbles on the path, which reminded her of a caterpillar climbing to a point on a leaf to eat during the summertime.

She listened attentively as she combed her hair. Suddenly she blanched and ran to the window. Opening the curtains, she saw him making his way toward her house. That year her father was in a good mood. Her maternal grandfather had a bumper harvest of persimmons and it was said that her father wanted to obtain some money to cover the losses at the glass factory.

She still remembered how he formally came to the house the following day to arrange their marriage. He seemed like a different person standing there before her in a brand-new suit. Pride showed in his expression, and he held his chin high like a hero. His serge suit appeared like the whole world before her. The fresh smell of his new clothes was wafted to her on the breeze; the nails on his heels clicked against the pavement. He was so young at that time, but looked older in a suit.

Although he was a little awkward and not particularly attractive, she liked his honesty. He was like a tree, quiet and real.

He never skipped a class in law school. He hardly ever asked for leave in half a life spent working. However, he gradually aged and walked like an old ox dragging a broken cart. He took the bus to work early and went to the classroom early. All year round, he wore the same dirty and worn pair of black shoes, but he surprised people by polishing his shoes with pork fat during the war when oil was in short supply.

After they married, he hid away in a dim corner and buried his nose in his big book. He would not come out until she called him to eat.

She packed his shaving kit when they stayed at the inn. The strong but familiar odor, like old sterilized cotton, floated out of the bag to assail her nose. It was a smell he carried out of his corner for half his life.

For no particular reason, he embraced her in a panic. She thought it was because he was leaving by sea the following day. The mirror in the room reflected the sea, the silver waves swelled high above. They made their way downstairs, where the old doorman dozed at the counter. Outside on the street a water truck drove by and sprayed water near them. They walked into a long, quiet alley, waiting for the sky to darken.

The evening before she went to Keelong, her obstetrician told her that she had no problem, that her period was back to normal, and that her womb was as healthy as any other woman's.

Standing on shore, she waved to him. Her nearsighted eyes were attracted momentarily by his back as he turned to enter the cabin. The autumn sun shone beautifully; the sea breeze gusted, raising the collar of his serge suit.

They had been together for half their lives, but even when they parted, he was still so stiff, standing on the deck, avoiding her eyes.

"Go home, that's it, go home. Don't stand there. That's it," his facial expression seemed to say. He was a middle-aged man who had to go abroad for further study. His fate was a harsh one.

The day before, he'd taken her to the harbor.

"That's the ship."

He relaxed after he confirmed which ship he was taking the next day. Waves broke where the ship was moored. The crew members were swabbing the deck that was piled with ropes. Dirty water ran through the deck sluices. Water flew as the waves beat against the stern. The sun was going down across the harbor.

So, he finally drifted out to sea.

Their marriage should have ended at the harbor years ago....

His first letter from Japan suggested replacing a regular incandescent bulb with a fluorescent lamp, which was better for the eyes. But at night, if she wanted to do some sewing, she'd best use a regular light bulb.

Before he left, he told her more than once not to sew at night. He didn't express any concern about her health, much less that she would be on her own. He only said that the sewing machine was too noisy and might bother the neighbors.

His letters were the same—he was too shy to say anything directly. He was serious and old-fashioned, and, even when separated by the sea, still very shy. In two years of writing letters, he only mentioned going to Kyoto once on New Year's Eve, where he listened to the bells tolling from the Japanese temple, and how he wished she could also hear them....

At the harbor, they suddenly decided to go for a walk. Although it was night, a strange light shone over the sea onto the city. During the day, the waves were strong, the room was muggy, and the electric fan, though it ran constantly, was unable to dry the dampness, and the warm wind blew the dust from the street over everything.

When he traveled, everything was more difficult and he often wore a pained expression. However, they liked the quiet side of the harbor, so they got the idea, for the first time in their lives, to stroll together to the night market.

They had a snack at a stand in the temple yard selling braised eel soup, where the fiery tongue of the calcium carbide light nearly licked their faces.

The second time they had fun together was after he came home. They took a pedicab to see an orchid show at the Land Bank, where they unexpectedly ran into an old classmate of hers who was divorced, and whom he criticized for being loose.

The divorced woman bent over in her tight *qipao* to smell a phalaenopsis orchid. Her ex-husband stood ten feet away, quietly looking at her.

On his arm hung a gentleman's walking stick; his silver-rimmed glasses flashed, and two white circles covered his startled eyes. His straw hat, which he still wore in the main hall, seemed to flutter like a startled butterfly.

The Grecian-style building was impervious to the summer heat. The tall, smooth, cylindrical columns towered high above the spectators, making the air feel particularly cool and comfortable. There were few people, and their footsteps echoed in the cavernous hall. The divorced couple, ten steps apart, perfectly mirrored each other as they enjoyed their own favorite flowers.

The director of the bank knew that her husband loved orchids, and he had invited them to visit his greenhouse in Shilin. A week later they again took a pedicab, this time to Shilin. In the greenhouse they unexpectedly ran into the divorced couple again.

The husband's walking stick had disappeared from his arm and been replaced by his wife's arm hooked through his, her hand hanging in the pocket of his flax suit. Their pasts vanished like smoke amid their new infatuation. The sunshine streamed through the glass roof, and they walked shyly through the shimmering rays of sunlight to avoid anyone else. The last flower show in the Land Bank helped the former couple, and they were remarried.

Her husband sighed and was unable to imagine that an orchid show could actually . . .

"A dissolute fellow." He seemed to choke as he spoke, his face reddening.

She now felt that their divorce and reunion were actually sincere and honest.

And what about her own marriage?

She had just been widowed, and suddenly this question presented itself. How could she explain this? She had been married to him for thirty long years. One day followed on the heels of another. Thinking back on it now, she couldn't be sure of anything. True or false, her mind was unclear. How did she come to marry him at that time?

She remembered she didn't really like him in the beginning. But how did she stay with him for thirty long years?

Her marriage to him was fated. She originally had planned to date him at first and then wait and see. How did she know she would marry him just after their first meeting? It was during the war, and there were few chances to meet other men. She was bored throughout the summer, and went out to chase away the seagulls at some distance behind the glass factory. The vast sea was blocked by a grove of trees.

After they got married, she still didn't like him all that much. Every night when she went to bed, she loosened her long hair, which was like the mane of a running horse, and spread it over the pillow and buried her face in it. Her heart was far away.

Her husband snored, but she was unable to sleep.

In those days, when she went to bed, the young man who died of TB in the hot springs inn would suddenly appear in her mind's eye every night.

When she was a senior in girl's high school she had taken a trip. They stayed at a hot springs inn in Sichongxi, where she witnessed the young man vomit blood and die on the first night there. Since then, his thin and melancholy face had been imprinted on her life. He was found unconscious in the cypress woods, and was carried to the lobby of the hotel.

Having grown up in the glass factory, she had so longed for such a pale face.

Everybody in the inn woke up at midnight. The sound of footsteps and whispering in the hallway downstairs could be heard. In a hush, they announced that the young man had died in his room.

At midnight, the old hotel maid wailed as if her own child had died. She said she had seen so many people come and go in half a lifetime, but she had never seen such a fine young man as he, nor had she heard such a melody as he had played.

It was said that the young man knew his end was coming, so he left his lover without bidding her good-bye and had come to this remote area alone, waiting for death. He went to the cypress grove every day after mealtime to play the harmonica.

"The melody . . ." cried the old maid of the hot springs inn. His harmonica made her think of her son in her hometown.

The morning her class departed from the hot springs inn in the mountains, the cicadas cried in the cypress grove as the people of the inn busied themselves with the funeral for the young man. The bus followed the road around the mountain and emerged from the wooded area. The whole class in the bus loudly sang the graduation song. She looked out the window and when she glimpsed the sea, she almost cried.

She was shocked when she discovered that she embraced the images of her husband and the young man. Even during the day the sound of cicadas in her courtyard left her terribly upset.

Her husband took the *Mandarin Daily News* into the toilet. She was alone in the courtyard on the verge of tears as the south wind blew.

She was unhappy when she was alone, sometimes even very depressed. Confused, she blamed herself.

The cries of cicadas stopped, and the courtyard was quiet and cool on a summer's afternoon. She could hear her husband reading the newspaper aloud in the toilet, using the phonetic symbols provided for teaching pronunciation.

The law school students had complained to the dean about his unintelligible Mandarin. There were so many Taiwanese professors in the university and they all tried very hard to lecture in Mandarin in the classroom. "If only Japanese could be used in the classroom," her husband often sighed. His Mandarin had been garnered from the *Mandarin Daily News*. She wondered how much he could learn from it.

In order to rid herself of the image of that young man, she immersed herself in sewing. The creaking of the sewing machine drove away those impressions that annoyed her. Later she got into the habit of sewing at night.

Sitting in the taxi that morning, she was cheered by hearing the canaries singing in the noisy streets, and the weariness and numbness of the last several days disappeared. She seemed to hear a far-off call, and recalled the young man who had died at the hot springs half a lifetime before. How many years had passed? She had all but forgotten that shadow from so long ago.

Her husband looked especially young in his funeral portrait, which was immersed in the profusion of chrysanthemums on the altar, for she had chosen to make do with his passport photo taken before he set off for Japan. He hadn't yet gotten fat and looked thin and pleasant, as if he were smiling slightly for the tricolor offerings.

She'd never imagined that a face could show so much pain. After being struck and killed, her husband was carried home, his mouth hanging open. He was placed in the living room until he was fetched by the people from the funeral parlor. She washed his body and was surprised to find that it was still young and white. His mouth hung open and couldn't be closed. The pained expression on his face when he was hit remained. She couldn't bear looking at him and covered his face with her hand.

What was he trying to say through that open mouth?

She covered his body with a white bedsheet. Then after staring at him for a while, she began to feel as if she were treating him like an outsider, which was wrong. Though she kept vigil beside him, they in no way resembled a husband and wife.

Then she uncovered him and took away the bedsheet.

When he was alive, he appeared older in sleep than in waking. Now the pained expression actually made him look younger. Looking him over, she could tell he had struggled before death.

She remembered that he suddenly had spoken at the dinner table.

"I've decided not to buy it."

He had borne the same expression of struggle during his month-long obsession with the potted cymbidium at the Land Bank. The director had said he would hold it for him. But in the end, he couldn't bring himself to purchase it; he couldn't bring himself to pay the high price. He said he would wait till after he published his book and buy it with the royalties.

When buying something, he always bargained for the lowest possible price, and then would still end up not making the purchase.

She began to worry that his trigeminal neuralgia would flare up when he didn't buy the cymbidium orchid.

He wore such a pained expression. What had he been thinking the moment he was hit?

She hung the mosquito net at night, and he lay inside like he was sleeping as usual. A swath of cold, bluish moonlight streamed into the living room.

They had seen the same swath of light streaming through their window the night they stayed in Keelong. Returning to the inn after a snack in the night market, they were unable to sleep even after taking a bath. They opened the window and looked at the autumn moon in the rain-washed sky. Clear and bright, a swath of moonlight shone over the wet Taiwan-made roof tiles.

He is going away tomorrow. The idea crossed her mind and made her cry. She hurriedly hid herself in the mosquito net.

A few years after they married, he almost died of acute pneumonia shortly after his stomach started bleeding. He lost a great deal of weight in a short time.

His hoarse calling late at night woke her. He said he was going to die.

She touched him. He was cold and a bit stiff.

It was a chilly winter night and a cold wind was blowing. She wanted to cry for help, but there was no one around. In a panic, she held his icy cold feet in her arms and cried. Holding his dying body, she was stunned and didn't know what to do so late at night by herself.

She wept like Niobe, her heart racing. Despairing, she suddenly felt his feet move in her arms, as if life were returning to him. She hurriedly opened her own clothes and placed his feet between her breasts. She held him tightly under the quilt, knowing it was too late to heat water. In this way, her body warmed him until daybreak.

He was revived. Unbeknownst to him, life was like a river that flowed from her naked breast into him.

The indifference she had felt toward him after they got married vanished. She started warming to her husband's body.

She recalled how the flowers covered the ground behind the glass factory after the rain.

After that she kept thinking about going on a real honeymoon. She couldn't remember how long she had the idea before she said anything. When she finally told him, they went to the countryside to soak up the summer sun. In the evening they stood on a riverbank, looking at a distant gray water tower.

Her husband didn't like to go out. His classmates went to Taishui to play golf. He couldn't swim or ride a bicycle, and he didn't know how to jump across a ditch.

"A simple husband is good. He won't fool around outside."

Her classmates had commented on her husband, when they complained about the way their husbands fooled around with other women.

"Marrying a handsome face, you can never be at ease."

Her husband led a simple life and was not demanding. A fried egg in his lunchbox would make him happy.

With the approach of winter, she took his clothes to the courtyard to air out under the sun before packing them away in a box. She picked three grasshoppers out of his fresh clothes—they were the same green insects they saw flying near the water tower that bright summer day. That day in the countryside, he'd said he missed his mother. He didn't say anything else, but kept his eyes fixed on the insects flying around him.

The manager of the funeral parlor said it was easy to right his open mouth. "Just a shot." As he said, his facial features were restored to the way they had always looked, except for his two front teeth, which were knocked out when he hit the ground.

He lay in the mourning hall; his pained expression was gone, his open mouth was closed, but he would never open it to speak again.

In his coffin, his final smile was cold.

She had had a bad dream while taking an afternoon nap the previous day. In the dream he was alive as if nothing had happened, and was silently watering his flowers in the south window.

She fought with him. He kept silent, immersed in his work. Suddenly he moved to walk away, and she grabbed him tight.

Why? Why? Why?...

On her pillow, she was overcome with weakness. Turning over, she felt beneath her pillow for a bunch of keys, which she tossed toward the south window.

The jangling of the keys hitting the glass window woke her.

It turned out to be just a dream.

As his body was carried into the house, the keys fell out of one of his trouser pockets. She picked them up and put them under the pillow on which she slept for several days. They were keys for the house, the school study room, the glass bookcase, keys to open everything that he locked, only...

He always carried the house and school keys. Once in a while, late at night, she heard him as he inserted the key into the keyhole when he arrived home from the director's. It was the loneliest sound in the world to her.

If only we had a child of our own...

The day the Japanese woman said good-bye to her with her boy at the doorway, she happened to notice marks left by the woman on the boy's shoulder.

It was hard to imagine that such a gentle and proper woman could express such strong emotions when talking about her husband. Once outside, the woman turned, her hands on the boy's shoulders, and bowed deeply in farewell and pleaded:

"If only you would let us see your husband's funeral portrait, we could return to Japan with peace of mind."

She suddenly awoke at midnight after they had left and realized that she'd seen her husband's face in the boy's face.

The typhoon was coming, and the house was filled with the chirping of crickets. The wind whispered outside the window.

At midnight everything suddenly quieted down. Moonlight streamed through the window. A thin wet halo surrounded the quarter moon. There wasn't a cloud in the sky to obstruct the light streaming through the window.

It was deathly still. The day of the orchid show in the Land Bank, she also had heard the silence suddenly fall in the grand marble hall.

What was it? As if coming from afar, it was a constant drone, but only now did she sense its existence. Then she realized it was her own voice. She had been overly tired recently, and things had happened so suddenly. She wondered if it was her ears ringing. She listened carefully, but everything was so quiet in the dark night.

Silence reigned. She woke up and in the darkness she saw the boy's face imprinted with her husband's features.

First cold, then thunderstruck, she fell on her pillow and cried aloud.

Handling her husband's sudden death seemed like a dream—the police report, the hospital death certificate, the cancellation of his permanent residence registration at the district government office, the funeral parlor, and so on. She always controlled herself and managed not to cry.

But now, late at night, she had discovered the secret her husband had kept from her when he was alive. The dams of her eyes broke and out poured a lifetime of tears.

She couldn't believe how the Japanese woman had stealthily visited her with her husband's child. Never could she have imagined such a thing. She collapsed in bed. She seemed to hear her aunt calling out her childhood name, and then feel her forcefully shake her inert body.

"You've got to trust your gut."

Her aunt was right—men cannot be expected to take care of themselves.

His nearly grown child had leaned quietly on his mother in the living room that day. Occasionally he lifted his head, and his eyes, clear as a lake, betokened his shyness. Like his father, he would be a quiet man when he grew up, only handsomer.

The youngster was as handsome as a full moon. She could see the young man in every photo of her husband from when he was young. Arriving from afar in Taipei for his father's funeral . . . she could already detect an orphan's loneliness and confusion in his face.

She stood up, washed away her tears, and made herself look presentable.

She did not cry again.

Every night, when the moon gradually appeared in the window, she dressed and, following the moonlight, made her way to the funeral parlor.

Why? Why? Why? . . .

She had been keeping vigil beside the coffin and patiently waited for his answer.

Tell me.

Impatiently she hastily grabbed the coffin and leaned toward him.

The assistant manager told his boss that it could not go on like this....

"If it goes on like this, the deceased will soon be joined by the living."

Had they been a married couple? She sought the answer from his made-up face.

So, you had a woman and also a child.

When you covered your face and wept by the south window it actually had nothing to do with your trigeminal neuralgia. The silence you maintained every day had nothing to do with your character. Hiding in the corner, you avoided being seen clearly, except for the occasional flare of your cigarette butt. You terrible man, you were constantly thinking of that other woman.

So, you had a woman and a child. And you kept it secret. Why?

Tell me. Open your mouth.

"Ma'am, this..."

On the edge of the coffin, blood stains now appeared along with her countless fingerprints.

"Oh, you are so sad."

The manager suddenly remembered that a corpse had been destroyed once before. It was said that a widow demanded that her dead husband express his love as he had not done in life. Uncontrollable, she had opened his mouth. The manager was worried, fearing that the same thing would happen. He decided to take a difficult step. *I won't let it happen again.*

In all tact, he pleaded with her. There wasn't a moment to lose—the deceased was still in good shape. He would have to close the coffin and have a funeral. The typhoon had passed already; it was good timing.

He entered the hall.

"Watch out for the living," warned his assistant behind him.

The manager wiped his mouth, and with all propriety put on a determined expression. He walked down the dark, icy hallway directly toward her. Walking into the mourning hall, he lifted his head to look and was stopped there. He was moved by the scene he saw before his eyes, for the dead body in the coffin was still in good condition, which made him relax. Their worries were unnecessary.

What about her?

He looked at her. The way she sat made him more afraid of her than the deceased.

She was calm, but in low spirits.

Her body was there but her mind was elsewhere.

Inured as the manager was to death after dealing with it for half a lifetime, he was still perplexed by her and couldn't help trembling. He would never know that she had been called away by the canaries she'd seen on the street that morning.

The chirps of the birds guided her toward a faraway and unknown place.

Running Mother

TRANSLATED BY **YINGTSIH BALCOM**

The silent fear I felt when I looked at the vast dark expanse where the night and the sea merged in my dreams first appeared when I was little. It has stayed with me through my childhood and my youth, and into middle age today. It often disturbs me that I have been unable to free myself from it.

Feelings of affection disgust me. But nothing makes me feel more uneasy than the fact that I am now the father of two children.

My mother said I was far too quiet and introverted. So every night before I went to bed, I would take the thermos, and my mother would lead me across the dark street to the shop that sold seasoned millet mush at the mouth of the alley to buy boiled water. This was the social training my mother provided when I was little.

I bought the boiled water and handed over the money, then took hold of the now heavy thermos. During the transaction, my mother stood outside waiting for me by one of the stone pillars of the covered walkway. This was a required nightly class for me. I never once missed it, even after the drizzling rain started in December.

Taking the thermos from the counter, I turned around and saw the night suddenly deepen.

The street retreated far off into the distance. There were no cars or pedestrians. The covered walkway shrank into a thin, long line, stretching deep into the unfathomable darkness.

My mother, who had been waiting by the stone pillar, had disappeared.

I carried the heavy thermos. I was ready to cross the street alone, but my heart was pounding.

"Mom!" I couldn't help but cry out in fear.

Normally my mother would walk over to take the thermos from me as soon as I had bought the boiled water.

Just as I was about to cross the dark street, my mother peeked out from behind the stone pillar, half of her face visible.

"Mom."

Then she disappeared.

I wanted to bolt across the street.

Again my mother silently peeked out from behind another stone pillar; the half of her face that was visible was wreathed in a playful smile.

I ran toward her. However, for each step I advanced, my mother retreated one step. My mother seemed determined to leave me, but at the same time she seemed to be playing hide-and-seek with me. She was hiding behind the stone pillar, secretly smiling.

After what seemed a long time, she showed half her face again, silently smiling at me.

"Mom," I called loudly.

My mother simply started running; she ran down the middle of the street. She ran toward a darker, more distant place, as if she were running toward the sea. She ran so desperately, so stubbornly, and so determinedly that her long hair flew up in the air.

She left me alone at one end of the dark night.

"Mom..."

My calls pierced the ramrod-straight street. I knew that I could do nothing except shout as loudly as possible to pursue my vanishing mother. I just stood on the street. Immediately, the thermos in my hands was no longer a necessary heavy encumbrance.

My mother's footsteps receded down the asphalt road. Leaping up, one by one, they decreased as the distance increased, until they were a blur. Finally, along with my shouts, they completely disappeared at the other end of my dream.

"Okay, let's analyze this."

I described my recurring dream when I was little to my old friend, Liao De, who was a psychiatrist at the National Taiwan University Medical Center. I hoped he could analyze it for me. In his old Dutch-style house, we sat drinking Kong Fu tea, for which he recently had developed a taste. The setting sun shone through dense foliage of the tree fern into the window of the east wing of the house, onto the delicate clay tea service on the table. The house, which had been in the Liao family, was where he had devoted himself to the practice of medicine. A few minutes before, the whistle of the train going in the direction of Shuanglian gradually had faded in the air. I sank comfortably into the old rattan chair, wrapped in the languid afternoon. The vanishing train led me to the sea in my dream. Liao sipped his new tea and explained how hard it was to conduct psychoanalysis on a friend, especially a childhood friend.

"Do you remember the way your grandfather ran down from the second floor holding that feather duster?" Liao asked, picking up his small teacup, as he slowly sank into his rattan chair.

We hadn't seen each other for a long time. As soon as we met, we started to talk about the interesting things that had happened when we were young. The trees and flowers that Liao's family had planted with such care three generations earlier completely covered the house today. The train outside the wall now seemed very far away. The cries of cicadas were feeble and faint on that autumn afternoon, lulling you to sleep.

I remember that my grandfather never liked Liao. Perhaps he blamed Liao, who was two years older than me, for the scabies on my head. Naturally, when Liao was not around he scolded my mother, saying that the ugly scabies on my head were the result of her carelessness.

When summer vacation started, Liao would call me downstairs. I would put down my rice bowl, pick up an empty can, and run to school with him. There was an ancient banyan tree there from which hung a plethora of aerial roots. Believe it or not, if you climbed to the top, you could shake down hundreds of golden beetles. And even stranger were the brown beetles you could shake out of the wax apple tree that grew by the flag-raising platform. Grandfather said that the excrement of the brown beetles or cicadas or long-horned beetles that fell on my head gave me scabies. Liao also brought up how we had to have fun by catching cockroaches when we couldn't find the beetles, cicadas, or long-horned beetles at the end of summer. We would tie a long thread to the leg of a cockroach and fly it in the street like a kite.

"The children nowadays are different," Liao sighed with the tone of a professional. "They can have any toy they want, but they are not happy."

He said such children would end up in a mental hospital after they grew up. They are weaker than our generation.

"But . . ." I didn't agree with his view and was about to object, but suddenly felt tongue-tied. Then, altering the tone of my voice, I said, "Are you serious?"

Every winter, as twilight vanished, my eyes opened in that dream to that vast dark expanse where night merged with the sea. My heart pounded. The nights of my childhood were filled with an inexplicable fear. I would pull up my quilt and sink nervously back into sleep.

In those days we were living in rented rooms on the second floor of a building with a balcony facing the street. We would stand on the balcony and wave to my father as he walked down the street. My father wore a gray wool hat. As he walked, he turned back to wave to us. He slowly walked away, passing the doorway of the photo shop and then the New Stage. After the New Stage was the rear entrance to the Rear Train Station.

"Where is Dad going?"

"Dad is going to make money."

I saw Father just as he was passing the New Stage. Soon we were unable to tell if he was still turning to wave to us.

Father grew smaller and smaller, smaller and smaller. Then he disappeared. He never came back after that.

I vaguely remember Mother caressing me on Taiyuan Road.

One afternoon after my father left home, I fell asleep under his desk. My mother picked me up and put me to bed. I vaguely sensed that she wiped my dirty feet with a hot towel.

At that time, clear water flowed every day in the ditch beyond the covered walkway. When the sunlight hit the ditch, the red worms in the wall of the ditch started to sway leisurely, as if they were panning for gold. They didn't stop swaying until dusk, when the sun climbed out of the ditch.

At that time, Taiyuan Road wasn't called Taiyuan Road, but Shimokeifu-cho.

At that time, the whole street was very quiet, like an uninhabited island. The war forced us to leave Shimokeifu-cho. When we returned, it had been renamed Taiyuan Road. The betel nut palm in the courtyard reached up to the bathroom window.

"I remember that after returning home from being evacuated to the countryside, our house made me feel sad."

"Maybe you were afraid of losing your mother after losing your father."

After the war, when I came home from primary school, the combined odors of mildew from the window after the rain and camphor from the clothes chest and the sight of the slowly withering bright eye blossoms would choke me with sadness.

"But it was never like that before," I stressed.

I remember that before the war, as soon as summer arrived, a flying insect called a rice husk bug always flew into the bathroom. They buzzed up and down against the frosted glass window. When they stopped, their tails beat time as if they were pounding rice. I remember becoming excited as I squatted on the toilet and saw how the window reflected the sapphire blue color of the rice husk bugs.

What is more, flipping through the pages of my grandfather's perpetual calendar, I could smell the musty odor from previous generations. The odor of gasoline left in the quiet streets also made me inexplicably happy.

"Then when did it start—"

I was too impatient to let him finish his question, because I assumed I knew what he was going to ask, and I told him that my eyes opened to the dream for the first time toward the end of the war.

One morning after being evacuated to the countryside, I saw my young mother, who was holding a flour sack under her arm, jump like a grasshopper onto a truck slowly driving away. She went to another village to buy black market rice. The war had made my mother, who had graduated from a girls' high school, into a nimble-handed and fleet-footed woman like a grasshopper. Even now, as a middle-aged man, the very thought of it still terrifies me.

"But what does that have to do with that dream of yours?"

"Maybe it's the image of my mother desperately jumping onto a truck."

"Sounds like your mother jumped onto that truck so as to make a living."

"But, life really is terrifying . . ."

" . . ."

"It changed my gentle and beautifully refined mother into a grasshopper . . . good at jumping onto trucks."

In September, my grandfather took his caged myna bird, the one that later died in the bombings, and hung it out in the courtyard for the sun. The umbrellalike blossoms of the bright eyes fell, covering the ground under my mother's feet. My mother bent over and soaked her long hair, which she curled with a curling iron until it resembled hornwort, in the tea water. The bare white of the back of her neck was bathed in the sunshine under the eaves.

At night I buried my head deep in my mother's pillow. Sometimes the long whistle of a train at the distant Rear Station could be heard, which made me think of my father. I would breathe in the fragrance of my mother's clean hair. The vast dark expanse of the night merged with the sea would silently appear before my eyes.

However, everything always changes in an unexpected way.

I started stammering; my memories multiplied until I didn't know which was first and which was last.

"Speak, speak," Liao urged me.

At night I dreamed about quarrelling with my mother, starting from when I was young.

"Go on, go on."

Mouth wide open, I dashed toward my mother, shouting.

"Go on, go on."

Sometimes I couldn't catch my breath, and even cried while quarrelling with her in my dreams. I woke up in a cold sweat when I could no longer bear the weight of my anger, only to discover that I had been dreaming because I was choked under the weight of my own quilt.

In my dreams, my mother still ran away with such desperation.

One day, in the year of Taiwan's retrocession to China, I hurried to my uncle's home, where I found my mother.

My mother called me aside and pinched my leg without saying a word. She pinched me so hard, and wouldn't let go. I didn't dare cry out. I just looked at her in total confusion. My mother cried first. Then I understood that I had made her lose face. I had misbehaved. On the sly, I had eaten the sweet potato cake that was kept in the kitchen cupboard. My aunt made a big scene. Through the walls, I could hear my uncle as he tried to placate her. Then I understood that I had to be on my best behavior; and I had to be even better behaved in my uncle's house.

After I'd anxiously rushed to my uncle's house, he let me stay and keep my mother company. But this did not stop my grandfather from forcing my mother to remarry. Unlike when we were at home, my mother wouldn't beat me or scold me. She could do nothing but just silently pinch me. She was very much afraid of my aunt. The sadder my mother was, the harder she pinched. I clenched my jaw, swallowing the pain. But after a while I was unable to endure it and tears started from my eyes. The day my uncle decided to let me stay, without saying anything to my aunt, he went out the back door to borrow some black market rice from his neighbor. That night, through the walls, I heard my uncle and aunt quarreling again in their bedroom.

In my dreams, my mother ran with more determination.

Afterward, she ran away because she was afraid of the look on my face and my loud quarrelsomeness.

My nighttime dreams often continued into the daytime.

I was cruel to my mother every day. I even forced myself to recall all sorts of happy things to compensate for the resentment I felt toward her.

"What sort of things did you recall?"

"All sorts of beautiful things."

"Such as . . ."

"Such as the way her print skirt billowed in the air as she crossed the bridge."

"So you really miss your mother, don't you?" Liao continued in a professional tone: "To you, as a child, was your mother beautiful?"

"Oh, yes," I replied, "beautiful; more than beautiful."

My mother couldn't disobey my grandfather. The night she agreed to remarry, she suddenly scooped up my sister and me from the quilt and hugged us. I felt her tears against my cheeks. She didn't say anything, and I felt that her embrace no longer contained the least bit of affection.

"What if Papa comes back?" I asked her after her own fashion.

"What if Yansheng were to come back? How could I bear it?" she often retorted to my grandfather.

After arguing with my grandfather, my mother would go out and take me with her. I ran across the stone bridge, waiting for her on the other side. But she didn't want to walk across right away. She had to think about so many things. She wanted to be alone on the other side of the bridge. She leaned against the bridge with two hands on the stone balustrade. The water under her feet flowed fully. The rippling water imprinted by the moon was like a billowing skirt.

"Yansheng, Yansheng, all you can talk about every day is Yansheng. Don't you know Yansheng died a long time ago?" Grandfather always retorted.

Finally, Grandfather recorded that terrible day in his almanac with a red pen.

Waiting on my side of the bridge, I stared at my mother, who was going to remarry.

It was said that my mother often looked for bridges. She often sneaked off after midnight. She had to cross seven bridges, without crossing the same bridge twice. There weren't that many bridges in Taipei to make it easy for her. Every time she went in search of bridges to cross, she couldn't greet an acquaintance, nor could she turn back. Crossing a bridge, she couldn't talk, stop, and look. She could only walk, one step at a time, ramrod straight. If she were able to cross seven bridges in this way, her wish would be granted.

I continued to wait for her on my side of the stone bridge.

She had long ago fulfilled her wishes. But the terrible day that Grandfather had set for her wedding was steadily approaching.

My mother's skirt billowed as she crossed the stone bridge.

Step by step it billowed across.

Step by step it drew nearer.

She arrived.

Her body overflowed with warmth.

But in fact, she ran away from me step by step.

You didn't move from your side of the bridge. You were a blockhead.

You knew very well that you were incapable of even calling out "Mom."

You scrutinized your more than beautiful mother, who was about to be a bride again, walk toward you step by step and also depart from you step by step.

During the fourth grade, when I was in the middle of abacus class, the teacher summoned me and told me to take my book bag and go to the office, where my mother was waiting for me.

"Grandfather passed away," Mother told me on the way home. For a while I didn't know to express sadness. I replied in a hurry: "But I just dreamed of his myna bird the day before yesterday."

In my dream, my grandfather finally succeeded in teaching his myna bird to say "Good-bye, take care, come again" to a departing visitor.

The day before I went abroad, my mother packed for me. She managed to put together some photos from who knows where.

"Weren't these lost in the flood of '87?

My mother didn't reply. She lowered her head and looked at the photos one by one. She mumbled to herself as she looked at them.

"Your father would be so happy if he could see you going abroad to study."

You never imagined your father was dead.

It was Grandfather who divined it in the temple.

"I'm afraid he died in a foreign country," explained Grandfather as he read the quatrain on the bamboo divination slip. You had no way of understanding. You never felt your father's death in the slightest.

It was the death of my grandfather that ended our miserable life when my mother was being pressured to remarry after Retrocession.

The next day in the airport, my mother pressed something into my hand and told me to keep it safe. I opened it in the airplane. It was two photos of my father wrapped in a white handkerchief.

One of the photos was of my father carrying me on his shoulders. I was about three years old, and he was looking up at me. The photo was taken behind our house. The other one was also taken behind our house. My father, arms crossed, leaned leisurely against the brick wall, gazing into the distance with a smile on his face. The betel nut palm was only half a head taller than he.

My mother's family had a piece of a land that was made into a pool in which to raise eels. The eel business made some money. My mother decided to spend the money to travel around the world to fulfill her long-cherished childhood wish. She was already more than sixty years old at that time.

My sister told me in a letter that my mother planned to travel abroad in the spring. You had been teaching in a foreign country, and hearing this, you started to feel uneasy.

"I was afraid that she would start running again," I said.

"But in fact?" Liao retorted. From his anxious tone of voice, he obviously had had this question in mind earlier. He had been waiting for the right moment to say, "But in fact, you were the one who was running."

His words embarrassed me momentarily.

"You think so?" After a moment of silence, I continued, "I reckon it has been seventeen years."

"How do you feel coming back this time?"

"I am getting older, but my whole body is sort of like a Taiwanese tile that could shatter at any moment."

"How do you feel about your mother?"

"As a matter of fact, I asked to come back and teach because I was afraid my mother would run away again."

I recently had been upset about being asked to write a reference letter for a female student who wanted to study abroad. I hesitated to write it, because I found out she was a mother.

"Did you write it?"

"Tell me, if I did write it, did I help a young mother run away?"

The fact that I have two children still makes me shiver.

To me the children seem more fragile than tiles. I'm scared to death that I'll drop them and they'll break.

"But it shouldn't be that way," said Liao. "How are your children?"

"My children, at any rate, have no worries."

"Sounds like you're the one who has the problem."

"I think so too."

"Does your mother still plan to travel?"

"Not for the time being. She seems to sense that I came especially to stop her."

"Didn't you talk to her about it when you saw her?"

"No."

"Then what did you say to her when you saw her?"

"When I saw her, I just held her tight," I said. "I was afraid she would run again, run so fast into the vast dark expanse where night merges with the sea."

"Do you mean to say that your mother is the source of your misfortunes and no one else?"

Liao hesitated, as if he were probing as well as suggesting. It suddenly dawned on you, and you wanted to say, that his words were the result of his own experience. He was talking about himself.

No, perhaps it was just the clinical observations of a psychiatrist.

"If you consider it a misfortune, then . . ." You'd like to answer as well as argue for yourself. You'd like to persuade him and at the same time persuade yourself.

But he continued along the same lines.

"Then that is both fortunate and unfortunate." That was the first time you had an inkling of Liao's eloquence. "It's the beginning and the end. It's all indistinguishable—the beginning and the end, fortune and misfortune."

"Wherever you start, it all ends up in the same place."

"No matter which way you look at it, it's a mental burden." He knew you were willing to chime in, so he spoke more emphatically. Even after more than ten years, you still saw the same rigidity that had characterized him as a child.

"Which is enough to make you happy."

"Even if you had a nervous breakdown, you could come here for help."

"Even that."

"Then all sons the world over share the same fate, don't they?"

"All sons."

"The world is filled with such brilliance on account of the complicated mother-son relationship."

"…"

You were unable to respond, for no other reason than that Liao was right in front of you. You hesitated again. Could it have been that he was talking about himself?

When he was little, my mother often had him stay at our home to keep me company because he was an orphan.

Liao's father suddenly passed away the year after Retrocession. All alone, he left Jiayi for Taipei and lived on the family property, which was managed at that time by his second uncle.

The first time the teacher brought him to our second grade classroom, he stood in the doorway, looking very old, not because he was two years older than us but because he was still wearing mourning for his father. The teacher introduced the late enrollee to us in class. He stood numbly on the platform. His cold expression aroused our curiosity.

Leaning back in his rattan chair, he looked, with the same cold expression, past the Chinese ilex outside the window, past the wall, past the quiet rails, to the sky that was already darkening. On the eve of his graduation from primary school, his second uncle committed suicide. He sat numbly in the same manner for many days in the same rattan chair.

He was the master of this old Western-style house, the only offspring and survivor of a sad, unfortunate but renowned Jiayi clan.

The thick mud wall around the Western-style house once made him feel secure and comfortable. During the years from primary school to college, the double iron doors in the middle of the wall had been tended by one of his distant relatives. When we came to visit him, his distant relative would slowly limp out and force the door open. The two iron doors swung open on wheels that fit into iron runners in the ground. Once inside, we would be confronted with a deeply serene atmosphere pervading the lush greenery of trees that had been planted by three generations.

Now the metal plaque on which was engraved the words LIAO HOSPITAL had lost its luster. The hospital, which during its heyday had housed as many as fifteen patients, had suspended business. Lacking all joy in life, much like the house, he often stared at the rails. He remained absolutely still as if he were part of the lifeless building itself, passing indifferently through time surrounded by the shadows of previous generations that had occupied the place. He always appeared tired, even when he was engaged in a convincing argument with you.

As a child, I frequently came and went from this building. It was in the four years of our primary school together, sitting in this very place, that he talked as if he were trying to cover up something about his father, who unexpectedly had been shot dead in the Jiayi Train Station, and how he and his grandmother went to bury him.

The dust, the shadows, and the illnesses combined to create a certain inexplicable mood that hung over him. You might conclude that he chose to become a psychiatrist because he was forced to leave his mother as a child. His grandfather blamed his father's violent death on his daughter-in-law and drove her out of the family. After arriving in Taipei, Liao never saw his mother again. He knew his mother was trying to devise some way to see him, the same way he tried to devise a way to find her. But his mother never saw him, and he never saw her.

"Go on, go on."

When we were young and full of vigor, we dreamed about the pure and dependable love of our mothers. As our bodies and hearts are exhausted, the years we enjoyed with our mothers seem so remote.

"Go on, go on."

Who said that a mother's love is faultless?

"Is that what you felt after you got married?" asked Liao.

"Mother said the noise of her grandchild's cough kept her awake at night."

"Separated by the Pacific Ocean?"

"The noise her daughter-in-law made as she washed the dishes was so loud that it kept her awake."

"Is that then the reason you stayed overseas and were so reluctant to return home sooner?"

"She even hurried across the ocean for fear that her own child would be unable to feed himself properly."

"That time your mother did indeed want to run to you."

"She said that she was getting old."

Could it be that all mothers in the world are ambitious illusionists who seek to use love to control their children who have already left the nest?

But not everyone is inherently capable of indulging in this kind of love.

Who could enjoy a mother's jealousy more than a gentle childhood caress?

You'd have as many misfortunes as the joys you carelessly cast aside, and how many misfortunes did you have in the love in which you sacrificed yourself as well as others, and sacrificed others as well as yourself?

"Oh, a mother's jealousy is flickering in the son's eyes now."

Liao's sudden excitement made you more indulgent.

Jealousy and promise, hostility and kindness are neighbors often living harmoniously side by side, capable of becoming a mental burden anytime.

"Go on, go on."

Even the most serene and considerate moment can secretly sow the seeds of future regret.

Oh, the war between mother and son to destroy each other never ends.

"One moment she is running away from you; the next, she is running toward you."

"Rarely in the long years of one's life does she ever run just right."

"The direction and the timing often are upside down and deranged."

"When she should run to you, she runs away. When she should run away, she runs to you."

During the war, after my mother realized that my father would never return, she and her children bonded together for survival. Does that mean that she has sowed the most pungent seeds of love since then?

The image of your mother that you carried abroad with you all those years was not that of an old woman, her face full of wrinkles, stooped over, and whose legs were loaded with the weight of time, but that of a beautiful mother who was always running toward you.

"Is that because I cannot squarely face reality?"

"Those are unnecessary worries." Liao seemed to be easing his own anxiety.

"I hope you can analyze my bad situation."

"You miss your mother."

Actually it was Liao who took care of my mother during those years. When my sister was unable to get away and care for my aged mother or even take her to see the doctor when her gout flared up, it was Liao who took her and even supported her with his own hands. Liao treated her as if she were his own mother.

"That's just my recollection," I said. "I hope such recollections are not colored in the slightest with shades of regret."

"Making them just pure recollections?"

"Just pure recollections."

"Just let your memories lead you."

"Let my memories lead me."

Outside it was now pitch dark. The tea was already cold and astringent. Liao was not ready to turn on the light.

Just half an hour before, he had forced himself to get up, walk over to the hallway, and turn on a small lamp. The entire living room was concealed between light and dark. It seemed that we could cherish our memories and talk only under a dim light.

Liao sat alone here every day, absorbing the twilight with his eyes. I heard that this was the most effective way for him to relieve his mental fatigue.

The last train on the Tamshui railway line that night passed by. The train whistle faded into the distance, engulfing our speculations, creating an enormous space that made us feel so tiny, as if we had returned to the days of our childhood, when we lingered barefooted in the paddy fields around Shuanglian.

The small houses by the railroad tracks appeared even smaller whenever the trains came and went, and the lush, green fields unfolded, expanding to fill heaven and earth. The fading whistle revealed the mystery of the sky. Only at such moments did you wish you were a child again. The egrets were not alarmed; they languidly took wing from one field to the next to meet the train as it flew by and expressed, from the air, the chill feebleness of life. And even though the sun was still high, if you paid attention, you could see masses of dewy clouds move, gathering and diffusing, diffusing and gathering, before you all the way to the Yuanshan iron bridge. It was the best time to jump into the ditch to catch loaches and mudfish. After Retrocession, Liao and I played every day in this way. We didn't stop until dark, and then we dragged our muddy feet home. My mother would wash our dirty clothes.

A fear confronted often enough is no longer feared. A good many years ago my mother suffered so much from gout that she could not even get up because of the pain. She gradually gave up her dream of traveling around the world. My sister mentioned in a letter that the wind blew the sweet scent of osmanthus flowers through the back courtyard, which reminded my mother of the ditch at Grandmother's house. The osmanthus flowers fell into the dry ditch and attracted hordes of fruit flies that could not be driven away. As it turned cold, the fruit flies became restless, sitting wherever they fancied without the slightest fear of being crushed to death. She only remembered her mother's home when she was sick in bed.

"Living in the city for so long, there are many things I no longer see. I don't know if the fruit flies are still seen at your grandmother's place or not."

My sister related my mother's sickbed words to me.

The B-29 bombers no longer appeared in my recent dreams, but my mother appeared in them more frequently than before. In my dreams she was a slim and graceful young mother, not a bedridden old woman with a lingering disease.

Under the shade of the tree fern across the street, my mother waited, holding my lunchbox.

As the twelve o'clock bell rang to signal the end of class, I dashed out of the classroom.

I paused at the school gate; I didn't want to cross the street.

Therefore, my mother, her skirt billowing, crossed the street.

Step by step it billowed across.

Step by step it drew nearer.

And there she was.

Then I could sense the warmth of my mother's body.

I was reluctant to take the lunch box from her right away.

I struggled for a moment, standing there, not wanting my mother to leave, so that my classmates could see how beautiful she was.

My mother had perfectly curled hair like cedar moss.

I was already a middle-school student at the time.

Life's first kindness called unexpectedly and wonderfully just when you were frightened about losing something, as if someone came and calmly led you into a rich and gorgeous dervish's whirl.

However, this was only a recollection, you said to yourself.

After the uncontrollable excitement, you could only approach your two children.

You understood that you could not fight your children for their mother. You would say:

"Children, one day you will remember your mother."

In the confusion when you sacrifice yourself as well as others, and sacrifice others as well as yourself, we know not who will calmly enter the happy procession of the host in heaven. In such a vigorous age, who doesn't dream of perpetual joy? As the last whistle of the train was fading away, the vast expanse of dark where night merges with the sea appeared leisurely. Perhaps it was a good place for you to take refuge. You took in the twilight as if you were absorbing the memory of your mother's bodily warmth.

Your dreams made your sister feel uneasy.

The last letter from your sister across the ocean said she was sad and couldn't sleep, because you were exhausting yourself, body and mind, for no reason. She also said that after she tossed and turned all night, she knew your mother would be consoled if she knew about it. The next day she folded up your letter and put it before your deceased mother's spirit tablet along with the burning incense.

Clover

TRANSLATED BY **HAYES MOORE AND LEE YU**

When you saw him, your memory was stirred—you seemed to have met before. Where ... when ...? There had been someone like him, whom you met in a dream long before you knew him. Unable to stop yourself, you walked upriver into the golden rays of the setting sun, approached him, step by step.

He was alone, like a chest of drawers that had recently been moved from the corner of the room, ill at ease and out of place. He leaned against the rail lost in thought, his eyes roaming. He appeared shy, like a fire lit in the wind, reluctant, trying to extinguish itself. Yes, he was a pale youth who wanted only to stand alone at the stern of the boat. He was the sort of person who made it through his days in silence, as if he had grown nourished only by the wind. The first time you saw him was on the Mississippi River.

You had received an express letter from your sister at home and made a special trip to Louisiana to visit her childhood friend who had suddenly fallen ill. You planned to return to school in the north upstream via steamboat.

Tucked into his luggage beside him was a Chinese newspaper, something you had not seen in ages. The paper flapped pleasantly in the wind, as if his hometown were calling out. Feebly, you wanted to grab the paper he was about to throw away, but for a moment it felt as if the wind had grown wings. It was difficult to grasp. And he was at a loss. That was not so strange, for he had only recently left home.

You wanted to talk with him. And you were pained because a confused nostalgia appeared in your eyes. He had just recently come to this new land. You asked around about him and learned that he was going to school not far from where you lived, about half a day's drive. He was majoring in philosophy and history at a seminary.

"If all goes smoothly, we'll get there by sundown tomorrow."

He did not speak for a long time. Occasionally he raised his head toward the sky as if to predict the future from the splendid clouds. The Adam's apple on his thin, long neck was unusually large. That large lump bobbed up and down even when he was not speaking. Finally, as if his mouth were dry, he stammered, asking if the weather could be relied upon.

Clouds dyed red by the setting sun brushed past a nameless forest. The horizon was jet black. The wind on the river blew sharply, making people long for home. The sunset was fading. The beating against the boat's belly slowly slackened. Farther away, on the other side of the forest, the sun was hastening to set. The mist embraced the riverbank; that calm enfolding imitated the dim thoughts of people.

His body was traveling quickly, but his thoughts gradually became as calm as the vast expanse of the river. Silence and the evening light intermingled, as if mocking your busy, disordered life. The river below rose and fell ardently. Only at that moment did you realize that the delicate current was wholly for the consolation of a frustrated dreamer. Standing dumbly beside the rail, he was doing nothing more than begging the world not to test him once more against the desires and aspirations of his heart.

You had encountered his type before. It was when you were in middle school—the memory came back to you now—you were lying in a hospital bed and saw an internist. Every evening as the sun set in the west, he would lean on a railing in the corridor. Entranced, he would fix his gaze on the ground floor. That young intern had fallen in love with an empty corner of the hospital.

The river formed a silver belt, drawn out in the wake of the boat. The last light in the tops of the trees was receding; motes of dust floated. Bathed in the depths of this dim light, you were not sure when an old-fashioned church appeared amid a shady thicket. Its platinum cross captured the final rays of the failing light.

The two of you traveled in this manner without saying anything, following the Mississippi River north.

The next time you saw him was during summer vacation two years later, in New York. You drove across half of North America to work in that great metropolis. Unexpectedly, you ran into him on the street. The garret you rented was just a few blocks away from his place. During the day the two of you waited tables at different restaurants; late at night you rode the subway home. On your days off, he would occasionally come with weary steps to visit your garret.

He could not drink tea, and always asked for a glass of water. Raising his head, he would swallow the red capsules of his medication. You never asked what kind of medicine it was. Sometimes he would brush his trouser leg with his hand. You saw that he had ten fair, slender fingers.

He was too quiet. It was hard for him to speak. His words were all concentrated in those dark eyes of his. Whether it was just the weather or some anecdote about a cat, his eyes expressed everything in his heart. The large globes of his eyes would momentarily avoid your gaze. But that deep stare, regardless of how brief, would form strong links with its sincerity. If the spirit could move matter, then his flashing, evasive eyes could bind and lead you away. That year, he climbed up to your garret on a clear day and, using all of his strength, pushed open the window. You saw a face full of life's perplexities. He was not yet thirty years old.

You drove him from New York to the seminary. Summer had passed, and the clouds hung constantly over the mountains behind the campus. When the sun did not shine through, the mountain peaks were cold and desolate. Twilight came earlier and earlier. The weather was not really cold, but people were already wearing wool sweaters. The seminary campus was built in an old, monastic style. Over time, the thick round pillars and the lofty arches of the grand halls seemed ever more solemn and dignified. On the walls, twining vines preserved an ancient composure, but every corner of the campus was once again full of vitality as a new semester was about to begin.

The lights had gone on in the little college town in the valley. A haze of lamplight fused with the color of the sky. Time stood still. Voices floated up from the earth, but in heaven, joy was matched by a solemn tranquility. At this school, separated from the world, the evening light was unusually splendid and gorgeous. Like a glass of wine in each person's hand, it warmed your heart. Sitting outside by the street at a dinner table, through the blue smoke of roasting beef, he nodded to a professor sitting across the street. The bearded professor, you heard, was the very popular Professor Solomon. This coming semester he was going to take the professor's class on "The German Ideology."

You looked across and saw a haughty face accentuated by a thick beard. That serious expression seemed to be debating some philosophical question with the people sitting beside him. You could not imagine that a whistle could come out of this person's whiskers, although he was now drinking from his large mug of beer. Yes, most of the students at the seminary majored in metaphysics. From the spirited discussion over drinks, they most certainly were debating such questions. And so, this valley town surrounded by sunset was momentarily stirred by German idealism. Indifferent to nationality, it flickered across each face; it spiraled upward, heading for the spacious, open sky, and departed. Debating philosophy seated on earth gave life a transcendent quality. As a result, the atmosphere was suffused with a vibrant melancholy fainter than the alcohol. At the table, in the midst of grand arguments, in accents from every country, human shadows sank away. The glow of lamps among the people appeared only in the dark of night.

The idea of delving into the mysteries of metaphysics with foreigners had always been inconceivable to you. But to him, metaphysics was as natural as gnawing at one's own loneliness. Only after you became close to him did you realize that what was inside people was so dark and un-fathomable. Sitting quietly to one side as he was, there was something other than a marvelous ease in his silence when compared to those fero-ciously debating around him. The fear of inadequacy hung about him in the presence of so many ideas tossed around.

As you drove back to the quiet campus from work downtown, you gathered your scattered thoughts, for heaven and earth were changing quickly. And the beer you drank gradually gave rise to a fine nostalgia. Rustling trees in the twilight stirred your memories. A moment earlier, clouds had appeared in the sky with forms you recognized, interpreted freely, based on the town you left long ago.

Dew soaked your feet. You walked up the slope toward his apartment; looking back, you saw the lights in the tavern below you still burning. Occasionally you heard the faint noise from the bar. The entire town al-ready lay deep in the dark. The silent railroad tracks stretched coldly to-ward the south, reflecting the hues of night. Only in the depths of night did you have a premonition of winter's approach. At the end of each year, snow enveloped the Midwestern plains in icy layers.

By the first snow of last year a marriage was breaking up. You heard that Professor Solomon raised his wine glass at a Philosophy Depart-ment banquet, his face slightly flushed.

"So, you're the philosophy student from Formosa?"

With fear and trepidation, he waited for the famous professor to clink his wine glass with yours. Professor Solomon's wife, who felt like hiding, hurriedly left the gathering. She opened the door and departed, a solitary figure escaping into the cold of swirling snowflakes.

The professor's words were punctuated with hiccups. Later he said to this foreign student, "I'm sorry, you came at a very inappropriate time." He was a sincere believer. He would often tell his philosophy students that trying to disprove the existence of God was not only pointless but also futile.

When you got up at dawn, from his apartment window you could see a thin line of smoke rising from a granary far off in a quiet field. Only from this commanding point did you realize that there was nothing more to this small town than the businesses along the road to the seminary. The post office occupied a discrete corner inside the pharmacy. Next door was the bank, on the upper floors of which were an insurance company and Social Security Administration offices.

The smell of coffee permeated the apartment complex. When it snowed last year, the landlady had come knocking on his door to borrow some eggs and a little sugar. She stood at the door and asked him about his hometown. She was a nice lady. Her son and daughter had already grown up and left home. She lived alone on the top floor. Later, for no particular reason, she would often come knocking on his door. In front of a moody, taciturn youth, this elderly lady became talkative. Seeing him thin as a rail, she had suggested that he eat a serving of dandelion greens every day. She could stand in the hallway and discourse on any subject under the sun, instructing and advising him, mentioning the weather and criticizing life.

She complained of insomnia. She just couldn't sleep a wink at night, she would say. But in the morning when she opened her eyes, it felt like she had slept. She thought that she must have dreamed about being unable to sleep. This confused her.

"Dreams are so tricky. They might come and demand my life someday."

In the afternoon she wanted to visit the granary and came looking for him. She wanted him to go with her to visit the elderly man who had guarded the old, broken-down granary for so many years. He was eighty now. The deer he was curing reminded her of her childhood. She said she was herself once a country girl who harvested wheat. Every evening she would brew another pot of coffee, perfuming the entire apartment complex. As she talked about the elderly man at the granary, she mentioned his lifelong setback.

"Love is one of life's accidents. In the end it made him the way he is."

You stayed at his apartment for two days. On the evening you left, you stood together again on the dark, sloping path, watching the lights of the little town reflected on the sky. Afterward, you did not speak again until the start of summer the following year, when unexpectedly he called you long distance.

A nest of birds had hatched in his air conditioner.

"What should I do? What should I do?"

Flustered, he choked. "What kind of birds are they?"

"Could they be migratory birds?"

He had lost his presence of mind, similar to what would happen if you opened a book on metaphysics.

Once he said to you over the phone that he really did not need to go to New York to find work. The pay was not bad at the nearby nursing home. He heard that if you carried an old man's corpse from the nursing home to the crematorium, you could make at least twenty dollars.

He said he had to move. The place was too cold in the winter and too humid in the summer. It was not good for his health.

He ought to go elsewhere to study philosophy and history.

He suffered from asthma. Even on fine days he would carry an inhaler that resembled a spray gun. Sometimes he would put it in his mouth and shoot a mist with an irritating smell down his throat. He had a deep cough for someone so young. Each time he coughed it was as if he were going to cough out his lungs. His entire body thrown forward, he gasped for air to fill his emptied chest.

It sounded as if his body were bursting.

The school nurse advised him to find a Mediterranean climate; otherwise he would find it difficult to recover.

"Does your country have a Mediterranean climate?" asked the school nurse.

He said that if Taiwan weren't so humid, he never would have left. If he had not left Taiwan, sooner or later he would have died of asthma.

He considered the childbearing system described in Akutagawa's *Kappa* extremely reasonable.

Just before the kappa was born, its father approached the open reproductive organs of the mother, and, as if he were speaking by phone, he talked to the fetus inside the mother, introducing it to every aspect of the society it was about to enter. Then he asked for the fetal kappa's opinion.

Whether it wanted to be born or not was left entirely up to the unborn kappa. If it felt it would not be compatible with the society described by its father, it could decide not to be born and its mother would receive a shot and her large belly would immediately shrink.

If his father had let him know how things stood ahead of time, he would not have thought twice about it and would not have been born in Taiwan. He always joked this way when he had a coughing fit.

Gauguin could move from Paris and make his home in Tahiti because a sailor's blood flowed in his veins. Where had he read this? He had always admired Gauguin. The story about the sailor's blood and other stories like that may not have been true.

"Perhaps he had some hidden affair that prevented him from remaining in Paris."

He said that his lifelong dream was to be a village pastor, to have a small church of his own where he could contentedly preach the gospel his whole life. As a young man in his hometown, he used to look out through his dark window. He would see villagers walking down the stone steps of the church. Silently holding black umbrellas, in twos and threes they would walk out onto the village's freezing, rainy streets. The streets shone under the street lamps at dusk. Though separated from them by the windowpane, he could still hear those solitary shadows dragging heavy footsteps through the warm, light rain, lonely. For the first time, his chest swelled fully as he leaned toward the window.

At the seminary in the valley, he pointed to some distant mountain peaks and asked whether or not that was snow on top of them. A female American student who had had several pints of beer looked up and said, "It's just October, there can't be snow this early." It was too early for snow. After speaking, she returned to her beer mug.

"But you can't cry for a rainy street in your hometown."

From the very beginning, that female philosophy student took a liking to him. She gave him a linen shirt and wanted him to wear it every day. She sewed a clover on the front of it for him.

"Did you ever hunt for clover when you were a kid?"

She looked at him. Then she said to herself, *Hmm, it sounds like kids all over the world play the same games.*

Long live clover.

This made the female student happy all day long. When evening arrived, she wanted to spend the night with him.

And it really was snow. The snow piled on the mountain ridge, soft, agreeable. From a distance, it looked like a spirit descending from the air. At the hospital in Taipei, the patients vied to get a look at Tatun Mountain peak from the hospital window. There was a full-page report on the snowfall on the front page of the metro section. The entire hospital was in an uproar. The patients even forgot about their illnesses. They had never seen snow in all their lives.

The young internist alone leaned on a different railing, fixing his eyes on that empty space on the ground floor. Wearing his starched, stiff white doctor's coat, did he realize that white clothing was meant to keep the dust away? He had ten fair, slender fingers. The stethoscope would tremble in his hand, as if it were being used to transmit his own heartbeat. He leaned over you in the sickbed and you felt his cheeks burning more feverishly than a sick person's.

Fear and anguish would appear in his eyes at any moment; looking at the faces of his patients, he would ponder even deeper worries. You thought that something regrettable and difficult to talk about must have happened to him. But then one evening when the rays of a winter sunset suddenly burst forth, he walked with quick, light steps down the hospital corridor, all thoughts abandoned to the twilight, his heart wallowing in the twilight, his tired eyes suddenly taking on the distant tenderness of the evening sky.

In the summer of the following year, you saw him again in the hospital. A ribbed pattern of a stout banana leaf was printed on his white clothes. A draft in the hospital caressed his twitching face. He held a clipboard of medical histories in his hand as if he were holding a notebook. The smell of summer seaweed filled the corner of the red brick walls of the hospital. He hung his head in front of an old professor, as if he were silently apologizing.

You had just finished the paperwork for admitting your mother to the hospital. As you walked down the hall, you thought you saw tears rolling down the intern's new beard.

The old professor turned and departed. He stayed standing there alone, hanging his head, facing the wall.

Why did he want such a stern teacher?

You did not look at him again as you anxiously walked down the hall.

Life was being consumed. His silence had already reached a point where he could do nothing but destroy himself.

"No matter what," the head doctor had told him the previous year, "the patient comes first."

He was feverish to the point that when he walked down the corridor at dusk, something had already forsaken him.

He had forgotten himself in his love for that empty space. Whenever he had a free moment, he would lean against the concrete railing on the second floor, his stethoscope hanging at his chest. Holding his breath, he let his eyes roam.

On the day you checked out of the hospital, you looked over the railing and saw that empty space. It was a small corner that no one tended. It was spotted with traces of dead moss and covered with broken tiles and dead leaves from the year before. Many years later you suddenly realized that the young doctor was the type of person who had to wait for winter to arrive before he was able to love. Even now you were still drawn to those eyes that were like water.

You climbed the mountain behind the seminary with him; standing on a beautiful mountain path, you gazed down upon the entire town. The train station, bank, liquor store, church, nursing home. . . . A bit farther off was a long, narrow field. The alfalfa was already dry and the bales neatly stacked in rows. Even farther was that isolated granary. Against the morning sun, the granary's wooden walls were rust colored. On Sundays in the small town, the train station lay like a solitary child sound asleep.

Every time he climbed the mountain it was for the unimpeded view. When he stood before the vast wilderness, the emptiness expanded. His luminous eyes coupled with the scene. Time vanished. The open country before him would stretch out in silence, on and on, unbroken, until everything was revealed. Autumn's vast brightness and solemnity reigned over all. He knew that whenever he climbed the mountain he would be able to see a field without a human trace. Then he would look at the autumnal wilds with no expectations, and the scenery before his eyes would mirror the loneliness of his solitary shadow.

It was during that autumn, in the silence at noon, that you unwittingly sensed that you had already become his friend.

Sometimes his face would twitch. That would be the previous night's insomnia. It was at the start of your friendship. You were suddenly moved to pour out your heart. The two of you would lie together with open eyes, staring at the ceiling until daybreak. Later, when each of you turned over in search of sleep, in all likelihood he did not sleep.

With the footsteps of an insomniac, he climbed the mountain behind the seminary, his thoughts lured on by the silence. Every time he stood facing the open country, his appearance moved your heart and spirit. Then you would understand: the dream had to be dreamed while standing.

The decay of his hometown streets was inscribed on his face. His young body was the only defense for his own world. That day, the two of you stayed on the mountain the entire day, until the church steeple vanished in the twilight. When he went to speak, his gaunt body began to change, slowly becoming warm, kind, and delicate. Only at such times could he break free from the secret deep in his heart and reach a final peace with the spacious earth.

A window opened. He, a graduate student in a seminary, always waited for a voice to call to him. He was prepared to make contact with that strange voice when it came. But the waiting made him fall apart. He would look out the window to view the world with eyes puffy from lack of sleep. He had already paid a price of sorts for that fallow field. That year you had become very close; at any time, you could even hear his breath rattling in his chest. The autumn leaves turned red, and the sudden cold weather bound your two solitary lives together.

And that really was snow. The female student who had drunk several glasses of beer was wrong. Snow was piled on the mountain ridge. It was just October and snow had already appeared on the mountain behind the school. Snow had covered the mountain slopes. In December came one of the biggest snowstorms in the Midwest. He drove a day and a night to get to your place in order to escape the snow, but also to get away from the female student who had been pestering him. That was your guess.

The two of you had not seen each other for several months; he behaved as if he were in the presence of a stranger. He looked away from you, as if avoiding a needle.

He didn't know what to do with his hands. He hid them in his pockets. Every time he took them out, he knocked over something. He touched everything, and everything seemed to await his touch to shatter into pieces. Everywhere he touched, he left his damp fingerprints. His hands were always sweaty; even during the day, it was as if he had night sweats.

In later memories, that pair of lovely hands turned and fluttered through the empty air.

That pair of hands had freed a nest of young birds from an air conditioner in the summer of that year. Only when those hands held a book could they be said to have returned home. You recalled that the book he brought to your apartment that time was Hegel's *Phenomenology of Spirit*, the cover damp from his sweaty hands.

He lay in the guest room listening to Mahler's *Das Lied von der Erde*. Behind him, you sensed his eyes cutting through the air. His thoughts had drifted far away again. Too many things weighed on his heart. Listening to the music as he lay there, he sought himself. Occasionally he would cast a glance at you. The lingering intensity of his gaze always left you feeling apologetic because you had no way to respond. The previous year, his silence had alarmed the seminary. An autumn moon hung in the middle of the sky when he had suddenly run with tears in his eyes down a road covered with leaves. He ran straight home, alone. There was a harsh, cracking noise beneath his feet. The two of you strolled through the small town at midnight. Passing the pharmacy and the butcher shop, where the lights had been turned off, you walked toward his apartment complex. He had been moved by the vacant, soulless train station. Then he began to run. He didn't know how to take part in life. You knew he could not become part of the life in this small town.

Now your room was filled with irritating mist from his asthma inhaler. He loved snowstorms. The only time he drank wine was to toast the bold vigor of snowflakes. The entire pure-white sky formed a warm tent for him. The whistling wind outside made his silence even more transparent. Music eventually calmed him. That first time on the boat, you had noticed that, finally, beneath his feet, the Mississippi River also moved with such composure, such immensity.

He talked about his life at home. The apartment complex was suffused with white warmth, the light reflected off the snow outside. And in the silent night, only the branches nostalgically stretched forth their loneliness in the weak, cold light of the street lamps.

You could no longer describe that street in your hometown accurately. You stole some money when you were little; your father, who was drunk during the day, scolded you. You stood facing a wall, the foot of which was covered with pine needles; the river wafted the fragrance of pine resin to your distressed nose. Such scenes often appeared in the darkness of night as you recalled your hometown. You saw, as if in a dream, a shabby house on the bank of the Tamshui River where your ruined father leaned on an altar table, pouring himself drinks. With beclouded, drunken eyes he looked out the window, past the dense summer banyan shadows, staring at the Cheng family's red brick mansion on the riverbank. Young, you were already aware that your father was a failure.

And your cat silently snuggled against his chest, having become his friendly companion over the last few days.

Normally the cat would loll against the window, bored beyond belief. Sometimes its eyes would suddenly flash and then fade with the slow, dark descent of time. And so it would accompany you through another day. At times you disdained these American cats that could live their entire lives without once seeing a mouse. He would place the cat on top of himself to play with it until his elbows displayed bright red claw marks. The cat was happy—it would viciously claw at his flesh. And he was even happier than the cat—he had never expected that something could so easily sink into the narrow playfulness of his arms.

Sometimes the cat would walk away from him to crouch in a corner of the room. They would silently gaze at each other from a distance, calmly interacting with civility. Only at such times could you see in its eyes that a spirit had filled it.

Someone could be heard shoveling snow on the street. The sky seemed on the verge of brightening: the sun labored behind layered clouds. When you looked out the window, the scene had the look of a half-boiled egg.

Finally the feeble light of dawn shone on the snow. Overflowing with the dawn, the room abruptly lost the sealed-in comfort provided by the snow. The light quickly dispersed beautiful dreams. Cats are naturally more spirited than humans. It wholeheartedly wanted to pursue solitude and depart with him. The paw prints of the cat extended across the snow from the door and ended directly behind him. That was the cat's vow to follow you, regardless of the odds, its whole life. Only you, the owner of the cat, remembered its abortive truancy that day. It broke your heart. You had fed it for all those years and yet it was actually a dispirited animal with no home.

The last time you saw him was just after the new year, in early spring at the Chicago Botanic Garden.

It was after you'd entered the tropical fern house. He nonchalantly appeared from behind a hanging basket of ferns shining in the sunlight. Loneliness like cracks in porcelain remained inscribed on his face. Pale, he still looked so young, and now it was as if his shyness stemmed from some sort of irremediable regret. A giant tree fern spread beside him; bubbling water gurgled with the voice of his hometown. You saw each other at almost the same instant; neither of you was surprised, as if you knew that you would meet here. He just grinned and laughed. A piece of porcelain was about to break.

That day, the two of you lingered in the botanic garden until sunset. They set up a tea table in a small room full of skylights so that you could sit down and slowly sip your drinks. The sunlight fell on the small, round table top. Still, he drank nothing but water. He smoked silently.

Outside the French door, a large patch of moon-white dwarf narcissus flowers blossomed, nodding in the wind. A sign in front of the flower bed said that this type of narcissus was commonly known as "April Tears." He could no longer live here. He said he wanted to go west to Las Vegas to work for a while. The desert might be good for his asthma; besides, he would be able to save a little money.

His voice was resolute. The words he had been saving up while alone amounted to no more than a few lonely sentences.

He was destroying himself, is what you thought.

The way he focused his gaze outside clearly revealed that physically he had too many worries to bear.

He said that Professor Solomon had already ruined himself with alcohol after his wife left. Whenever he heard a horn outside, he always looked out, thinking that she had come driving back.

You recalled the small town where the seminary was located. You recalled the excited passion aroused in the professors by the autumn sun, how they welcomed the festive happiness of a new semester as they drank beer.

But Professor Solomon, even when drunk, still insisted that arguing about the existence of God was futile.

"If one had such ideas, it would be better to join the Salvation Army."

When he lectured in class, a tremor would pass through him. He faced the ultimate metaphysical questions, and his eager expectations won the love of his students. He would open his textbook to the most moving page and point out the wounds of life for his students.

"Human beings must seek suffering."

One day while taking a bath, he suddenly pricked up his ears. It was the sound of a car horn outside. Like a horse in the middle of a battlefield who hears the bugle call, he turned, climbed out of the bathtub, and ran outdoors. You heard that Professor Solomon stood completely naked in the middle of the street.

And he had decided to leave that small town. He gazed out the window, drinking water. He paused to find the words. Several times, as he was about to speak, he swallowed his words. He gazed up at the sky and suddenly looked odd. You knew that he was eating at himself in the dark again and was troubled because at that moment he was unable to treat you with warmth. Yet while sitting there quietly, you sensed that he had already begun to travel.

Go west, to Nevada. Go to Reno, or even a little farther, to Las Vegas. Leave this inland area, and go to a place where there is no humidity. Now the desert was the only place he sensed he could live.

It was already spring, the perfect time for travel.

And still he continued to gaze up at the sky while smoking, predicting what was to come in the splendid clouds.

It was true, such weather was unreliable. Last year after the beginning of spring, there was another large snowfall. Snow, more than five inches deep, froze the newly blossoming hyacinths, crocuses, and snowdrops.

Early spring clouds floated by overhead. The quickly lengthening shadows had fallen and dusk had overtaken busy Chicago.

He walked down the street. Fading sunlight lingered on the tops of the skyscrapers. The street had already arrived at the intersection of day and night. The mute buildings were drawn to his faint shadow. You noticed that the Chicago skyscrapers actually possessed very simple lines that wanted nothing more than to stand upright in the air.

You walked beside him, encouraged by solitude, the bustling crowds forgotten.

After you went your separate ways in Chicago, you buried your head in your books. Your dissertation had reached a point where you could no longer continue to put it off. Your advisor told you that you had dragged it out for nearly ten years now. If you continued to do so, he could not help you anymore. This warning finally awakened you.

In order to dispel the accumulated anxiety, you spent entire days in front of the typewriter. "Trying to interpret a polysemous narrative from a single point of view is rather. . . ." Evening was approaching, and the last light of the sun gleamed in the study. Tranquility froze into a chilly loneliness, occupying the apartment for singles where you had lived for ten years. When you couldn't write, you often thought of things your younger sister had said.

In a letter, your sister said she finally knew that the only warm place she would have in her entire life was the home she'd had when she was young.

She said that as soon as she had married she knew the emptiness of life. Marriage scared her. Your divorced sister had returned to live with your father.

Your sister also said that for a while she had had extremely negative feelings toward your father. When your father drank, he would still raise his hand and slap her. "Am I a child? I've been married," said your sister. Then she was filled with regret. "The way I treated our father, I ought to be beaten." Your sister did not want it to be that way, so she took care of him and paid for a set of dentures for him.

"Well, now he can eat peanuts again when he drinks."

While your sister was getting a perm, she suddenly could not bear to sit there any longer and began sobbing. She was extremely scared, if Father continued to drink like this . . . and the police had come to the door. "Who knows what Father says when he gets drunk?" Her letters often complained that she had not been a good sister to you because she didn't understand anything. She was horrible at everything. All she wanted to do was look after her father, but she couldn't even do that.

However, your sister continued, with someone looking after him, the wrinkles on his face didn't seem as deep as they used to be. Father kept saying that he saw through life early on and had no fondness for it. Your sister asked if you remembered when your mother was alive. One day your father was drunk and wanted to kill himself on the railroad tracks. The next day when he awoke on the icy tracks at dawn, he suddenly discovered his conscience.

One windy summer evening, Father sobered up and began telling a story from the past about himself and your mother. This made your sister so happy she cried. Before falling asleep, your sister took a large fan out from under the stove. She ran about the room in excitement, hitting the madly flying cockroaches. "These crazy cockroaches," your sister shouted as she hit them. Her voice was filled with emotions stirred by the past. That was when you were in elementary school, when you and your sister still slept in the same bed. That night you smelled the odor of cockroaches as you sank off to sleep, your chest swelling.

The day you went to the hospital to have your appendix removed, your father was sober.

He was alone in the courtyard with his head lowered, mumbling something. He did not accompany you to the hospital—alcohol had so poisoned him that he was too flustered to walk down the road. The internist carried you to a sickbed in a third-class room. As you lay there you could hear the electric heater humming at the foot of the bed at regular intervals. The sound provided you with warmth in a sickroom that lacked sunshine in winter. Your mother had bought the heater for your operation. She hesitated for a long time before buying it, and wasted a month's worth of charcoal for credit.

The following year it was your mother's turn to be admitted to the hospital. Your father was drunk again. When your mother died in the hospital, your father was at home and still nothing more than a drunk. That internist suddenly knelt down and turned up the electric heater for your mother. However, your mother's body had already grown cold.

And the young internist had already reached a point where he could do nothing but destroy himself.

Every time a patient died in the hospital, the life within him was diminished. Soon those trembling hands would be unable to grasp the stethoscope at his chest. In the cold of winter, the young internist whose beard was just sprouting would exhale, producing clouds of white mist before him. He was eating himself up. Sometimes, with a pair of feverish eyes, he would hurriedly leave through the hospital corridor. Without the least hesitation, he strode to meet pain. Life was like a gust of wind that unintentionally blew down a handful of tender leaves.

At a morning rally once in middle school, amid the shouting of slogans, a warm ray of winter sunlight fell across your head, and thoughts of that intern from several years back momentarily made you shout louder than everyone else. You suddenly felt that every time he walked into the ward, his face was as gentle as moonlight. There in that moment of excitement, standing in a row with the others, you shouted from the bottom of your heart:

"Long live ... Long live ..."

Later you would know that someone like him would most likely not achieve happiness as a doctor. You would also know that someone like the doctor would most likely not achieve happiness as a person.

At times you wondered if the internist was still alive. He would be over fifty, and should have been a father. Every time you thought about it you said to yourself, *He is, at this precise moment, swimming through life. He is trying to solve some difficult problem he is confronting. It was destined that he would lead a difficult life. He loved that blank space by the wall so much.*

You finally prepared to leave the country. In a dark corner of the stairs, the landlord grabbed your hand. He tightly held your hand and said that you were just like the sun at midday, your future was immeasurable. He also wished you success with your study abroad, that fortune might fill your home. The desk lamp out, you came back to yourself. The dull, winter scenery of middle America had already dozed off to sleep outside. You closed the window blinds; the window of your home shone in the total darkness of your room.

Only after your mother died did your father think to scrape the strip of paper used to protect the windows from breaking during the war off the panes of glass. Late one autumn afternoon, sunlight streamed through the freshly washed windows, and through the glass you could see a row of houses, built without construction permits, bathed in the shadows. Neighbors were releasing their pigeons on the rooftops one last time before nightfall; one flock after another flapped in circles over your head, reminding you of something. Following a shadowed ditch, you hurriedly left the little alley. In the sunset, each house had started a charcoal fire outside the door. You wandered aimlessly on the streets until the shadows of the buildings appeared in the night and sparks shot from the fires in the dark and dirty alley.

Winter was approaching. Standing at your apartment window, you saw a group of black people walking along the street. The sound of laughter reverberated down the quiet asphalt streets of the small town. America had long ago become their homeland. Their footsteps were light as they walked down the street despite the winter cold—that elastic bounce of their gait seemed to move in time with music. They shone in the sunlight. From a distance, they looked like a herd of gorgeous horses; in this mighty new land they galloped, raising clouds of dust.

You walked, following the street. The elm leaves had already fallen; the sky was endless. You walked along the train station platform, leaving the narrow sidewalk of the neighborhood, finally passing the elementary school that was closed for winter vacation, leaving everyone behind as you entered empty ground. A foreign country, a small town hidden in a pine forest. The river became shallower, revealing the dried, corroded riverbed. As you walked, you thought about the dissertation you held in your hand, going over in your head again your advisor's most recent comments. The last few years you'd felt no urgency to finish writing it. If you did not finish it, the truth was that you would not even be able to keep your temporary teaching position.

Occasionally a weak ray of light appeared before you; you thought that your dissertation, which had kept you occupied day and night, had taken a turn for the better. But then the light vanished, and what you saw was really the snow settled on withered limbs. You surely must have felt at ease in the small town. After all, you had idled away much of your life there. Wandering off to a foreign land the way you did was no longer something unexpected in life. On weekends in the small town, the only thing you did to pass the time was tediously peruse your sister's old letters.

After you parted ways in Chicago, you never saw him again. The phone in your home became quieter. You discovered that when you were by yourself, whether it was walking along the street or busily handling affairs, you were always listening to his silence, feeling that it was the most convincing metaphysical argument. Now your slow memory would only awaken with winter. One day right after you got out of bed, your mouth was filled with bitterness, the cold entered from the cracks in the window, and suddenly you found yourself thrust amid the scent of his body.

His thin and melancholy form never ceased to make you feel that loneliness was fostered from the cradle.

Those roaming, unsettled eyes told you that even when he was standing still, he was still traveling rapidly. His sole aspiration in life was to live in exile in some far corner of the world. That summer, he used all his strength to open the window in your New York garret simply to see a corner of the sky.

At home he wandered all day along the village's sole street. His hometown was composed of a cluster of small villages. Resting at the foot of a mountain, they always looked sparse and solitary in the sunlight.

Country life echoed in the valley. In the vast, icy American Midwest he once proudly spoke of those familiar sounds from his childhood.

The sound of the village women's wooden buckets dropping into the well, the calls of greeting through bamboo groves after breakfast, the sporadic sound of nails hammered into caskets in the shadow of the trees—some echo always floated through the sky that was such a melancholy blue. Sounds, just like rays of light, illuminated his youthful life in the village.

He could not vainly ignore time. He could not let himself be idle. He needed to do something with this life. Ever since he was a child he had pushed himself. In a fine, warm rain, he had walked down the only street in the village. After a few steps, he had already reached the end of it. So he turned around, wanting to go back and knock on every door. He wanted to embrace every person who came out and wail.

He walked alone in the rain. After falling sick, he knew that his asthma would linger, accompanying him through the rest of his life. With him the days passed quietly and calmly. His village was finally outfitted with electric lights. The night the lights came on everyone was crazy; he heard fearsome echoes in the air. Not long afterward, the villagers began reading the Taipei newspapers and began to have thoughts like those in the papers. Then he got the idea to leave.

At the bus stop, when he squeezed in among the sweaty, smelly reservists, his asthma flared up immediately. Before he departed, his hometown showed him a face from the window of a speeding bus that was completely unknown to him.

He abandoned the world in this manner, startling even himself.

When he spoke of this on the mountain road behind the seminary, his face still harbored certain doubts.

You planned to climb up high, so you always left your apartment early.

Only after he left did you get the idea of copying his gaze to look at the end of the world.

You would go through the rundown elementary school, walk past that empty land to reach the slope.

You waited patiently until the scenery before you gently unfolded, the way memories of him did.

Mud, withered trees, distant houses. . . . The frozen sky unyielding and the clouds slowly pressing on your chest. Each time you climbed the slope you thought that everything would be written on the wide wilderness. And the branches, from which all of the autumn leaves had fallen, lifted the veil on an affectionate vastness for you. The breeze penetrated to the bone, and through the smokelike haze you were unable to pinpoint the sun. It was only at noon of each day that the sun would pass obliquely overhead. Human shadows left no trace, the mud had frozen solid, the wide wilderness was blanketed with white snow. The entire American Midwest lay forgotten outside the human realm. You believed that you had completely adapted to the land in which you sojourned. You resolutely held fast to that famous saying: as long as there is a place to live, there is life. Without him beside you, you finally understood that to gaze leisurely at the scenery was more important than life itself. He once so loved the narrow fields of open country behind the seminary. However, his steady gaze at the sky, his aimless walks, and those worries that nagged for no apparent reason were all the time diminishing his life. He did not care about the pain in his lungs and would let the cold air flow through his entire body. He would rather cover his mouth and cough in the wind and wrap himself tightly in an overcoat and walk resolutely toward the mountain slope. Every time that lonely figure appeared against the sky it was like a crescent moon suspended on the horizon.

The few hurried meetings you'd had with him had already become a sumptuous banquet of the past. At the beginning of winter, you smelled the fragrance of holidays past in your solitary existence. The scenery spread before your very eyes. You felt close to the open country, that smiling decline. The sky gradually took on the warm hue of mother-of-pearl. In your rapt stare, the sparseness of the winter scene was everywhere possessed with abundance and beauty, to the point of flourishing. You suddenly saw with penetrating insight that his constantly sorrowful eyes originally shone with the brilliance of the peach blossoms filling his homeland in May. This sudden illumination was like a joy fallen from heaven, dazzling and bewildering. Standing before the wide wilderness, you were convulsed with a spasm, and your legs could no longer support your weight. Scenery tortured people. The sudden rapture left you physically spent, as if after coupling. In the broad, open space of this foreign country in winter, you knew that there was no one close to you save yourself, and the scenery was the only thing to look forward to. Yes, it would not be long before there would be another snowfall with flurries on the plains before you. Every year it was the same. Snow came carried by the north wind, wailing like a madwoman, then blanketing the plains in silence. You didn't know how you'd get through the latest snow season. Every year you had fewer strategies for handling the winter. At that very moment, intoxicated by that convulsive spasm, you desired only to leap into those swaying bare branches to be embraced by the warmth of the wide wilds. Oh, spirit was still able to move matter. . . . Then the gusts of wind would be stilled, space would be made mute, and at that time, the clouds would be superfluous, rising and falling like memory. Sweet intoxication like a thousand years of blessings. And what he so avidly pursued at the seminary was nothing but this metaphysics.

Thinking you understood what it was he cherished, you were overjoyed, until that day. . . .

You received a parcel from your sister in Taipei. You opened the box of instant noodles and were about to throw away the newspaper packing, but your cat thought it was a game. It had been waiting patiently for quite a while—you had been ignoring it the last few days. Now the cat could no longer keep from leaping into the pile of paper, its back arched, pawing the air playfully. You could hear the crisp paper being shredded as it played. You happened to glance at a piece of paper the cat had torn away with its claws. There, in a small insignificant corner, was some news about him: he had been sentenced to prison for sedition.

Snow Blind

TRANSLATED BY **FOSTER ROBERTSON AND LEE YU**

The Sun Goes Down

The elementary school principal grasped the boat tightly. Stooping over, he pushed it into the sea.

White foam rushed around him; the wind blew toward him. The faint, scarcely audible lapping of the sea rose from under his feet. His pants were rolled up, exposing two thin legs. His head was lowered; his face could not be seen. His undershirt hung loosely over his shoulders. Two patches of dark hair were visible under his straining outstretched arms.

A few minutes earlier the principal had dragged the boat down from the dunes to push it into the sea. Beyond the sea wall, the water suddenly swelled enormously. The lazy clouds of the morning had since disappeared from the sky.

If we were to paddle around in the boat after it rained, the principal had to get the craft into the water before the rain fell. Once the sand was soaked, there would be no budging it no matter hard it was pushed.

The distant horizon line had now lost its grand equilibrium and displayed a quickening sense of alarm. The sky looked as if it were saturated with ink; the sea was sluggish and heavy. Whitecaps swelled, broad and uneven, and appeared to have lost the will to rush to shore.

The horizon, the sea, and the beach became quiet, each calm and self-contented. The wind suddenly subsided. The shrill cries of the sea birds, heard a moment before, suddenly vanished from the air. The rain would soon shatter the static order of things.

The principal dug his toes into the sand, the balls of his feet straining for leverage to push forward. A long trail of footprints cut through the sand like an iron groove, well defined and lovely. The footprints, interlocking, one in front of the next, ran from the dunes to the water's edge. Before lunch, while the principal's wife squatted in the courtyard picking water spinach, she told your mother in her soft voice how the principal's kidney problems had not improved since retirement. He still suffered from kidney stones.

Your mother now stood beside her on the embankment. As the principal tightly gripped the boat and struggled to push it a step forward, the two women gasped in unison. The two women held each other's hands tightly; they had been close friends since their days in girls' senior high school.

The sand stretched out beneath their feet, past the principal, and into the sea.

The principal was about to push the boat into the water.

Slowly, ever so slowly, the principal pushed the boat forward till it intersected the water line.

The bow of the boat moved toward the horizon line to form a T-shaped conjunction. The yellow dog that had been following the principal now barked excitedly.

The principal pushed the boat with all his strength, bending and forcing it forward. Beneath the leaden sky, the concentrated strength of his body held promise.

After one last burst of energy, the boat floated freely on the water, as if it had fulfilled its long-cherished wish of returning home to float on the sea. The principal's thin hair was matted with sweat; his rolled-up khaki pants were soaking wet. He steadied the boat in the water with both hands. Bent over, quietly solemn, just as he had been when he stood at attention facing the wall to recite the "Founding Father's Last Will" during morning assembly each week.

You stepped away from the window and buried your nose again in the pages of the old book bearing the Government-General of Taiwan's seal of approval.

. . . never passed the official examinations and, not knowing how to make a living, he had grown steadily poorer until he was almost reduced to beggary. Luckily he was a good calligrapher and could find enough copying work to fill his rice bowl. But unfortunately he had his failings too: laziness and a love of tippling. So after a few days he would disappear, taking with him books, paper, brushes, and inkstone. And after this had happened several times, people stopped employing him as a copyist.

Wearing *geta,* the principal climbed the stairs. Hugging the wall, he passed the blue-and-white advertisement for Medicine Deity Magic Water. The wind blowing off the ocean in the morning forced him against the wall. Stuck there, he was unable to proceed any farther.

"*Sensei! Sensei!*"

Hurrying from the Taipei train, your mother ran after him, shouting "Teacher! Teacher!" in Japanese.

The principal turned around. The two bottles of Black Pine Soda he carried shattered against the wall.

His hoarse greeting was obscured by the distant sound of a fishing boat engine starting up. On the stone steps you could see the rows of moored fishing boats tossing on the waves. The air was filled with flies waiting for the bonito boats to return to the port at Nanfang'ao.

"Let's go to the port to visit your elementary school principal."

Just after the high school entrance exams, your mother complained that the cramming had made you so pale and thin, "white as a silkworm." She wanted you to go to where the principal lived to get some sun.

A fishing town, endless summer days, and the smell of rotten fish wafting from the sea. The asphalt road in front of the Fisherman's Union Hall was strewn with nauseating brown seaweed.

Hearing your mother say you would soon be a high school student, the principal looked up from his bowl of bonito soup, embarrassed because he could not make a living in the fishing village. At noon he was nagged by his wife and stepped out to buy more soda.

A school principal and he can't even carry two bottles of soda. His wife harangued him until he stepped out the door.

The principal's *geta* clattered along the quiet country road. Before long he was again seen hugging the same crumbling wall, climbing the steps. This time he carried a block of ice tied with a straw cord.

The seaside swallows built nests under the eaves. Their continuous chirping made the principal's wife happy. Coming and going, she was careful lest she scare the birds away. Every morning and evening she lit a special stick of incense and stuck it in a crack in the wooden wall by the doorway.

The crack was soon filled with ash. Each thin stick, the color of eggplant, pointed upward toward the roof. In the morning, as one stepped over the threshold, one's nose was assailed by the heavy odor of incense, the same as at a temple.

"Things will get better soon."

"It hasn't happened yet."

"The kid is good here." The principal tapped the side of his head with the back of his chopsticks. He wanted to change the topic of conversation to you so that the two women wouldn't keep going on about his fishing.

The sun was still climbing. The sun shone through the begrimed window, providing a bit more light on the dining table. The principal always looked so sad, as if spending his entire life mourning for his brother. The grown-ups stopped talking and ate. You could hear the muffled sound of the sea outside.

The sun stood directly overhead, shining down on the water. Seagulls: one, two, three glided down without beating their wings to land on the posts. The distant headland stood guard, and the horizon was already darkened by several clouds. The coastal scenery no longer attracted you. You were wrapped up in reading the book approved by the Government-General of Taiwan.

After lunch, the principal pursed his lips around a toothpick. Walking, he said to you that there wasn't much around the house to amuse you. He opened the glass doors of a bookcase and pulled out an old book. It was the only Chinese book in the house. "Read this." You took the book. Bookworms had already eaten holes through the pages. Each page had a little hole in the same spot as the page before. On the spine you could still make out the words: Approved by the Government-General of Taiwan. The rest of the words had been eaten away by the cockroaches.

Holding the book, he bent over you. As he turned the pages he seemed to be lost in thought, slipping into reverie. He chewed betel nut, which oppressed you.

"Take this and read it."

By the bed, the principal took off his undershirt. Skin darkened by the sun, he nervously pulled a clean shirt on over his head. He left his khaki pants on, though they were soaked with sea water. He hadn't taken a breath since he pushed the boat into the water. The two women sat at the table in the deeper darkness of dusk, chatting about women's health problems. You occasionally lifted your head from the book. No wall divided the room; no screen. The house resembled a storage shed. Flypaper hung from the roof beam. The soft sound of the women's conversation permeated the house with memories of high school. Breast cancer had already taken away some classmates. Surprisingly, so-and-so had absconded with the private banking cooperative funds, ran away, and disappeared. And the doctor, who had made an incorrect diagnosis, the principal's wife said, had worried her for so many years. Raindrops began to fall obliquely against the windowsill. The principal walked over and closed the window. Then, taking a chair, he bowed slightly and made room for himself, joining the conversation at the table. After changing his clothes, the principal suddenly took on the bearing he'd had when he was in charge of morning assembly. You lowered your eyes to find the place where you left off:

After the Mid-Autumn Festival the wind grew daily colder as winter approached, and even though I spent all my time by the stove I had to wear a padded jacket. One afternoon, when the tavern was deserted, as I sat with my eyes closed I heard the words:

"Warm a bowl of wine."

It was said in a low but familiar voice. I opened my eyes. There was no one to be seen. I stood up to look out. . . .

The rain, as expected, poured. The principal's wife stood up and took some basins and large bowls from the kitchen. As if it were second nature, she put them down one by one to catch the water leaking from the roof. *Du-du. Da-da.* The rain dripped into the containers. And so-and-so's son in America had an automobile accident; it's a shame, he had almost earned his Ph.D. The roof tiles had not been laid evenly and the center beam was askew. You watched the rainwater fall through the cracks in the roof tiles, watched it fall to the floor. Oh, talk about him, he always changes his mind, she complains about her husband. His indecisiveness spoiled his son's chance to make a good marriage. The principal sat silently to one side. *Du-du. Da-da.* All he thinks about is that yellow dog; he doesn't even care about his own daughter. *Du-du. Da-da.* Eventually you saw light coming through a few places in the ceiling. But again, you shouldn't count on your children for anything anyway, she advised your mother in conclusion. *Du-du. Da-da.* The rain fell harder. Yet the seagulls were heard all the louder outside.

They had lived in a little side alley off Dihua Street, which was considered an old Taipei neighborhood. Upstairs in the old house, the green mosquito net in the bedroom at the top of the stairs had faded brown. The narrow street was dull gray; coal cinders covered the ground. The air was filled all day with the smell of laundry water. In the morning you awoke to the sound of the water pump. The neighborhood women were already washing clothes by the well. Circling around behind to avoid them, you hurriedly ran out of the alley to school. You escaped from the suffocating smell of laundry soap.

At sunset, the well turned very quickly into a dark and shadowy place.

Your mother was once so frightened out of her wits by some guy who exposed himself there that she rushed back home, her basket of wash only half done. The white soapsuds dripped and dripped all the way from the well into the house. Mother's face was still pale with shock when we sat down at the table that evening.

As you climbed the dark, dank wooden stairway, the footsteps and the greeting of the principal's wife reverberated through the old wooden house. The oblique rays of the afternoon sun shone through the alley. The shadows of the eaves were quietly imprinted on the walls. The women finished washing clothes. At the end of the end alley were a series of stone steps atop which sat two wooden houses facing each other. The house near the river belonged to the principal. Opposite it was an abandoned house. Coming home by boat from taking shelter in the countryside, you heard the grown-ups whispering that the owner of the house had died. The windowpanes had all been shattered during the bombing raids. Dust covered the sharp points of broken glass in the windows. When you looked over from the second floor of the principal's house, the two empty windows stared mutely at you like a pair of empty eye sockets.

When Taipei was most severely bombed in July, the owner of the house could no longer stand the unending roar of the B-29s day and night. He hanged himself on the second floor, leaving behind his wife, ill in bed downstairs. Coming home from the countryside, you heard the monks chanting even before you jumped off the boat. Wave after wave of enemy planes passed overhead; from the bomb shelter you heard the solemn chanting of "*Na-mo Ami-ta-bha Bud-dha. Na-mo Ami-ta-bha Bud-dha*," reverberating throughout the neighborhood.

You could recall the days of mourning in the alley. When the war was over, the bedridden wife died too. The daughter, who was of a marriageable age, was left to carry on alone.

After her parents passed away, Miniang suddenly changed from a snot-nosed schoolgirl into a shy young woman. But the house was devastated. Weeds grew everywhere. Bachelor's buttons bloomed on a pile of dirt in front of the door. A wax apple tree, which had been knocked over by a bomb concussion during an air raid, leaned against a window of her house, where it flourished more than ever before.

Miniang grew up quickly when the bombs were falling day and night. Perched up on a tree limb, you couldn't figure out how it happened, no matter how hard you tried.

You climbed up in the tree. You vied with the neighborhood kids for the wax apples. Her father would not have allowed it, if he were still alive. The wax apple tree, after all, belonged to her family. Sunlight seeped through the green shade in flickering and shimmering points of light. Miniang stood outside her front door. As she combed her hair, drops of water fell from the ends. Her unbound, freshly washed hair was fluid as a river. From up in the tree you peered down. Her pearl-white skin ran up the back of her lowered neck and across her shoulders and sneaked down her unbuttoned collar.

Pa-cha! The tree limb broke. Exploded. The principal, who was squatting in front of his own door repairing a bicycle, immediately looked up to see what caused the noise. You saw his startled face. Ah, it wasn't a bomb, just a branch of the wax apple tree.

Men are all alike. That's what the principal's wife said, when your mother told her about the time the man exposed himself by the well. What she really wanted to talk about was her husband.

"I'm leaving. I'm leaving," said the principal.

Later, it was Miniang who left. The house became dark and abandoned.

"He wouldn't dare! Had he the nerve, I'd just let him go." A few years later, the principal's wife adopted such a rational tone when talking about it.

Retrocession arrived. The alley was once again choked with the smell of laundry soap. The sun had scarcely started its afternoon descent when the red dragonflies began flying overhead. They darted from one person's head to another and back. The whole afternoon they repeated the same monotonous routine. Snails crawled in the shade of the walls. On one side, the principal was downstairs fixing his bicycle. Across the street, Miniang leaned against the upstairs window, languidly combing out her freshly washed, undone hair. One drop of water, and then another, fell onto the stone pavement below. The two of them were always the same, silently engaged in their own business. From downstairs you could look up and see that Miniang was still in mourning, wearing a band of blue cloth from which a Qianlong period coin dangled from the fair skin of her wrist.

The alley. A quiet afternoon. The air was motionless. A quiet summer day throbbed languidly with the pulse of a beating heart. It was so hot! The atmosphere was oppressive. Miniang leaned out of the window.

Believe him . . . and quietly stand by his side.

The principal turned the pedals with his hands. The rear wheel began to turn. *De-de-de. De-de-de.* It made a pleasant sound.

Everything was like a wave. Throw yourself into it. Come on! All the water in the world's oceans. You could drown. Be careful! Drown yourself in the soundless air of the afternoon at the end of the alley. Ah! It was so hot.

Suddenly Miniang stepped away from the window. Disappeared into darkness. Gone. A silent open window.

A shadow like an aircraft carrier heaved into view in the downstairs doorway. The principal's wife came outside. Dragonflies continued to dart back and forth without a sound in the alley. The principal didn't move. He squatted there as before, occupied with turning the pedals—*de-de-de. De-de-de.* It was so hot. That summer . . .

The principal's wife held a basket of peapods. She was going to string them in the shade of the doorway. The fragrance of Miniang's freshly washed hair lingered in the air, caressing, caressing.

Angrily, the principal's wife got mad and turned. "Good-for-nothing! Good-for-nothing!" In a huff, she picked up her basket and stalked to the back of the house.

"I'm leaving. I'm leaving," said the principal.

An evening of lingering warmth. . . . At the open doorway was a column of ants, one behind the next. The wings of dragonflies were carried along by the column. As soon as their dismembered red bodies were seen on the ground, they were carried off into the cracks in the walls.

Gone....

The principal stood under the awning of the tofu store. He looked grim, solemn. He carried a small bag and an umbrella. Under a dazzling autumn sky he stared blankly at the passing cars.

"I'm leaving. I'm leaving this suffocating island all by myself.... Going far away from here.... Far, far away from here. I've wanted to do this ever since I was young."

Dihua Street had become a long grassy path between fields. The war was over. The alley was deserted. At the time the principal was not yet a principal but a municipal educational inspector. Oh, if only life were like a shadow, growing shorter with each passing day. He looked down and stared at the sight of the autumn sunshine reflected off the tile placard of the tofu store.

The principal's wife remembered the hustle and bustle of Dihua Street before the war. Under the covered walkways along the street were mountains of goods from Canton. Preserved golden shrimp and dried oysters infused with the smell of sesame oil. The principal's wife, then a private teacher for the famous Lin family of Taizhong, sat in a rickshaw and was whisked like the wind through the streets. The pampered daughter of a good family, she was about to marry a talented student from the Normal College. Sober and dignified, she entered the gate of the Chen family, elegantly accompanied by several cartloads of dowry. She was in the bloom of youth, proud of her smooth, uncallused feet. The first time she used talcum powder after bathing, he seemed surprised. She couldn't believe that a student from the Normal College in Taipei had never seen talcum powder before.

But what did he get out of it? Rumor had it that the principal and Miniang had walked side by side along the floodgate. She herself didn't believe it. If he had the courage, then let him go. In Yaziliao someone ran into the principal together with Miniang squeezed in among the shoppers at the market. At that time, she had nothing to say. Sundays he was always in such high spirits as he picked up the shopping basket and left early in the morning. No one would ever take him for a philanderer. He was a municipal educational inspector, after all.

"I've lived long enough. I've lived long enough." Shortly after entering the Chen family, she no longer wanted to go on living. "Yang Zixian could be considered farsighted for taking advantage of the wartime chaos to hang himself." What the principal's wife was talking about was their neighbor, the father of Miniang. However, he wasn't all there upstairs. Everybody in the alley knew it. Reciting the sutras for seven days and seven nights was sufficient to control a crazy wandering ghost.

The principal's wife now preferred to live in the countryside rather than in Taipei. How peaceful life had been, living in the countryside for safety during the war!

What did he get out of it? In the one-story house in Nanfang'ao, the principal's wife squatted in the courtyard. Picking water spinach, she pressed her wrinkled, powdered face close to your mother's face, and spoke of that one summer afternoon ten years ago.

She stretched her neck, and in whispers concluded that he, in fact, was still a good person. Night and day in the same house together for nearly a lifetime, how could she not know him?

The principal straightened his back and put on his hunting cap, ready to leave for the office.

A fine-looking municipal educational inspector.

He carried his bike over the threshold. Bending down, he clipped his trouser legs with clothespins. Everything was fine. He slowly pushed his bike down the stone steps. Yet before he was able to glance at Miniang's room in the house across the street, his wife rushed through the door and hurled a basin full of old dishwater on his back, along with a few curses.

Sweet pea vines clambered over the crumbling wall. An array of pale pink, purple, and powdery white petals faced the light of dawn. The sky was a deep blue, which it rarely was after Retrocession. There by the wall the principal brushed off the dirty water and wrung out his cap. Everything was settled. He jumped on his bicycle and dashed off. Like a puff of smoke, he disappeared at the end of the alley.

The one who felt more embarrassed, in fact, was the principal's wife. She was the only person in the alley who was addressed formally as "Mrs." She was a woman with status.

Once on the Tamshui train during the war, as the scenery flashed by, you chanced to see an old woman dashing from a house, holding a stick, chasing ducks. The train sped on. The image of the old woman merged in your mind with that of the principal's wife. It stayed with you all the time you were growing up.

When your father was alive, he always said that among Taiwanese people, the principal was a rare educator. He had been determined, ever since he was young, to become an elementary school principal. When necessary, he spoke Japanese as refined as that of any colonial civil official. You still remembered the principal's voice when he turned and recited the "Founding Father's Will" each morning in assembly. At each retroflex sound of the Mandarin text, he would conscientiously curl his tongue and fluently produce the correct sound.

Stars glittered in the sky. The principal and his wife had patched things up. Dressed warmly, they strolled arm in arm along the floodgate. On their way home, the principal dropped by for a chat; sometimes he brought a couple of squid. At that time your father was still healthy.

The squid were cooked over the brazier. The grown-ups sat around the fire and talked about what had happened in the past, about the first Taiwanese pilot. Your father's face was red from the cooking fire, looking tired and puffy as if he had just gotten out of bed. The Samuelson-type Gaoxiung plane flew high among the clouds. A rainbow ten thousand miles long. The aspirations of the Taiwanese people. The will soaring. Flew across the sky of the colony. When you looked down from on high, it was said, the land of the Chinese people was lush and green. Fate seethed in turmoil. A decade of Wilsonian idealism burgeoned there. And too many Taiwanese were studying medicine. The Cultural Association was in need of determined intellectuals.

A wind from the river blew over the earthen wall to the second-floor window, carrying the aroma of roasting squid. A sound of an explosion was carried on the gritty wind. The Gaoxiung plane crashed. The body of the first pilot was carried from the wreckage of the airplane beyond the parade grounds. Filled with emotion, the young principal had attended the pilot's funeral ceremony.

A smile finally appeared on his melancholy face. Bell ringing, the postman turned his bicycle down the narrow alley to deliver the contract. Soon you read in the paper that the Provincial Department of Education announced his appointment as the first principal of your elementary school after Retrocession.

Yet he continued to clip his trouser legs with clothespins, and left home every morning on his bike.

Walking down the hall, you students were no longer required to bow at the door of the principal's office, regardless of whether he was in or not. That was the first rule he changed after he became principal.

One day, he taught the science class for an absent homeroom teacher. He lit the Bunsen burner to demonstrate how to make soap in the classroom. His manner of speech was reminiscent of the martial artists who sold medicinal plasters near the traffic circle. If you can make soap like this, then you don't have to go out and buy it. How much does a bar of fragrant Heavenly Scent Soap cost these days?

The principal's face was smeared with chalk and grease. Fat and sodium hydroxide. His hair fell forward over his face. The soap set up in a rectangular mold. But the classroom was now full of greasy smoke. All the students coughed. Gradually everyone lost sight of the principal, who was still busy with the demonstration at the front of the classroom. You had no appetite for dinner even though your mother made rice topped with a piece of pork fat. That was the time the principal nearly set the whole classroom on fire. The teacher in the next classroom rushed over. Dense, greasy smoke, resembling a dragon, curled out of the window. The next day at the flag-raising assembly the principal's hands, hanging at his sides as he stood at attention, were thickly bandaged.

"You broke your word!" The principal's wife screamed as if it were something big like an air raid.

When was it that the principal broke his word and began chewing betel nut? It must have been before your father passed away, because you remember your father saying, "He is chewing the shadow of his older brother who died." You had finished elementary school by then. You often saw the principal near the floodgate in the evening. He squatted by the river's edge, hunched over and silent, his head looking like it was going to touch the Tamshui River. Only when his cigarette burned his fingertips did he come back to himself. He hurriedly tossed the butt into the water.

The melancholy reflections were disturbed by the evening ferry. Only then did the principal stand up and leave.

A boat cut through the still surface of the river. Its wake widened quietly, lapping between the rocks, churning up white foam. The dark water, laden with filth, returned to the heart of the river. The Xinzhuang boatman spat into the water. In a thin, twilight river mist, the boatman stood alone at the ferry station. He mumbled at the departing passengers. Anyway, that was his life. "So sorry. There's a little water in the boat, but it won't sink. So sorry."

Clover grew on the silken path home. The clover grew all the way from the river's edge to the embankment. The principal climbed the steps of the floodgate; he picked a sprig of jasmine and used it as a toothpick to remove the betel nut stuck between his teeth as he walked home. He grew depressed; the image of his drowned brother floated before his eyes. The principal's wife let him linger by the river. Alone and absent-mindedly staring into the distance, he killed whole evenings that way.

In his youth, he despised nothing more than older people noisily chewing betel nut. The sloth of the subtropics. On the narrow-gauge train of the sugar factory, amid the repetitive clickity-clack of the train, he and his brother had both sworn never to chew betel nut.

"Fool!" The principal's wife screamed the moment she detected the pungent smell of betel nut on his breath.

His big brother's face was imprinted against the green lacquered wall of the carriage of that narrow-gauge train, amid the clickity-clack of the train. Several years later, near the end of summer, his older brother traveled north, returning to his medical studies at the university in the capital.

His brother talked without ever getting to the point. Finally, just before they arrived, he told him what was on his mind.

"I'm afraid that I can't continue with medical school any longer."

The clickity-clack of the train. The shining green wall. His brother's face.

"Don't let Mom know."

That was the last thing he said to you when you parted. The principal didn't finish that semester, but rushed home for his brother's funeral.

He had committed suicide by drowning himself in the ocean. There was no note, not a word for the principal. His brother's clothes and a book were found on the beach.

The principal patiently chewed strips of dried squid. It was hard to chew such things now. He sat by the cooking fire; his nostrils still flared when he talked about his dead brother. There was a tight knot in his chest that he was unable to untie. The body was never found. Their mother's heart was nearly shattered—there was no spirit tablet by which to remember her son at the cemetery or the temple.

One of his books was found on the beach. Did that prove he had taken his own life?

The principal's hair was peppered white; he still couldn't understand it.

But after that his brother was never seen again; it was as if he had vanished off the face of the earth. But that did not prove that his brother was really dead.

The principal sat by the fire. As soon as he mentioned his dead brother, the endless guessing began once more. Then he saw his father's brooding face; he waited for a response from his father. The living room was silent.

His brother rushed out the medical school gate and ran toward the street with tears streaming down his face. His white coat was blown by the wind. That anguished image is what the principal could never forget.

That very day he had just brought the household identification book from home so that his older brother could transfer his permanent residence to their second uncle's house in the capital.

The street was empty. Chestnut trees formed a dense green canopy. The red brick buildings of the medical school stood majestically in the bright sunlight. It was a gorgeous afternoon. As a third-year intern, he had just finished an obstetrics class. Suddenly he collapsed.

His brother wanted to run through the streets. His white coat danced playfully in the middle of the street like a ghost in daylight. That running form, so bewildered, was imprinted forever on the principal's memory.

He was unable to pull himself together in front of his younger brother. He lowered his head and twitched. Suddenly he was stupefied. The younger brother continued to hold the household identification book. The two brothers sat in silence on a stone bench in the park. At noon on a day in May, the younger brother began to tremble. He didn't know how to hand over what he was carrying to his older brother.

"Was a woman giving birth really so frightening?" his father asked.

"I remember the only thing he said when he ran out of the medical school was, 'Who could have dreamed that giving birth was so ugly?'"

The principal, who had never let his harmonica out of his hands when he was little, finally gave it up. He gave up not only the harmonica but all music.

His father used a pair of brass chopsticks to stir the charcoal in the brazier. The fire crackled up. In the middle of a winter night the room gradually took on a warm glow. The principal unbuttoned his jacket, staring at the charcoal burning red in the brazier. As if making an announcement, he said he would spend the rest of his days like a mute.

You remembered the weekly assembly when he faced the wall and recited the "Founding Father's Will" in a loud, clear voice.

The cement Fisherman's Union Hall cast a gray shadow on the asphalt road. A number of people rested in the building's shade. Some played chess, some ate herbal gelatin. The fragrant smoke of New Paradise cigarettes hung around the people gathered there.

Black clouds rose over the ocean. Soon there would be a sudden cloudburst. Every day it was the same. Sunlight would occasionally break through the clouds to fool people.

The foreign priest rushed by on his bicycle. His black cassock rose behind him on the wind. This strange sight had appeared on the streets of the fishing port the previous day. That black cassock appeared at any moment like a dragon, causing the pedestrians to stop and stare. It was said that the priest was busy preparing for the funeral of a young couple who came to the port to commit suicide.

The principal's *geta* clattered on the quiet street. "There's no need to see us off. There's no need to see us off." Your mother was holding some pickled fish wrapped in newspaper, which the principal's wife had thrust into her hands before you left. The new asphalt road. The empty fish market. The deserted streets. Flies buzzed languidly in the air, waiting for the fishing boats to return. The flies wouldn't land without the stink of fish; they just buzzed overhead. "There's no need to see us off. There's no need to see us off."

"When the weather gets better, I'll come up for a visit. This kidney problem is still giving me trouble."

The train was still in the station. The principal stood at some distance on the platform.

Smoke from kitchen fires rose above each roof in the fishing port.

"When I get some time I'll come up. I'll go back to Taipei."

There was an ant nest in the old-fashioned refrigerator. The principal's wife had constantly complained to your mother about the refrigerator over the last couple of days.

"We'll see. Maybe next year, when we get to Taipei, we'll buy a new one. I'll surely come up when I get the time."

"There's no need to see us off. There's no need to see us off. Go on home, please."

You spent one night in the principal's house and ate bonito every meal. When it came time to leave, you were suddenly very happy. When your mother wasn't looking, the principal, who was standing outside, hurriedly pressed a banknote into your hand. He didn't say a word; he just blinked his still inflamed eyes, showing the red of his eyelids. The swallows flew out from under the eaves, chirping.

"Take it. Take it. Buy something you like."

He pressed the money on you.

"Take it. There's no need to tell your mom."

On the train you touched the bill in your pocket.

You felt a tinge of regret. Yesterday afternoon after the rain stopped you didn't go out in the principal's boat. Instead you shut yourself up inside to read.

The train began to move. There's no need to see us off. There's no need to see us off. You looked out the window. The principal, a life of passion, stood on the platform, like someone out of a sad song from before the war.

"It's the right time to go home; you'll avoid the rainstorm. Yes. Yes. Next year I'll come up and visit."

"There's no need to see us off. There's no need to see us off."

He lived by the floodgate in Taipei. When the principal went out, he'd jump on his bicycle. So dashing. . . .

The air at the port portended rain . . . caressing . . . caressing. The principal's face faded from view.

Gone. No more smell of bonito. No more sharp betel nut smell. The shadow of the deceased brother. Chewing. Chewing. It was the right time to go home. The rain would soon be there.

In the carriage, your mother scolded you. Amid the clickity-clack of the train, by the dim light, you continued to read the book the principal gave you.

"You had better pass the exam!"

Looking up from the book, you must have looked pretty bad.

Your mother couldn't stand it anymore. The reason for taking you to the principal's house was for you to get some sun. You already looked as pale as a silkworm from preparing for those exams. Yet in the end you spent two days reading again! You didn't even accept the principal's well-intentioned invitation to go out in the boat.

What your mother wanted to say was that if you didn't pass the entrance exam this time, she would be very worried.

You spread some newspaper on the floor and sat down on it. Squeezed among the legs of the other passengers, you couldn't take your eyes from the book.

Kneeling quietly, you suddenly felt very contented.

The sea outside the train window no longer attracted you.

Now the scattered promontories were waiting far off on the level horizon line. The waves no longer rose and fell. You hastened home on the northbound train before the rain started. In what way was this unfair to the principal?

In the swiftly moving train, amid the legs of the grown-ups, you suddenly felt depressed. You didn't want to have anything to do with a single person, including your mother. If only you never had to stand again. Let your hands be muddy and even your legs broken. With that book in your hand you sank ... sank.

"Be careful, look both ways before crossing the street."

"You have to take care of yourself when you are away from home."

After you lost your father, your mother's nagging was always slightly tremulous.

The cicadas of early autumn....

A Sunday after Retrocession. Taipei under martial law.

In order to get some tofu for his mother, who was ill in bed, the principal took a bowl and felt his way along the wall to the door.

"Be careful crossing the street...."

The principal walked alone down the covered walkway. He wanted to cross the street.

A military policeman at the mouth of the alley shouted, ordering him to halt. "What the hell are you doing?"

The principal stammered. He said he was going to the tofu shop across the street. He would cross the street and come back right away.

His mother had been sick a long time. She had called to him from her bed asking for some tofu. He would just cross the street to the tofu shop. He'd come right back as soon as he bought it. He'd cross the street and come back right away.

Whack! The military policeman slapped the principal across the face.

"What kind of time is this? Eat tofu, eat tofu."

Dihua Street was empty without a soul in sight. The sharp sound of that slap echoed like a memory down the deserted street. *Whack! Whack! Whack!*

In the World

Walking up the sand dune shaded by mimosa trees toward the apartment parking lot, your head was pounding. A worm was devouring you. Your temples were splitting with that throbbing sound. You had suffered from a splitting headache all day long. Images of car crashes flashed before your eyes as you drove.

You smelled something pungent. The aroma of pistachios. Three geraniums by the kitchen water tank shone with promise in the desert morning sun. Outside, in the distance, the freeway stretched off in silence. Farther off in the distance, the white light rose off the sand, blocking everything from view.

You suddenly realized that the sound throbbing in your head was the static on the line when your mother called from across the Pacific. The connection was poor. The static continued. Your headaches were inherited. When you were little, you often saw your mother, who was approaching middle age, wearing Salonpas pain patches on her temples. Your mother's voice sounded faint and remote on the trans-Pacific call, vague and intermittent like some event from the past.

The heat from the ground assailed your head. The sky, like an immense sheet of tinfoil, reflected the heat and light onto the ground. The throbbing sound rose incessantly from the bottom of your heart.

One day that throbbing sound became the first ray of light in the desert dawn. You had settled down in a city built amid a jumble of rocks. You learned patience.

That year, a strange sound woke her. She climbed out of bed. She thought it was perhaps a mouse chewing on wood or wood borers eating holes in the wall. Finally she realized that you had been grinding your teeth in your sleep.

It was a strange sound.

What kind of sound was it?

You yourself found it strange, talking in one's sleep.

Every day you started at one end, cleaning one bathroom after another; she started at that end, vacuuming one room after another. You both started downstairs and finished upstairs. At noon you'd both finally meet in a room upstairs.

You were dressed in the white uniforms of the housekeeping staff. A shy greeting. You each did your own job. You scrubbed the white ceramic toilet bowls with a round metal pad; you heard her turn on the vacuum in the next room. Before long there was a crisp snap as she put clean sheets on the beds.

Two weeks later when you met again, the two of you sat on the freshly changed sheets, stealing a little time to chat. You asked about each other's schools, what you were studying, and when you left home to study abroad. 1966.

After a while, everything had been asked and there was nothing left to talk about. Then you both lay down on the freshly changed sheets. You dared not turn on the air conditioner for fear the owner downstairs would hear you.

Lying down, you could smell the odor of ammonia on each other.

Her hand moved away from the large bruise on your chest. It still looked like a map, a map of the United States. The bruise, which was the color of pork liver, covered your ribs.

"Now we are here." She pointed to a place on the bruise. Your chest twitched immediately.

"When summer break is over, I'll go back to here." She pointed to another spot. "Salem, Oregon."

"And you," she said, "you will return here, to Oklahoma."

Her hand moved down the bruise.

You fell asleep and woke again. You dreamed of screw clamps, wrenches, hammers, screwdrivers, electrician's tape . . . and all sorts and sizes of nails.

The first day at work the owner threw a heavy toolbox in front of you. "From now on you will be responsible for this." You opened it and found it packed with tools you had never touched before in your life.

"Xingluan, don't worry yourself. I'll take care of you."

"Yungyue!"

She had a pair of dark, intense eyes. They looked straight at you now.

The first time you saw her was in the line of people looking for work. She turned her head, and you saw her dark, intense eyes looking into the distance.

The sun set on the other side of the casino. Neon lights began to light up the desert. Summer vacation had just begun. Chinese was heard everywhere in line. The hiring agency was glad to take Chinese students because they were honest and hard-working. Ever since they were shipped over as coolies to build the railroads over a century ago, the Chinese had maintained a good record.

Everyone went to work in the casino. You two were sent to a motor lodge to work as housekeeping staff.

On the second day at work, the owner asked you to move an old air conditioner. You hurt your chest badly. A huge bruise appeared the next day. You never expected it would be so heavy. Yungyue's mouth left a wet trace on your cheek that looked like the slime trails left by snails on the shady wall in the alley during the summer.

"Lu . . . Xun." Flipping through that old book of yours, she asked, "Who is he?"

"A writer."

"Is he good?"

"Yes."

She flipped through the book a couple of times and saw a hole in the identical spot on each page made by a bookworm. She closed the book and put it back.

"Xingluan, don't think so much."

Every day after work, you longed to hold her breasts, which were like chilled fruit. Coming in out of the sun, her body was feverishly hot; only her breasts were still agreeably cool. The swollen fluid body filled your hands. You touched the essential core of all things. Your ten fingers worked, making the tip ends stand erect like words of promise. If you chose, you could let them drip milk on the desert. Filled, your hands grew warm. It was like sunset at home, like the smoke from the kitchen fires, like the roof tiles ... work.

Summer vacation was over. Her dark eyes were more intense than ever. Before going your separate ways, the two of you joined an organized tour of the Grand Canyon. Accidentally you stepped on her birth-control pill and crushed it. And she, as serene as a virgin, without so much as a word, knelt down quietly and picked up the powder with her fingers, to make sure she took a sufficient dose. Given the devout way she stooped to pick up the pill you had trod into powder, the hotel room took on the aura of a church.

"Yungyue."

On the tour bus you clasped her ten fingers.

"Xingluan."

She was a soft-hearted woman. Her nails were as soft as water. If you pressed on the tip of a nail it bent, pliant as a willow. When you had nothing else to do, you often spent time together examining her nails. On each one was a frosty crescent halo. She told you, as her grandmother used to say, that only soft-hearted people have soft nails, and all ten of hers were soft.

The bus climbed above the Colorado River. The colorful strata were visible on the canyon walls.

Passing down a brown mountain road, the bus headed for the Petrified Forest.

You knelt before her. Her head rested weakly on your shoulder. She sat on the toilet and moaned as if she were breathing her last. Her hair was wet with sweat. After the heavy menstrual bleeding, her face was blue. In the desert night, her face was as pale as your mother's face the day she ran home after the man exposed himself. The toilet flowed like a mountain spring. Her face surged.

A desert basin stretched on without end from Montgomery.

Cars and trucks from the city, shiny as beetles, traveled silently, one after another, on the highway toward the gambling town. Vacations were short. Now the sand became lonely. Calm came late to the plain. You stood and looked off into the distance, waiting for the sinking sun to meet the horizon, forming a T-shaped promise.

You loved the desert. You had no plans to leave.

"What are you waiting for?" she asked. "But, going to the Hopi Indian reservation is a good idea. You can see some Indian cave dwellings."

On sleepless nights she squeezed the blackheads on your face with her fingernails.

"A scarcity of water is the most significant aspect of desert history." The voice of the tour guide in the dusty wind suddenly sounded like an echo from a distant mountain.

You hadn't yet said good-bye, and she said she would miss you, like an old song.

At the Indian reservation, she reminded you of Amah Wu.

She sat by the window with her hands folded. She craned her neck, looking out the window, then she rested her chin on the back of her hands. She must be exhausted after the heavy menstrual bleeding. She looked out the hotel window at the sand. It looked as if only the distant mountains covered by the clouds had received any rain. The flatlands were bone dry.

In your teenage years you always thought that this kind of casual encounter would happen only on summer evenings. In those days you had your heart set on having a wife as beautiful as Miniang.

"Who is Amah Wu?"

"A soft-hearted woman Lu Xun wrote about."

Standing on the balcony of the hotel, you suddenly realized that nobody could have eyes as innocent as Amah Wu's. Even Ah-Q on his way to the execution ground wanted to sing a song for her.

Such eyes were only for gazing at the stars.

"The Colorado River meets its main tributary, the Gila River, at Yuma. The river bisects the desert." The voice of the tour guide still sounded remote.

The tour bus stopped. She was not very steady on her feet. You were right behind her. When she took a step you followed. Her skirt was stained with blood.

At the Indian teepee, she suddenly began to hum an old song. You bought a pendant of turquoise in the shape of a tongue.

You helped her put on the necklace; then there was another tongue on her chest.

See the river flowing on and on.
See the great river flowing east, never to return.
... like flowing water
Like that great river flowing east, never to return.

You wanted to leave, to go far, far away. You never wanted to return to that narrow little alley. When you were little and had wet the bed, your father dragged you down and beat you with the feather duster. You were soaked through with that rank smell. The only person you spoke to was that woman.

The next day that woman looked distracted. In silence, her head lowered, she took the bedding outside to wash. She never said a word, feeling it was her fault. With never a word, she lowered her head and washed the bedding by the well. That woman was your mother.

It was the first time in your life that the memory grieved you.

You wanted to leave, to go far, far away. In whatever street or alley you found yourself, there was always the smell of urine waiting for you. The clacking of your *geta* as you walked behind the railway warehouse was a desolate sound. The ground was still, baked by the noon sun. A thick mat of ivy covered the concrete wall. The smells of shit and piss were always waiting for you. But the most ridiculous thing on Dihua Street was the dilapidated foreign businesses, still decorated with eighteenth-century rococo ornamentation. The relief sculptures, once as exquisite as a song, were now as ugly as a drunken old woman, due to the odors of dried mussels, dried golden shrimp, marinated bamboo shoots, and dried scallops from the dry goods shops.

"Be careful when you go out. Watch out for cars, Little Axin...."

A mother's final farewell. Cicadas in early autumn.

Thoughts of life as you imagined it overseas crowded in one after the other.

"Native American civilization . . . can be traced back to 25,000 B.C. This is one of the key sites of the great cave culture. . . ."

A large shady space spread beneath the canopy of mimosa trees. You fled from the incessant chatter of the guide. The early September light shone through the densely interwoven feathery foliage overhead, like a blessing. Gone. Parted.

A line of large, deep footprints formed a track without beginning or end.

Off in the distance, the forms of the tourists moved in a disordered fashion against the horizon, like a black sawtooth silhouette, as they gathered around the Indian vendors.

After the sun went down, the delicate golden sand of the desert offered its spacious, endless surface. The scene gradually receded. Your heart felt calm. You heard the muffled sound of waves. The wind lifted the priest's black cassock. During the summer that year a young couple drowned in the sea. The prayers of the foreign priest.

Now you could look straight up at the blue sky without blinking. Night was about to fall. A moment of peace, like an old song. Broken off. Separated. Tomorrow . . . or the day after.

"In shallow parts of the river, you can see the glint of copper below. Copper is still the major mineral resource of Arizona . . . followed by molybdenite."

A leaf fallen on the desert shriveled in the scorching sun. Blown across the sand, its shriveled shape etched out cold, distant memories. Then it was swallowed by the shadows. That large and solid, but crumbling, wall of the narrow alley. Sweet pea blossoms swaying in the morning breeze. The voices from the city that never stopped, day or night. Your decision to leave for faraway places.

Separated, broken off like this. She had given her all, then she gave even more. She learned to kiss to her heart's content in broad daylight and in public like a foreigner. Under the mimosa trees, she turned to you; her tongue played in your mouth. Like a snake in the desert, bidding farewell. A voice without words swept your heart. You wanted to leave for faraway places.

The sound of Taipei. Fog rose over the Tamshui River and wouldn't disperse till noon. The fortune stick that your mother drew in the Temple of Lord Guan predicted that you were fated to leave home, indicating that after a certain number of years you would meet your woman in a motel room in the desert in a foreign country.

Dragonflies flew through the air on delicate and weakly beating wings. Flower buds burst forth amid the moisture. It was the sticky season. On the river danced fragments of light. A pair of red shoes with gold buttons hurried down the slate steps, carrying a disturbed heart. In a flash they disappeared.

Later, the red shoes reappeared by the floodgate.

Leisurely the silvery light trod on the river. One person. Trod out the hidden bitterness of a bride.

There was a story about the red shoes too.

When you were little and thought about those striking red shoes at night, your heart beat faster. You curled up under the quilt and felt that someplace you were unaware of, something was happening.

Everyone in the alley peeked out from behind dark windows.

Miniang's father had just received the first paycheck of his life. He went out by himself to Rongding to buy a pair of red shoes with gold buttons for Miniang's mother, then his new bride.

Her mother caressed the shoes, then put them on and looked at her new shoes in the mirror.

They were far too bright and ostentatious for her to wear outside.

At first she was delighted. Then, suddenly, while looking in the mirror she became quite angry.

Spending so much money! Buying such flashy things! The shoes came off and were tossed away.

"Go give them to your woman. I'm not a geisha to wear such things."

When Miniang took the shoes out of the bottom of the trunk and put them on her own feet, they fit quite well.

The shoes were still brand new.

Even then, when the red shoes appeared in the alley, the neighborhood women around the well began to whisper about them. They said that Miniang was just like her father who hanged himself; she was just as crazy but would probably come to a quicker end.

You could see those red shoes shining through the dense foliage of the wax apple tree; then they were gone, rushing toward the river. By the light of day they were an irrepressible red; on stormy nights, the shoes seemed to sprout delicate wings like those of a dragonfly—they would skim past your window without touching the ground, and no secrets were safe.

Early every morning, the principal's wife anxiously hurried the principal off to work.

On Sunday afternoons, the principal found excuses to fix his bicycle at his doorway.

There was a rabies epidemic in Taipei. Every dog was muzzled. All barking stopped. The afternoons were quiet, the summer days feverish. Hearts were restless. Dazzling points of light shimmered on the river's surface. How warm it was. The whispering silence was disturbing, the fragrance of hair ... caressing ... caressing.

Watching Miniang as she walked alone by the floodgate, the principal could not bear just thinking about her any longer. Come, all the water in the seas.

Miniang no longer buttoned her blouse all the way to the collar, exposing her pleasing neck. That pair of red shoes was always out, regardless of the weather.

Now, when she saw people, a dark look spread over her face, like a jellyfish pulsating in silence. The gold buttons on the shoes shone anxiously under the streetlight.

Under the dense feathery foliage, you finally held Yungyue in your arms and buried your face in her hair, looking for her neck that ran down into her collar, as if searching for some lost treasure in the desert.

The sun went down in the distance, yet the sand remained warm. Your temples throbbed; you longed to leave the surface of the earth, to leave the harsh, boring desert. You sank, no longer able to see the dim, monotonous outline of the dunes. Sank . . . to the bottom.

You wished for a sudden downpour to drench your feverish body and drive away the throbbing sound that never left your head.

You took your seats on the bus again. Already you had nothing to say. She leaned against the window. Traveling across the desert, it sounded like the ocean. Separated. Broken off just like that. Shaking your head, you sought to shake off the lassitude produced by the heat. Countless points of white light shimmered on the river's surface outside, forming a granular track.

Hu-la-li
I shout for that great river,
See it lift up billow after billow
See it flowing on and on.
See it flowing east, the great river, never to return.

Miniang finally left home. She never came back. Her house still stood at the end of the alley, facing the river. But the rooms were empty, just two years after Retrocession. Miniang's house was abandoned.

Summer was over. The crickets in the kitchen went on annoyingly. At night you could hear the withered wax apples fall. Miniang had been gone a long time when you suddenly heard her voice. You hurriedly opened the window. The river murmured. You remembered the rain of the night before. Lying in bed, you wondered if that hadn't been the sound of her returning footsteps. But that was a sound from the alley. The wind off the river was heavy. The fog off the water filled the night sky. Miniang's love was longer and deeper than the alley.

You shivered in bed. Suddenly you were grown up.

The next day, when you looked out the window, you were sure you saw the principal bending over.

Her panicked footprints were everywhere—the well, bits of coal, the crumbling wall, the air permeated with the smell of soapy water. Her voice could be heard everywhere. You embarked amid the thunderous sound of waves on the river. Full, round flesh; strange waves. You rushed toward a beautiful, unknown future.

I am going now. Rushing off.

I'll come back to visit you.

When will you come back and see the reeds growing by the river?

Start the fire. I'll take off my shoes.

Warm myself. At least my aching back.

No one ever saw those red shoes again. Only the women doing laundry by the well all insisted they saw with their own eyes what happened that night.

A year later, bats swarmed out of the broken windows of her house.

On summer evenings, when the sunset clouds rolled through the sky, you saw those winged mammals circle over the river and flutter quietly over the roof of the house.

Homeland

There was a freeway outside. As the cars returning home at night came around the curve, their headlights shone through the window, tracing indistinct images on the wall.

The electric cord hanging down from the ceiling was covered with a layer of greasy dust. The colored lampshade was filled with the desiccated remains of winged insects.

The shadows traced on the wall by the headlights grew larger and larger . . . becoming a blur. Suddenly they all fled in a panic to the upper left-hand corner of the wall.

The disappearing shadows were accompanied by a roar entering through the window.

A car passed the apartment building.

The following car then traced another and similar set of images on the wall.

Before you could identify the shapes, they began to change. They got bigger and bigger . . . still bigger, then dim. The next minute, the shadows fled toward the upper left corner, fleeing upside down across the ceiling. Zoom. Again, zoom. Zoom . . . zoom . . . zoom.

You welcomed the rhythm, and poured a glass of lemonade made from canned concentrate. You sat down quietly at the table. Concentrating, keeping the changing shadows on the wall company. Keeping time in your mind, you waited for the accompanying roar.

The shadows careening along the wall invaded your mind. Lying in bed, you were too excited to sleep. This was part of your life in the desert. Black-and-white images left an afterimage on the retina, moving as the shadows moved, without cessation. You got up the next day, and as you stumbled on your way to the parking lot, you recalled the humiliation of wetting your bed in the middle of the night when you were little.

Walking down the dirt road to school, you suddenly needed to use the restroom. Your stomach grumbled. The glass of cold milk you drank earlier that morning had reached your intestines. You rushed to the restroom as soon as you arrived at school. Making students sit for a whole class period wasn't unusual. The school doctor said that Asians couldn't drink cold milk on an empty stomach unless they were constipated. He said he couldn't count the number of cases he had seen just like yours.

The light reflecting off the desert entered your lungs. Everything inside you was lit up. No shadows remained. In this vast desert, so valued by entomologists, you didn't have to worry about contracting some awful disease.

In the seminar room, the stale smell of cigarettes was mingled with the smell of the toothpaste used by the Japanese professor. Your confused thoughts abruptly came to a halt. The crucial moment of the day—waking—culminated in this seminar room shut off by closed blinds. Your daily routine then began. Fragments hovered in your mind . . . throbbing . . . never coming together. The Colorado pine stretched its sturdy branches and needles at the end of the wooden building. Its trunk, struck by lightning, prepared to hold back, single-handedly, the heat that pressed down from the sky. It was the start of another day.

"This, then, is the victory of the desert," said the Japanese professor.

As you walked down the hallway leading to the classrooms, the scenery appeared before your eyes.

Forlorn trees, dried-up rivers, the horizon line, and the sun shining overhead. The freeway vanished into the heat waves that produced no shadows. Through the canyon was Las Vegas, the city of gambling. The Japanese professor lifted his hand and gestured in the air. He had no intention of going through the canyon.

He described to you with such enthusiasm how he'd traveled through the canyon the first time. Coming over the mountains, his chest swelled. From the mountain road at night, the great expanse of lights that was the city that never sleeps was spread at his feet.

From that moment on, he never left the desert.

Now, even alcohol couldn't wake that flame in his heart. For some reason, the Japanese professor became filled with regrets.

At any rate, it was the sort of place where one could survive. Every year you had to busy yourself with filling out the application to renew your teaching contract for the next year.

The chairman of the department asked what possible problems there could be, seeing that you had been there so long.

As soon as he spoke, he felt he had gone too far. So he smiled skeptically, which might have meant that he couldn't see any reason your contract would not be extended—since you had been there for so many years. But, since it was an annual contract, it was best to fill out the forms quickly each year.

An organism rather like a tadpole appeared on the television screen. It had countless hairlike legs growing from under a hard shell, and it swam freely in the water. In the dry season it knew how to bury itself in the sand to survive. It would reappear again after the rainy season started. After discovering the remains of dinosaurs in the Grand Canyon, archaeologists were surprised to notice the traces of the long and continuous history of this kind of organism in the desert.

Everyone in the apartment complex sent flowers.

"Poor woman." The wife of the Japanese professor signed the woman's death certificate and sighed. After the cremation she inherited a whole roomful of plants bequeathed by the old woman, as specified in her will. When you entered the apartment, the wife would bow to you in the most solemn Japanese way. Every time you left, she would see you off at the door and at the same time bow and say, routinely, that because of your honorable visit, the apartment was blessed.

Now she had a roomful of inherited plants. The apartment was full of greenery. Her face would occasionally appear among the pitcher plant leaves. She serenely described to you how the old woman smiled before she died. The old lady finally had a funeral. After she escaped from Poland, she had worried that she would not be able to be buried properly in a coffin. Her whole family had died in the gas chambers.

"Poor woman." The Japanese professor's wife would always conclude her descriptions with such suitable words.

The Japanese professor, by relying on a thick international yearbook, was able to imagine himself a citizen of the world. He knew every detail concerning the great current events of the last couple of years. He would say, in the voice of a wise man, that the thoughts of the human mind should be like the fins of prehistoric fish, trying their best to swim out of this desert and into the wider world.

When he was drunk he wept like a child. He would ask you to imagine his position. His grandfather was a Yottsuya samurai. His father was a businessman who managed the first shop in Edo to export paper umbrellas. As for himself, a good Edo man, how did he fall so low as to live in this desert? He would drop into the old-fashioned leather sofa, his face tanned by the sun, looking as frightened as a child who could not find its mother.

The mist rose in the valley. February rain. The distant mountains were washed with the delicate, light-green color of young golden moss. It was like the sea surrounding the fearsome foot of a mountain. The gorgeous month of March reigned over the lonely desert. Your thoughts were confused. You shook your head, hoping to shake off the lassitude. The moldy smell of dampness accompanied the black clouds from the horizon after the rain fell. In an international long-distance phone call, your mother said that Taipei had become a huge metropolis.

"Little Axin, you won't recognize it when you come back."

Like young fiddleheads appearing overnight.

The sunlight at noon had become scorching hot. A static, crackling sound was heard, just like when the police radio broadcast "The Ten-Thousand-Voice Chorus" at home, and just as moving. At your end, you suddenly smelled the milky fragrance of your mother's body, the nursing smell that stayed with her even after the children were weaned.

When your father was still alive, he had tried so hard to speak elegant and refined Japanese. It made your mother, standing beside him, confused, appear a bumpkin. She stood there, speechless.

In your senior year you prepared for the monthly exam on the dining room table. You loudly declaimed the speech of Brutus after the assassination of Julius Caesar. "Friends, Romans, countrymen, lend me your ears!" Yet another foreign language. Your mother's face was strangely contorted, as if drained of blood. She was proud yet humiliated—the reward for a lifetime of hard work.

The principal turned on the radio and listened to a radio drama. He learned to express his innermost thoughts in correct Mandarin. Evening fell. The awful odor that had settled in the alley after Retrocession never disappeared.

You woke to find yourself in the seminar room, and realized that it was the sound of the Japanese professor, mindlessly tapping the long fingernail on his little finger, that woke you. Melancholy warmed your thoughts. Muffled voices from the radio disturbed your afternoon sleep. You recounted your dream to the Japanese professor with whom you had shared a room for over ten years, but he didn't say a word. He merely stood up, walked over to the window, and opened the blinds. He wanted you to take a good look at the landscape outside, in order to recover your wits.

The glaring light hurt your eyes. A wasteland, gradually eroded by loneliness, became an expanse of pure and harmonious sand under the burning sun. The Japanese professor shook his head and said that he still couldn't figure out how he had become a desert wolf, something that others found incomprehensible.

During the rabies epidemic in Taipei, every dog had to be muzzled; none was allowed to open its mouth on the street. All of a sudden, not a dog was heard barking anywhere in the city. Dogs became one of the quietest animals. They tucked their tails between their legs and followed people in silence, blinking their puzzled eyes and sniffing around with their muzzled snouts. Even their paw prints appeared mute.

The principal held a bag of rice to his chest and walked quickly home. It was the first time he had been able to buy Penglai rice after Retrocession. The funeral offerings for his old mother, who had really missed the rice, had long passed. The rice spilled from the bag, which was unable to contain it.

A yellow dog, following the trail of rice on the ground, entered the alley behind the principal. If the principal quickened his pace, the dog followed suit. As he neared his home, the animal was still close behind him.

The principal halted and the dog halted too, lifting its head to stare mutely at him. Even more rice spilled out. Flustered, the principal became nervous and used a leg to prevent the dog from following but without making any noise, to shoo it away. But the dog misunderstood the gesture, taking it for an attempt at play, and followed more happily when the principal resumed walking. The principal stopped at the door and so did the dog. He didn't look back, but brushed the dog's belly with his leg. The dog whined agreeably behind its muzzle. The principal had no choice and when the dog was not paying attention, he quickly slipped through the door, spilling more rice before turning and closing the door behind him.

The next day the principal's wife was heard complaining loudly beside the well that he wasn't even capable of bringing home a bag of rice! He took money away but brought home an empty bag, not to mention a little yellow stray. To waste their food! The principal had not intended to keep the dog. But the following morning, it still stood outside as if waiting for the principal to open the door for it.

He looked worried all the time. The principal was puzzled by the dog, but also pitied it. When you got home after school, the principal could be seen dozing beside his cigarette stand. After falling asleep, he still wore that worried expression. The dog stuck quietly by his side, watching the stand for him. Occasionally, when he woke, he read the classified ads of the newspaper while nervously chewing betel nut. His sunken cheeks were sucked in as he chewed. The year he retired, he'd opened a little cigarette stand in the alley. In another year, he took his wife and that yellow dog and left your small alley and moved to the fishing village.

During his last year in Taipei the principal got a set of false teeth, which suddenly made him look much younger. Now he was frequently seen in the night market near the traffic circle. If someone happened to run into him there, he looked a bit frightened and embarrassed, and would quickly look away. He loved to sit at the crowded stands and have noodles and pigs' feet.

When the principal's wife didn't want the kids to understand what she was saying to his mother, she would switch to Japanese and say that the awful smell of betel nut was always on his breath, and it never entirely disappeared. She had already warned him that if he didn't kick that habit, he need not ever think of sharing her bed again.

"Let him sleep wherever he wants to!"

There, by the roadside stand, he lifted his head and bought a bottle of liquor, which he gulped down. He was trying to wash away the smell. He soon disappeared after paying.

In a little while, he reappeared, around the Paradise Pavilion. At night, standing in the covered walkway, he timidly peered at the teahouse across the street. He walked hesitantly and nervously back and forth across the street before finally hiding in the shadows behind one of the columns. Although it was just a few steps from the traffic circle, the area was dark and deserted. There was no streetlight there and not a single car was on the street.

You couldn't say how many times you had seen the old principal sneaking around the area. Yes, you had heard that after Miniang left home she didn't really leave town. She had been seen around the traffic circle.

That was years later, after you left. She sat in front of the teahouse and stared blankly into the distance. She looked peaceful and untroubled, without a single want. When you passed by on the other side of the street on your way home from school, you always stopped and stared at her from a distance. She no longer recognized you. You couldn't keep your heart from racing. Your mouth suddenly went dry. You couldn't believe that that beggar woman with a dirty face in ragged clothes was Miniang.

You loathed the women washing at the well. They gossiped every day and never stopped. You didn't believe that Miniang was crazy. Her father hanged himself because he was afraid of the air raids. What did that have to do with her?

You were already a high school student, yet your heart still pounded whenever you passed the teahouse. The beggar woman in the filthy quilted jacket, who was said to be Miniang, was unbearably fat and oafish. She had given birth to several little beggars, who now surround her. On wintry evenings, she held her family tightly together in her arms, tucking everybody under her ragged quilted coat. Later you swore you saw that pair of red shoes in her bundle.

Your heart skipped a beat. You had just pulled a book off the shelf with your index finger. The bookstore was a long, narrow stand. The odor of old books was mixed with the strong smell of lumber used for illegal construction.

In a circulating bookstore on Roosevelt Road you opened the *Collected Stories of Chang Ailing*. The thick book stood out among all the thin volumes of knight-errant adventure tales like some bastard child. Under the dim light you read the story titled "Nights and Days in China." The brown paper cover of the book had not yet been soiled by the grubby fingers of readers. On the smooth pages, white as pearl rice, was printed:

We sink down under the heavy struggle for three meals a day. The watchtower's first drumbeat rights everything.

It calms all hearts, the mutterings of the downtrodden subside. To sink all the way to the bottom.—China, at the bottom.

The passage occurred when the heroine of the story walks through the market, holding her basket. In her heart she silently wishes that all the hustle and bustle of her countrymen would fall quiet.

The lines were indelibly imprinted on your mind. In your desert apartment pervaded by the smell of pistachios, you wished you could possess the supernatural power of sinking downward. Sinking to the bottom—the very bottom.

Seven students stared silently at the blackboard. You tried to put the writings in chronological sequence for them. The creative process flows like a stream; the further it flows, the more it branches out.

The students stared, wooden faced. The one girl student among them produced a billboard smile, as if straight out of an advertisement for Tide laundry detergent. Before the final exam, ingratiating expressions suddenly appeared on their faces. The Indians who camped beside the Colorado River welcomed tourists on the bus with the same submissive looks.

"Now, please turn to page 79."

"Pistachio," said the only girl student in this desert. She presented you with a bottle of green ointment. Though it was sealed, you could still smell the scent. She tossed her head of free-flowing hair.

"Thanks, but what is it?"

"Pistachio."

You looked it up in the dictionary and found: "Pistachio (bot.), of the genus *Pistachia* of the family Anarcardiaceae. The species *P. vera* yields the pistachio nut and flavor. A light, yellowish green, it is eaten dried and used in confections. It also produces an aromatic oil used in the preparation of various orally ingested pharmaceuticals."

"Now turn to page 79."

The students all lifted their heads and looked at you.

"This was in 1919. The writer's creative powers were in full play. Three years later, in 1921, he reached his creative peak. . . ."

On the faces of the students were the submissive looks of Indians.

"Now, let us begin reading on page 79."

All heads lowered, they looked at their books.

Withered brown needles hung from a dead limb. The bark was split open. The tree had lost its erect majesty under the scorching sun. Every time you stepped down from the podium, you looked out the window and saw that solitary tree.

The forest was from the dawn of time. The broken limbs were petrified, the annual rings formed concentric rainbows. The brilliant sky was cut into pieces by the bare branches thrusting up into the sky. The roof line of the administration building paralleled the distant horizon. Millions of points of light flickered rhythmically on the horizon. One day you would forget the earthy smell of the humus of your homeland, as well as the smell of snail slime. You walked alone and silently into the gray shade, concealing yourself in the parched darkness, watching the conjunction of the setting sun and the desert horizon. A caterpillar fell from a tree and climbed coldly up Lu Xun's back and neck. Was that in 1918?

As you took a TV dinner out of the oven, you were disturbed by the ringing of the telephone. The weather forecast for the country was on the screen. Inland areas were already flooded. Floods in Nevada had already caused hundreds of millions of dollars in damage....

"Little Axin." The static crackled. Your mother was calling long distance from across the Pacific.

Her voice seemed muffled by sleep. She sounded distant and unclear, but as loud and clear as a childhood memory. "Little Axin. It has been seventeen years. Recently your mother has been—" then the static began....

Floods in the mountains in Nevada have created an exodus to the cities. Thousands now are homeless. The television news report continued. "Little Axin, do you still remember your elementary school principal? Yes, Principal Chen—" once again static.

Come spring, the Colorado River will be at an all-time high.... Principal Chen, who lived in Nanfang'ao ... and should be good news for agriculture and water usage in Arizona ... said he had started home after eating a bowl of fish soup in the market ... more static ... even though the excess water is creating floods in various parts of the country ...

he collapsed in front of the Fisherman's Union Hall . . . more static . . . and died.

A student was struggling to read page 79. You stared absentmindedly at the solitary tree. A student struggled, reading haltingly, but could not complete a single sentence. Only when he encountered a retroflex syllable did he show some confidence, curling his tongue effortlessly. Suddenly he stopped, but there was no period. The sentence did not end there. The student intended to continue but couldn't pronounce the word. Just imagine a car falling into a ditch.

He couldn't go on. The other students lifted their heads. Six pairs of colored eyes stared beseechingly at you, signaling for help.

Today you didn't feel like rescuing them. The student who was asked to read the paragraph mumbled timidly. He didn't project his voice. He mumbled as he looked at you. Finally the wheels of the fallen car pulled it out of the ditch. He started to read loudly again.

The other students were relieved when he continued pronouncing the Chinese; they buried their heads once more in their books. Even in the third year, the students were unable to distinguish the four tones of the language. Almost all of them read with English accents, slowly spitting out the sounds of the characters. The twenty-square-foot classroom was filled with halting whispers.

. . . never passed the official examinations and, not knowing how to make a living, he had grown steadily poorer until he was almost reduced to beggary. Luckily he was a good calligrapher and could find enough copying work to fill his rice bowl. But unfortunately he had his failings too: laziness and a love of tippling. So after a few days he would disappear, taking with him books, paper, brushes, and inkstone. And after this had happened several times, people stopped employing him as a copyist. Then all he could do was resort to occasional pilfering. In our tavern, though, he was a model customer who never failed to pay up. Sometimes, it is true, when he had no money, his name would be chalked up on our tally-board; but in less than a month, he invariably settled the bill, and the name Kong Yiji would be wiped off the board again.

Before the semester ended, the campus was already as deserted as during summer break. The buildings were covered with a layer of dust. Every summer vacation, upon entering the school, you felt the tables and chairs in the classrooms were another year older. Wood, like human beings, also aged.

The time for final exams had arrived, and every student looked dumb. Seven people looked up at the podium as if they had suddenly developed an interest in Lu Xun. You seethed. *Don't expect me to give you any hints about the final exam*, you shouted in your heart. What you would really wanted to say was what your mother had said: "You had better pass the exam."

It had been seventeen years, your mother reminded you. Yet here in the desert there was no indication that you should leave.

The ocean whispered. The whitecaps rose and fell irregularly. Before going to the dunes to push the boat down to the sea, the principal opened the glass doors of the bookcase carefully, as if he didn't want to disturb the cockroaches hidden inside.

The cockroaches awoke and scattered in all directions, embarrassing the principal in front of his student. Yet the fly-encrusted flypaper that was hanging everywhere in the house did not seem to bother him.

"Come here. This is the only Chinese book in the house."

The principal got up from the edge of the bed, which was draped with a mosquito net, walked over to the bookcase, and pulled out the book.

Flipping through the pages, he fell silent, recalling the past.

"There isn't much around the house to amuse you, so take this and read it."

You took the book and read on the cover full of bug holes: *Selected Works* by Lu Xun, bearing the Government-General of Taiwan's seal of approval.

That's how you first came to know the name of Lu Xun.

Against the enormity of the night sky, the Japanese professor lifted his glass. Raising his arms, he sighed and in a harsh voice said, "What kind of life is this?"

"Come, let us drink to that writer of yours. To . . ."

"Lu Xun."

"Yes, to Lu Xun."

The shortest distance from the seminar room to the apartment was a straight line. You supported the drunken Japanese professor and staggered out of the seminar room. Ever since he'd had his hemorrhoids taken care of, he'd stopped threatening to leave the desert. His wife and the head of the department had stopped saying anything to him about hiding liquor in the seminar room. He had been unusually pensive since that time. When he did talk, he lowered his head and went over his family history. From his father in Edo, he counted back to his great grandfather in Yottsuya. His older brother, who had inherited the umbrella business, was said to have gone bankrupt and disappeared after having embezzled funds.

"Even if you went back to your own country, you wouldn't be able to teach your Lu Xun."

He often said something provocative like this to persuade you to be content with the place. Overhead, the constellations divided the sky. Their silent tranquility was more deceitful than lightning and thunder rending the sky.

During the day he constantly shook his head, as if he wanted to shake off last night's hangover. Slowly, he asked you if you still thought about that woman named Yungyue. Then for some reason he changed the subject, as he walked out of the shade and proceeded into the sunlight.

Head lowered, he started thinking. Every morning his wife wouldn't let him out the door until she had polished his shoes to a high sheen. The dyed hair on his head had gradually faded to a dry yellowish color.

He trod across the waves of sand, across the shadows on the sand and across his own shadow. He stammered that perhaps one should open an ice cream shop in the desert. Every day he waited for that most enrapturing moment when the setting sun intersected with the horizon line in a T-shaped conjunction. He waited for the moment when the alcohol devoured the day, though the desert night was never able to completely erase the white of day.

In the depths of the night, the sky retained a white glow. The sand underfoot was visible all the way to the horizon. You were on an old track. Every time you finished teaching "Kung Yiji," you suddenly felt disabled, as if you had lost the use of your legs. You imagined yourself as Kung Yiji, crawling out of the classroom with a pair of muddy hands, and even imagined yourself, legs broken, crawling across the ground, the only way to walk from the classroom to the parking lot without shame. You would never forget your trip to Nanfang'ao. No matter how much your mother scolded you, you remained squatting on the floor of the train, reading your Lu Xun, letting yourself sink down among the unsteady legs of the other passengers.

The wind whipped up the desert sand, obscuring the conjunction of the setting sun and the horizon line. The weather forecast called for high winds all night long, quieting by morning, when the sun would shine again on the desert.

Now the sand drifted, creating an infinite number of scintillating points of light. Everything was blurred. The last class of the semester was over. You walked toward the parking lot and in time your chest shrank to the shape of Kung Yiji's as you prepared to meet hundreds of miles of glittering golden sand with a heroic and disabled gesture.

You drove into the blowing sand. Suddenly you changed your mind and decided to give each student the highest grade. Everyone would get an A. Six men and one woman. Each had a sturdy body: they did fifty sit-ups and thirty push-ups each day. They would go to work in the local casinos after graduation.

They had no use for Lu Xun. Actually they couldn't even make a simple sentence in Chinese. Perhaps they signed up for the class because they heard that they could get an easy A. They had stuck it out for four semesters and made it to the advanced course on Lu Xun.

You could teach any class you liked, but this school, after all, couldn't really compare to a normal university. The department chair was an old man, very easy to get along with. In class, what often appeared before your eyes was the powerful way they pulled themselves up and over the high bar.

Summer vacation. The deserted city. Unable to take the heat, the birds had departed for other states. You had to wait until December to hear their beautiful singing again. You saved some money, but you had nothing to do.

During the vacation, all you wanted to do was nurse your weary mind. Now you could breathe in the scent of winter clothes that had been stored in the closet. Before leaving home, your mother packed coats, sweaters, even a quilted jacket in your suitcase. You hadn't worn a single one of them even once.

Be careful when you go out. Be sure to take care of yourself.

Sticking to the same track, you could still hear the muffled sound of the sea. You fondly handled the old book approved by the Government-General of Taiwan as you rested in your apartment built among a jumble of rocks in the desert. You opened the book, and on the flyleaf you saw written: "Chen Kun'nan, fourth year of the Showa period."

You raised the book to your nose and sniffed. You wanted to smell the sand.

The book definitely did not belong to the principal, because his name was Chen Xin'nan.

Therefore Chen Kun'nan had to be the name of the principal's older brother who died.

This must have been the name that the young principal arranged to have struck from the household identification book when he returned it to the colonial government office.

You held the book up to your nose and breathed deeply. You were already able to smell the raw scent of the ocean sand. Now you were convinced that when the principal's brother drowned himself, he left that very book on the beach.

Your momentary excitement created a profound sense of depression.

You concluded that what you had been missing all your life was an older brother who died, one who might have shared his pain with you, making it a part of your life.

Oh, that there might have been a time when an older brother dressed in a white coat ran across the street in tears, his coat lifted on the air, his hair blowing, his desperate footsteps, his heart all tangled up in a knot, his disintegrating character, rushing out of the magnificent red brick medical school building.

In a high wind, you saw that spirit wailing by daylight as evidence of your future happiness, leading you to do something with your life.

Too late, too late, you always said to yourself.

The whole idea of being determined to do something with your life was abstract and foreign to you. In your elementary school composition class, you always panicked at the topic of "My Goal" and didn't know where to start; and looking up, you were confronted with an impenetrable emptiness. You would arbitrarily choose among being a pioneer on the frontier, an engineer, a pilot, or a rural school teacher. And to demonstrate your seriousness, regardless of which future you chose as your goal, you would always end your composition with a line, solemn as an oath, as your resolve: you swore that on National Day the following year you would hoist the Nationalist flag over the city wall of Nanjing.

Too late, too late.

Across the park, to an asphalt road on which there wasn't a single car. In those days the medical school stood high and floated magnificently above the thick summer morning fog. The lush chestnut trees swayed. You often stopped there on the way to college to wait for that form in a white coat lifted on the air to run playfully toward you.

Looking down from the upstairs window of your house, you understood why you stared so intensely at the back of the principal who had lost his brother.

In the days when he was an inspector, he would push his bicycle out of his house very early in the morning to go to the municipal government office. He would walk along the wall full of life, through the fragrance of rice washed to cook, step by step into the sunlight.

Too late, too late.

The chest of drawers smelled of mothballs from Taiwan. There was not a single piece of furniture in the living room, no carpet on the floor, the curtains were drawn. The apartment had been like that before you moved in. In all the years you had lived there, you had heard a knock on the door only once. It was a well-dressed black person preaching door to door. He courteously left you a copy of the Bible.

You didn't want to waste time moving. Besides, the landlord's wife already promised to provide a brand-new Simmons mattress. In the cruelest time of the summer, when everybody was fleeing the scorching sun, you prepared to sink into the blowing sand—sink to the bottom, sink into sleep, to nurse your weary mind.

In the endless days of boredom, the one thing that could not be relinquished in this American police academy in the desert 5,000 feet above sea level was perhaps how you saw yourself in the pitch dark—promise not yet squandered—running along the riverbank when young, facing the hoards of bats, flying silently at the horizon amid the splendid clouds of summer evenings.

Brightly Shine the Stars Tonight

TRANSLATED BY **JOHN BALCOM**

I. The Body Occupied

> Drunk, I take off my treasured sword
> Having traveled far, I sleep in the high dwelling
> Waking suddenly at midnight
> I get up to stand before the bright dwelling.
> —LI PO

1

A bare-chested child played marbles under a tree outside the park wall. Nearby, at the foot of the wall, two or three coolies, straw hats covering their faces, were taking a noon nap. An old woman selling ice seemed to doze as well. Once in a while, she would mechanically flick her flyswatter, as if she had completely forgotten its function. Under her stand, a yellow dog panted, its tongue hanging out. Not a single other soul was to be seen on the near side of the railing running along the park. The sun was high overhead with no apparent intention to begin its descent; the streets were devoid of any of the activity one normally associates with a city.

Brick buildings lined the opposite side of the street. The glass panes of the upstairs windows reflected the lush greenery of the park and the dazzling light of the sky. The shops downstairs were quiet and without customers. Some of the shop clerks dozed behind the counters. Not a single pedestrian was seen under the covered walkways in front of the stores.

The motorcade made its way slowly through the streets: chess pieces moved without a sound on a chessboard. The cars were silent, as if propelled by means other than motors. The motorcade proceeded in single file and, whether going straight or turning, it never varied speed. Never appearing in a hurry, the cars moved forward calmly and firmly, as though controlled by a chess player who moved according to a well thought-out plan, whose game was played 30 percent at the board and 70 percent away from it, who kept silent during a match. The streets in broad daylight seemed filled with the same imposing air of concentration that is witnessed during a chess match. However, this game did not attract a curious audience. A great strategy or cruel calculation was going to end without anyone being aware of it. The motorcade turned out of the park and slowed a bit before silently slipping onto a main thoroughfare and resuming its previous speed. The cars moved at a leisurely pace as if according to plan, heading directly toward their appointed goal. The final destination was visible. What remained of the game soon would be brought to an as yet unknown conclusion.

The image of a chess game came to him, not simply because he had glimpsed some people playing chess from the car window but also because of all the time he had spent—unimportant as it was—thinking about his own life in recent days.

This day was no different from any other day.

Except that the windows, linked together one after another, reflecting the endless silver light of the sky amid green shadows, changed infinitely in a flash, as if his fate were clear. He suddenly wanted to stand aloof from the world. He recalled the time, ten years before, when he had observed a solar eclipse in the mountains.

His enthusiasm had waned after seven days in the mountains. During the eclipse, it was difficult to distinguish between day and night, victory and defeat, and life and death. Light and shadow swallowed each other, and all earthly forms were transformed into nothingness. Time grew desolate and distant; fifteen minutes felt like a thousand years. Events from the past appeared before his eyes merely to withdraw swiftly from his vision like flickering illusions. He remembered that from his commanding position on the mountain, he had been contemplating the achievements of half a lifetime. He was too dejected to finish the game of chess, so he decided to stay on the mountain.

2

The motorcade arrived at its destination. The double iron gates slowly opened; the pulleys screeched as the doors followed their prescribed arcs. Only his car left the asphalt road, passed through the iron gates, and drove down a long, dark driveway, a chess piece moved to its expected place by an invisible hand. The three other cars—his car was always the third in the motorcade—parked along the road outside the wall.

Rolling over the gravel, the tires produced a faint crunching as the wide and quiet driveway entered the dense shade of the bleached banyan tree limbs, as if entering a dream. The ancient trees formed a dense green canopy making the Japanese building a unique and blessed spot. Once again he mistakenly felt aloof from the world.

The street outside the wall was the only thoroughfare through the city. During rush hour, the deafening roar of the traffic was like the continuous beat of war drums. But the surrounding wall was like a natural defense. Once inside, one could hear the chirruping of birds in the ancient cypresses. Just recently he had realized that only inside the wall could he stop and enjoy the birdsong. In half a lifetime he had walked thousands of miles and crossed mountains and rivers, but rarely had he found a place such as this. Did he really like the place? He didn't even know now.

A man appeared in the quiet, spacious courtyard that had been designed with such care.

Approaching through the sunlight filtering through the tree leaves, the man destroyed the whole discreet situation of a chess game. Halting by his car, the man opened the car door for him. He got out of the car and walked into the mottled light. The somberness filling the air around him forced him to change his perspective, slightly altering his mood. He wanted to look after the plants and savor the ingenious design of the courtyard.

He did not need to go out every day. When they wanted to interrogate him, they would send the motorcade for him. There were no questions that day. The person presiding had read out official documents to him, that was all. Perhaps that was why he felt differently before entering the residence.

Reluctant to leave the flickering sunlight in the courtyard, he slowed his pace and took his time to go inside. The guards stood at some distance. Watching him or not, they never moved. Their stillness amid the flickering sunlight created a strange and inexplicable scene in such surroundings.

He walked toward the door. One of the guards gestured silently to him from afar, perhaps giving a salute. The protective walls served the same function as the motorcade on the streets, and the guards surrounding him were charged with his protection.

But who had time to trouble themselves with asking about who they were?

Occasionally, he asked this question for others. The pedestrians were surely surprised seeing the strange motorcade appear and disappear on the Taipei streets.

However, who would have the time to bother asking "Who is he"?

He walked up the flight of steps and crossed the threshold. A huge horizontal placard inscribed with the words SPIRIT SWALLOWS DREAM CLOUDS in four huge characters hung high over the door. He could recite the words without lifting his head. As he ascended, an entrance hall suddenly opened before him. With feigned high-spirited steps, he measured the deepening interior. The huge square supports for the beams and the jutting eaves were visible, and the dense and towering trees outside only made the interior feel all the more open and radiant. The rooms of the house were open yet secluded. Each time he left or entered the building, he couldn't help but admire the artistic ingenuity of the architect.

3

Originally the Lizhi Society had been the Japanese Naval Club housed in the Zhaonan Building. The huge wooden building was hidden in the lush shade of ancient trees. The stone wall that faced the street screened the profound mystery inside from the pedestrians outside.

Occasionally the wind would bend the trees, revealing the green tiles within. During the Pacific War, Japanese officers would take their R & R there. They would relax and make merry, and, after eating and drinking, they surely would exclaim that it was a world apart.

After ascending the steps of the entrance hall, he entered the wooden-floored corridors. His every movement invisibly linked him to the guards around him. Without turning his head, he could intuit how busy they were, deploying their chess moves behind his back. Silently and without a trace, they made their moves, shifting imperceptibly like the sun.

He had been here for more than ten months and still was unable to picture the entire building. Judging from the dusty air, no one had stayed there since the Japanese left in haste. The beams and window lattices were still clean, but the paper doors had yellowed. Amid the intersecting wooden corridors, he felt that he would lose his way at any moment. Passing several halls and rooms, he turned left, following the west passage, passed three more rooms, and came to the foot of a spiral staircase. Bamboo blinds lined the entire west-facing passage. Returning late, he sometimes would see a stretch of dim light.

His footsteps on the wooden floor were not unpleasant. His movements were precise and controlled—he walked stiffly upright through the ever-changing light and shadow. He was, after all, still himself, calm in mind and heart. This was a source of happiness to him. As a young graduate student in a Japanese officer training school, he had become accustomed to paying attention to his own bearing. In the temporary office, as he sat listening to the documents being read to him, he had remained entirely impassive, not moving in the slightest.

Calm and dignified, he walked through the corridors. He communicated with the high beams and responded to the passages stretching under his feet as if he were part of the ancient building. At least, that is the way he saw himself each time.

Those following him gradually decreased in number. Starting from the entrance hall, a sentry would take up position every five paces or so; by the time he reached the stairway, each guard, like a chess piece, had taken up his position and only one remained a few steps behind him, following him up the stairs. The ten steps in the flight of stairs led to the second floor, which was open and bright.

He never turned around or looked back prior to entering his room. He merely gestured by raising his hand. The guard would simply stop behind him and salute without dashing forward to open the door for him. It was his impression that the person behind him, the last and closest guard, saluted him. It was always the same, even today. He never looked back so as to retain a good impression.

This guest house suddenly quieted down, and, as if some important matter had been concluded, everyone relaxed. However, the guards inside and outside had to fulfill their duties, their responsibilities incomprehensible to outsiders.

4

On this day, he stayed up alone in his room thinking late into the night. The world that he had constructed for so long rose before his eyes.

A military song about a defeated army woke him in the afternoon. He realized he had fallen asleep in his rattan chair. For a while he didn't know where he was; he stood up and felt top-heavy. He washed his face with cold water, trying to remain calm.

The armed forces of the Republic of China had made a complete retreat from inland. Some time ago the newspaper had carried the words, "Heaven should obey the wishes of the people," but he wasn't sure of their exact meaning. Was that the proper way to describe the common people who had followed the government across the strait to Taiwan?

The defeated soldiers retreated in surging waves, and common people, who followed, had become wave-tossed flotsam.

The song lingered in the air before he woke and brought recollections of his dusty hometown, time, and dreams.

It was a large living room of about eight *tatami*, which already had been removed. He figured that all *tatami* in this guest house already had been removed because no one ever took off their shoes when they entered. He wondered how long it would take for those who'd fled calamity to be able to lead peaceful lives. A low tea table stood in the center of the living room, flanked by two rattan chairs with seat and back cushions left by the Japanese. The silk covers of the soft cushions were embroidered with flowers and birds. The living room faced southwest, and a patch of clear sky could be seen when the *shoji* was open because the surrounding area contained nothing but single-story dwellings. Standing on the balcony, one could see the train station in the distance across the vast open space. The pleasant whistles of the midnight train could be heard.

At dusk, a mysterious light attracted his attention.

He rose from his chair and walked in the direction of the light. He saw his own reflection, but it took a few seconds to dawn on him that he was standing in front of his mirror. But he didn't move away with this realization. Looking at himself in the mirror had became an important activity while living in seclusion in this small room. He was satisfied with his reflection even without scrutinizing it.

Outside, he was big news now, and attracted everyone's attention. It was in the midst of chaos that he was able to return to the simplest life in time. He knew that everyone had withdrawn from the mainland. He had no telephone in his room and hadn't seen a newspaper in days. Once, when he had been a guest at a mountain villa, a Taoist presented him with a couplet: "Two stalks of bamboo outdoors; a patch of sunlight indoors." Then he continued: "You of course know that the answer to this riddle is the character for *simple*." At that time he was in a bad mood because he had ordered the death of Zhang Fei, his trusted follower, who betrayed him as an informer for the Blueshirts, following which he resigned as provincial chairman of Fujian province. He was bored and felt all worldly affairs were illusory. As he said farewell before descending the mountain, the Taoist eased his anxiety by saying that the hundred years of a life amounted to stepping over a crack and was not worth mentioning. What was important was simplicity and quiet. "Simplicity and quiet are good."

After ten years of constant improvement, he was confident that he could see the purity that would come when he had given up everything.

Although this may have been what he said, one evening—he couldn't recall how many times this had happened—he felt a sentimental attachment to the world. The sound of a radio outside, the sound of footsteps beyond the wall at midnight, and even the sound of a braking truck somewhere off in the distance made him happy, left him feeling elated with the beauty of life.

He knew it was a very serious matter. Afterward, he had to double his efforts to calm down and pull himself together, which was not too difficult for a soldier who had experienced life and death in battle.

He sat at attention in the living room without thinking anything until dawn broke.

5

The mirror was already in the room when they billeted him there. He was exhausted at the time and didn't particularly like the long mirror. Hanging as it did in the narrow hallway to the bathroom, the mirror shouldn't have had the slightest impact on anything in the living room. But from its corner, it reflected him at all times—his haggard image and useless life idled away—no matter how far away he was. It seemed as if he were always encircled and always breaking through an encirclement.

The bright mirror reflected his disorganized thoughts. Through foolish memories and frivolous thoughts, he vaguely perceived illusory shadows in the still mirror. Sometimes he felt heroic; at other times he felt his life had been caught in meaningless actions. His memories seemed insignificant today. In 1924, the thirteenth year of the Republic, he'd been appointed commander of the 1st Infantry Division by Sun Chuanfang. He won every battle on the Jinpu Road. For seven days and nights, he never dismounted to speed across the Huai River. He was barely forty at the time. At the battle of Renqiao, he surrounded Zhang Zongchang and destroyed his Russian armor.

The Jiu River flowed through a valley of peach blossoms and green willows. The remnants of the enemy troops were retreating; the soldiers deserted, abandoning their weapons as they tried to save themselves. In the ensuing panic, many were trampled underfoot and the casualties were immense. Some of the routed soldiers, who clung to tree branches or wood planks, called for help from the river; corpses were heaped up on the riverbank; the floating bodies filling the river were swept away on the current. In a fleeting instant, it all vanished into emptiness like a dream flowing away. Riding his horse, he entered another dream, until his nephew, who approached from behind, woke him. The river surged as usual, the wind howled, and the distant valley was filled with smoke. Peach blossoms covered every path for a thousand miles. It seemed as if the landscape were completely untouched by the recent war. He could not stay; he turned and hastily led his troops north. He set off from Lingjia Bridge in the morning. His woman wrote from home about the pains of giving birth. He forded the river and entered Xuzhou, where he was promoted to commander of five allied provincial forces from Zhejiang, Fujian, Jiangsu, Anhui, and Jiangxi. At the same time, he was also appointed as provincial chairman of Zhejiang province.

But time waits for no one. Before he could even take a breath, he fell out with Sun Chuanfang, who pinned him down with massive forces at Meihua Bei. In the midst of a sandstorm, buffeted by wind and thunder, the sky darkening around him, he fell into the hands of his enemy. He was sent to Nanjing under escort on a starry night. He still carried the letter from his wife. She bled for half a year after giving birth, perhaps because she didn't rest in bed long enough, insisting on washing clothes by riverside in the middle of winter.

At the headquarters of the five allied provincial forces, Sun Chuanfang, heavy of heart, lay in bed smoking opium. His bodyguards encircled the headquarters and sentries were posted down to the river. Enveloped in opium smoke, surrounded by sycophants, as the light of day began to stream through the window, Sun, the reputed commander-in-chief, lay on his side in a warm bed, facing the wall, with his back to him. He hated this guy from Zhejiang and hated those people from Zhejiang who had just come north from Guangzhou even more.

"You are against me! You have an army but are biding your time, waiting to see. Are you planning to join with Huangpu?"

The Northern Expeditionary Army's unstoppable push toward Wuhan was creating a sensation everywhere. Suddenly Commander-in-Chief Sun's mind was filled with murderous intent. "Stay here and rest." The softness of foreign cigarettes contrasted with the harshness in his victor's voice. He was taken out but didn't go back to Xuzhou; instead he became Sun's prisoner awaiting execution. He was locked in a dark room at headquarters. It was only during this period of time that he first began to appreciate common life. All day long he looked at the blue tiles and white walls of the other houses from his window. His woman wrote asking him if they should build a brick wall after the thatched shed was completed behind the house to serve as a windbreak against the wind from the river. He stared blankly out the window. The entangled skein of life and death was as incomprehensible as the lines in one's palms. Sun Chuanfang had the foresight of a prophet. He was right about him taking no action, but he had been mistaken and had not seen that he had long been weary of war. Still young, he could not express that weariness and had to endure more of the tortures of war. At first he was just startled and confused; later, after becoming Sun's prisoner, he had no more chances to see him. In jail, he kept thinking of the momentary red glow from Sun's opium pipe when he inhaled. He realized his fate hung on Sun's changing thoughts.

Sun Chuanfang changed his mind and set him free. He expressed his wish to resign and return home. Walking up to the observatory on Mount Zijin, accompanied by two or three trusted followers and several dozen retainers, he embraced the beautiful scenery from on high, thinking to wash away the foul odor from his body. However, seeing Mount Zhong towering above the Yangtze River, he was suddenly inspired and completely forgot his recent narrow escape.

A dream took shape in his mind's eye. His life once again hung in the shadows.

Before an armillary sphere, he sank deep into thought. He observed 300 constellations and 1,449 stars. The movements and revolutions of the sun, moon, and stars were like the hidden orbit of fate. A picture, an augury, a dizzying sight. He could hear the clear and forceful sound of his bodyguard's boots on the flight of steps. The white clouds floated leisurely in the sky, the plants were still, and he suddenly found himself bewildered.

The southern troops had massed, and as they approached they raised clouds of yellow dust. The northern troops of Feng stealthily approached the capital through the pass. The battle between the South and the North was about to commence. The whole nation was stirred by the winds of war and everyone was waiting for the storm to break, sweeping up the innocents. He didn't know why, but his plan for dominance, as yet unrealized, was, in his imagination, already fading. He clenched his teeth and returned home. Under the eaves of his home, his thoughts wandered; he had no set ideas about life. That afternoon he slept his first good sleep since he'd been freed from danger. He dreamed about several birds. They flew low in the sky and their chirping could be heard from the eaves.

He seemed to exist between sleep and wakefulness. Soon the clear, crisp days of autumn arrived; the sunlight was pale and distant, as if the country had not been sundered. Taking off his uniform, he put on a padded cotton coat and cloth shoes. With the sunlight on the wall, he gradually felt warm and secure staying at home. Naturally affectionate, Heaven and Earth need not resort to arms. The national heroes, ancient and modern, could not compare with the common people and their lives. He never knew that he could be so astonishingly happy about the world of men.

He was sound asleep and dreamed that his trusted fellows counterattacked and broke off from the regular army. They encamped that night by the riverside, and from their scattered conversation it was clear that they were dreading the next day's fight to break through the enemy encirclement.

He was awakened by the hoof beats of his nephew's horse. The young man brought his appointment as the commander of the 19th Route Army of the Northern Expeditionary Force.

He opened his eyes.

His dream was broken.

He was unspeakably annoyed when he discovered that reality had caught up with him. Suddenly he found himself in a dilemma.

However, he was in the prime of his life. How could such a bright future pass him by?

That night, he sat alone, deep in thought. Later he could only express himself in writing: "Advance without thought for reputation; retreat without concern for punishment."

To whom did he write?

To his wife, of course.

The following day he made ready and left home, charging off to another battle in another place with his nephew.

6

Sequestered as he was in the secret room for a long time, the mirror gradually became his close friend and companion.

The old mirror became unclear. The discolored backing, which looked like cotton balls, showed through in several places, which only served to accentuate the mirror's reflectivity. Every day, after the fall of dusk, he would automatically walk to the mirror to keep his assignation, which seemed prearranged for that hour. Outside the window, the colored clouds changed constantly in the subtropical sky, making the mirror as deep as the sea. Standing before it, at first he didn't know what to pour out to it from his heart.

He would concentrate on his reflection and the scene in the mirror in order to rid himself of external turmoil and disorder. He would inspect and speak to himself, and then straighten his collar and tug at his sleeves to look his best. He would slip into his memories as if entering an illusory world in the mirror. That's how he killed his time. Considering his life coolly for a moment, he knew it was in utter disorder. His dreams lay broken on the ground where anyone could trample them.

The mirror didn't really know him well. It was curious about his life experience, his military life, his administration, and how he made enemies and friends, as well as his beautiful dreams.

When he returned home to be the chairman of Zhejiang province again, he made a speech comparing himself to "a tired bird coming home to roost." How old was he then? Sitting in his office the first afternoon, he happened to smell the fresh aroma of the salted tofu that his woman set out in the courtyard. He hadn't seen his wife in several years. He wasn't really old or tired. Comparing himself to a tired bird was nothing more than emphasis. Their viewpoints were always different from his anyway. Naturally they had their opinions just like he had his. When he expressed an idea, a principle, or a fantasy in an offhanded way, he would be surprised at himself later. For more often than not, such expressions would be seen as shortcomings to be exploited by others. He disliked the continuous infighting, and there were times he regretted not having forces at his command, but more often he regretted having a large force at his disposal. He could carry out his ambitions only in his imagination.

At the age of twenty-four he saw a historical picture scroll of his motherland's glories and cruelties for the first time in the dormitory of the Japanese officer training school one snowy morning. He could faintly see himself scurrying through the world of the Republic, the starting point of his career. It stretched off into the future as vast as the sea. Later, that future rang with his accomplishments, and his dreams had become his nightmare. He had lived his life without foresight or guessing; even today, when he looked back, all he saw was the uninterrupted, disordered traces of dreams. When he was thirty-one, he was a representative to the office of the Commander of Northern Governmental Affairs. He entered the narrow gate of no return when he got involved in the military affairs of the Republic. As long as he had troops at his disposal, he rushed about, fighting all over the country; even when he had no troops, he still would take risks. For more than twenty years he had drifted along in this way. At fifty-seven, when he was chairman of Fujian province, he adopted a second son to be his successor, and so bid farewell to the Republic and retired to his home. But within five years, he had to arrest his adopted son and have him executed outside the west gate of the city of Fuzhou.

In truth, he treated the young Zhang Fei as his own child, and even though he knew he had been sent by the Blueshirts, he never suspected him of disloyalty or of secretly plotting rebellion against him. When he discovered the betrayal, he had him eliminated without a second thought, as if he were an outsider. But he felt old and sick and, although not prostrated by illness, he felt disheartened for the first time. He felt no joy in life, his mouth felt as if it were filled with sand for a long time afterward. The illness, like a worm hidden in a fruit, was forever lodged in his heart. When he was fifty-eight, he went to the mountains to recuperate as a guest in a villa for seven days. The host of the villa tried to comfort him and cheer him up with a couplet by Tan Sitong: "Drinking and overturning the world's affairs; in wind and rain the heart of the famous mountain never changes." At sixty, as General Secretary of the Executive Yuan, he opposed Kong Xiangxi, who was an extremely popular and powerful financial oligarch. He had nothing to rely upon save his dreams. His woman sent an express letter to tell him that the fires of war had spread to his hometown, and mirror grinders were hard to find. She had put the bronze mirror and a desiccant powder into a clay urn ready to bury in the corner of the garden in case of some unforeseen event.

At sixty-five, he was made a general and became the chairman of Zhejiang province again and the commander of provincial security. He still engaged in veiled struggles with the Blueshirts. His woman wrote in a letter,

> All the men who left home to study or to fill an office, or even to run off to the far corners of the earth, said they did so for world peace. But as far as I can see, all of you only have a keen interest in waging war. I fear that the war in coming years will be a source of constant anxiety for several generations. Though it is said that war is natural, outside, every indication is that this is the end. Can't you make the Yangtze and the Yellow River clear and clean like the beautiful sun and moon in the sky? If this is the state of things today, don't panic at the crucial point nor become disconcerted through fear and worry about what others think.

The letter continued,

It was the time to sacrifice to our ancestors several days ago, but my period also came. You know that it is improper for a woman to cook during her period so as not to enrage the kitchen god. But there is no help at home anymore, and our daughter, though grown up, cannot cook yet. I just had to disregard the superstition and allow myself to cook two dishes for our ancestors. Every time Tangsheng's mother forded the river and crossed the mountain, she would drop by for a chat and some tea. She entreated you, since you are his uncle, to look after Tangsheng who is away from home and exposed to the elements. I told her that Tangsheng now is the commander of a large military unit and that his uncle has to rely on him and be taken care of by him. Tangsheng's mother mentioned that without your guidance and support, Tangsheng, who lost his father when very young and always looked up to us as his parents, certainly would not be where he is today. I tell you Tangsheng is always very filial toward us; please treat him as our child, so that his mother won't be worried.

II. Waking from the Nightmare of History

One must have acute senses to savor destiny.
—Montaigne

7

Though closed up in his room, he did have things to do. His attention moved with the sunlight, from the dawn light on this wall to the twilight on that wall. He considered his life, from his youth to his present situation. Each day was short and he was in a calm state of mind, scarcely ever frustrated about his fate. "A soldier has no regrets" was his motto.

His uniforms, toilet articles, and even his bearing, like his time, were arranged in perfect order. His wife, as he recalled her, was very neat too, brushing her hair to a lustrous sheen every day. She never let him see her brush her hair when she let it down. Her decorous appearance was the perfect complement to his military bearing.

Thirty years of change and hardship that eluded understanding, whirled like the wind, spread like the clouds. It was all unfathomable regardless of his observations or predictions; there was absolutely nothing empirical he could rely on to understand his fate and that of his people. The military songs sung by the defeated soldiers on the street were like a gust of wind that despoiled the fruit from trees cultivated for decades.

He didn't participate in the great purge within the party in the sixteenth year of the Republic; he was the mollifying officer in the area north of the Yangtze River who incorporated the remnants of Sun Chuanfang's troops into his own force. The following year he went to Germany to study in the towering and solemn Heidelberg Museum, which washed away the bloody smell of warfare from his country.

Who am I?

He broached that question for the first time as his footsteps resonated in the exhibition hall.

Did he try to stop the hasty flow of time?

Even now, after more than ten years, he still found the question difficult to answer as he examined himself in the mirror.

The German strategic officer who accompanied him then pointed out a picture on the wall of a snake biting its own tail, and smiled knowingly.

"Isn't that the most faithful image of life?" asked the impulsive major general with enthusiastic politeness.

He came from a distressed country and his sufferings would never be understood by outsiders, but the picture and the German officer, whom he had met in that foreign land, made him feel warm like old friends. A dreamland where few people appeared to tread opened before him. But he didn't want to pause lest the foreign officer think there was something weighing on his mind.

In all the years of military campaigns and administrative work, he'd never once felt his life was his own. He was swept up in the moment and too busy to attend to other things. But who was he? Later, he never had a spare moment to care. He went from place to place, south to north, before finally ending up in the guest room at the Lizhi Society. On the second floor of the headquarters in Linjiang, his nephew, Tangsheng, in a heroic tone of voice with a melancholy hometown accent, recited some lines of poetry that dealt with the eternal regret for leading a life one had not chosen. That was the thirty-eighth year of the Republic.

His nephew had just assumed the post of commander-in-chief of the garrison command of Nanjing, Shanghai, and Hangzhou with a huge force under him. Not having seen his nephew for a long time, he thought the young man appeared more distinguished and dignified than ever. Owing to his high position, he seemed to have grown more confident, a key player at a critical juncture in time. When he spoke, his voice was sonorous and forceful, as if he intended to carve his own likeness in the hard stone of history. Seeing him, his uncle was both startled and admiring.

He was then the provincial chairman of Zhejiang province, with no forces at his disposal. Given the dangerous situation on the other side of the river and the unpredictable future, he was anxious to see his nephew. He took a break and was driven to visit him. He was not then old enough to have lost confidence in his own dreams.

Nanjing was no longer the same place from which he had escaped. The city was located at a forbidding strategic point, and since it had once been the capital of the empire, even the residences of the common people were stately and permeated with a peaceful atmosphere. Now he came again, Mount Zhong pressed against the border, the Yangtze River flowed into the distance. On the market, the currency amounted to waste paper. Popular feeling was anxious. The great flight of the Republic was about to unfold. However, the moon above the river was beautiful. Gazing from his window, he watched how the water suddenly surged at Pukou and then flowed smoothly, following its ordered course to the sea. The slackening flow was plain to the eye under the celestial mirror of the starry night. He was momentarily moved. The world of men clamored, heaven and earth were capricious, friends and relatives came together and parted once more. He had no son, he had only his nephew.

8

The following year, on the Taiwan side of the strait, he recalled that he was first able to bend his will to his dreams in his nephew's headquarters.

In those days, the end of time already existed outside his dreams. Two armies vainly strove for supremacy, reducing the beautiful rivers and mountains of the country to scorched earth. Even so, he was a general and he sat facing his nephew, who was also a general. He ought not to have considered such things, much less that absurd dream of his, which perhaps would only serve to create difficulties for his nephew.

However, he was sometimes pressed by worldly affairs and his temperament to address the relative superiority and inferiority of this absurdity. He didn't plan to conceal his dream from his nephew, whom he treated like a son.

That day the political situation had reached a head. Without the slightest hesitation, he strode into his nephew's headquarters and clasped the hand his nephew proffered. Recalling the incident later, he decided that it was precisely at that moment when he completely entered his own dream world. This was a matter of course; there was no turning back in the pursuit of justice. There was no comparison between the rise and fall of a generation outside his dreams and the endless pleasure in his dreams. He possessed a beautiful picture scroll that he wanted to share with his nephew, but suddenly he found himself tongue-tied and didn't know where to begin.

At that critical moment, all he wanted to do was to shout: "Stop for a moment!"

One's achievements cannot be planned; there is no need to be so hasty in everything. It had absolutely nothing to do with fear or despair.

Don't you see that since the founding of the Republic there has been nothing but turmoil? Those who attend the military academy in town do so solely to learn to use the army to realize their schemes for success. They are cruel and greedy, and become accustomed to the killing. Their meager talents take them here and there for any odd job whatsoever. The country is filled with soldier-bandits and military officials. The top is dominated by the secret societies, and hooligans govern the country. Those below are hangers-on of the influential. Tell me, what are the prospects in this job?

But his nephew had other thoughts. He talked only about the divine land, and sighed, gazing toward heaven. He recalled how the enemy had driven millions of hungry soldiers for several years from the cold and remote frontier fortress across thousands of miles of desolate land. First they swallowed the northeast after entering through the pass and ignited the fires of war in the vast divine land; at that moment, they were plundering and pillaging as they pushed toward Shandong, Jiangsu, and Anhui. On their own side, the blood of the army of Huang Botao had been spilled at Zhan Zhuang; the commander had committed suicide for the country. General Huang Wei lost Shuangduiji and was captured. The forces of Qiu Qingguan disappeared in a flash. Two armies, competing for victory, faced off across the river.

He had no intention of discussing the situation after the fact, of starting from the beginning. He wanted to tell a different story, of other risks, of another decisive battle. The vision and plan were probably greater and bolder and more difficult than the decisive battle before them.

It was a strange night; for no reason he disclosed his suspect identity. His dream, which he never ceased propagating, was like a swarm of butterflies emanating from his mouth. He couldn't restrain himself, he couldn't hold his tongue. He remembered how he'd unrolled that beautiful picture scroll for his nephew and how he had been moved by his own ingenious words. Finally, after he was able to calm down, he explained how uneasy he felt about the millions who were once again being driven to death with the same beautiful lies and about the decisive battle that would reduce generations to poverty from which recovery would be difficult. One impulsive act would plunge the people into an abyss of misery. A hopeless picture of a world of refugees was taking shape and nearly complete. Talk of the decisive battle was cheap and expressed a soldier's true colors, which he viewed as childish. You and I must not keep making the same mistake; we have to make a choice right now.

Tangsheng was unable to follow what he was saying. Certainly he did not want to disobey his elders. Tangsheng constantly said that the Republic would be successful by relying on his uncle's wisdom in handling human affairs. He indicated to his nephew that things could not be taken lightly; the country could be put right in an instant or a single slip could lead to regret. When it came to victory and defeat, a commander ought to let go and see the light.

Unexpectedly, Tangsheng's expression changed. He spoke resolutely, saying, "I will not sacrifice myself lightly." The tone of his voice expressed his will and seemed to warn his uncle, and even hinted at a rebuke. Their conversation reached a deadlock. His nephew, realizing that he was the source of the deadlock, softened his tone: "I'm afraid it won't make me a buddha overnight." He was referring to himself, but seemed to hint at his uncle as well. Recalling the incident later, he appreciated his nephew's kind intention of reminding him that given the situation, there was only one thing he could do.

Actually, Tangsheng was as uneasy as if he were on the front lines, and with the air of someone trying to convince himself, he said, "Never give up hope for peace as long as there is the slightest hope. Never sacrifice yourself unless it is at the critical moment." He found the words irritating, as if to say such things was utter nonsense. Perhaps his uncle had pushed him to throw out such slogans in a panic. When he reflected carefully, he found his words were not without reason. The first line, which mentioned peace, while acknowledging his gratitude to his uncle, also indicated that as long as the country existed, avoiding war was not a solution. The second line, about sacrifice, showed his consideration of the overall situation and that he could not reject his position as commander.

He had no response to make. His nephew ended the conversation at this point. Dizzy with excitement, he asked his nephew to bring some wine and changed the topic of conversation.

9

Inside headquarters, uncle and nephew sat face to face, their mood changed as they temporarily forgot about the war. There were only four small dishes on the table. The young man often toasted his elder. It was his handsome nephew who made the food and wine delightful. Not having seen him in ages, he thought Tangsheng did look heroic and daring, as some suggested. At the same time he was gratified that his nephew had the courage to take on this mission in his position. After several rounds his nephew was at ease and he was relaxed. All he wanted was sincere and mutual understanding between them, and then everything would be all right. The living room was peaceful; past kindnesses and old grudges, military honor and official rank as well as success and failure all became figments outside the window. The moonlight shone through the window, bright and beautiful. Their earlier dispute had vanished; everything was fair and reasonable. The young man really understood that etiquette was to be striven for.

Unconsciously, as if he had opened his heavenly eye, he sensed a clear and resonant sound all around, inside the room and outside. Leaning back in his chair, he was speechless. He became quiet and distant. His nephew, noticing this, joined in his pleasure, sinking into silence and thought.

A moment later, the headquarters building was quiet.

After a long while, he finally said, "Someday I will weary of war and will return home, closing my door, and just read."

The quiet was followed by dead silence.

The atmosphere became tense, but he thought he was perhaps being overly sensitive.

Then he indicated that he had left home and spent half his life in government service, but there was no longer any reason to do so. He wanted only to go home and lead a hermit's life in his later years. He hadn't told his nephew this in a fit of pique, but still, he was afraid his nephew would think so. So he added, "I say this from the bottom of my heart."

But his nephew became angry again. He stood up and said in a stern voice:

"Without this war, there will be no peace in this country." He gave his uncle a tongue-lashing in the strongest terms and in a willful tone of voice meant to suppress his uncle's thoughts.

He didn't back down. Seeing that his kindness was met with refusal, his temper flared. He wanted to express his true feelings while maintaining a persuasive gentleness. Was he crazy? He asked his nephew and then explained that his determination to withdraw from office in no way diminished the clarity of his mind. In making his request, he hadn't asked for the impossible, like cooking sand into rice or scattering beans to sprout into soldiers or cutting a river's flow with the flick of a whip. *Fine, whatever you receive, you pay for in the long run. Just make sure you are right and think thrice before you act and you'll be able to beat the wind into a sword or tattoo the sky with a dragon! Some wild ideas are not to be scorned.*

10

He was a little tipsy.

He was swept along on a rapid current, and before him loomed the treacherous and gorgeous splendor on the eve of calamity. His thoughts surged ahead. Because they'd parted at loggerheads, he wanted to bare his heart to his nephew in writing.

He laid out paper, ink, and inkstone on Tangsheng's work desk. His mind was a blank for a while; he was unable to think of any good lines. After wracking his brain, he focused his mind and, holding his breath, proceeded to write a quatrain:

Numerous tragedies have beset my career,
For how the wheel of history turns there is no seer;
Time's passing diminishes not my love of country,
A love so strongly suffered becomes a hell for me.

Reading these lines, Tangsheng was delighted. The disagreement between them was at once cast aside. Uncle and nephew (no, father and son) both drank and talked cheerfully once again.

It was late at night. The headquarters building stood among the homes of common folk. A single blue light burned inside. A great decisive battle was going to be fought, so be it. Drunk, he dozed.

His nephew helped him up to his own room.

He dreamed of the dusk at his old home.

He also dreamed of a stream. He saw himself move with lightning speed. The remnants of his troops broke through the encirclement, trying to escape being surrounded again by Zhang Zongchang. He finally slipped the noose, but his favorite cavalrymen were trapped in the Dragon King Temple.

At the time, he was undaunted by the battle because he was still a young man full of vigor. But reappearing now in his dream, it was different—all the tricky and dangerous situations were there right before his eyes.

However, he was awakened by the sound of his own laughter.

He sat up in bed. Great was the manifestation of Heaven's way, but that longstanding sadness remained in his breast. It was his own sadness and that of the people. Just think of how tears and blood had flowed in silence for thousands of years, and they would flow just as silently and naturally in the future. He suddenly saw himself and others in a different time and place eating the same bitter fruit. It was the same every generation—imprisoned in the circle of history, there was no exit from this rounding maze.

He awoke from his stupor.

The great river cut off all human talk.

The sky above the command headquarters was full of stars; outside it was gloomy.

He was moved by the loving care of his nephew.

He said to himself that he hadn't come to drink or debate the war, all of which he had lost interest in long ago. When uncle and nephew met, they should be able to talk and say anything with no ulterior motives. *But what possessed you to openly talk about your intentions of withdrawing troops at this critical moment? You had a well thought-out plan, but your nephew didn't. If he were caught unprepared, not only would he have a hard time dealing with you, but also his military career would be on the line.*

He sobered up completely. For the sake of lasting love between uncle and nephew, he couldn't push him too hard.

At dawn, he tidied up and left quietly.

On the way back, the clouds hung low over the river. Along the shore an atmosphere of war prevailed, and the people were restless. He sat calmly in the back seat of the car that sped west. Outside stretched the vastness. He recalled clearly that it was then that his majestic and beautiful dream ripened in his mind.

III. It Is the Shadows That Pry

.

As soon as you are born you fall into a dream, just like falling into the sea.

—Conrad

11

If he returned to the past in order to drive the evil out of himself, then he succeeded. But success had not come as easily as he had expected. Any intelligent organism that attached itself to the body was a predator that fed on another's blood, and the only way to lure it out of its lair was with another piece of flesh. So he gradually grew emaciated. Life in his small room wasn't exactly tranquil—that is, until he woke from a dream one night at midnight and discovered that the evil that had endlessly gnawed at him had been expelled from his body.

It was a good sign; he felt relieved and happy. He suddenly realized that the suspicions clouding his mind actually had disappeared for a few days already, and the reality before him, like the troops he once commanded, obeyed his instructions and orders.

Now, all he had to do was close his eyes, and the wind would stop blowing. What this meant was that he needed only to force himself inside himself and he would hear nothing at all. He flew out the window, but his shadow would not appear on anyone's roof. In other words, he knew the lithe freedom of the birds. He could be as still as a tree or float motionless like a cloud in his room.

Opening the *shoji* door, he stood under the eaves. He didn't cast a glance at the garden below or the street beyond the walls. The lights were out in every household: Taipei was silent and still. The light faintly flickered in the western sky, where, a little earlier, the setting sun had found its way home. He calmly measured his own breathing, unable to detect the slightest respiratory movement. Nor did he need to know how long he had been standing on the balcony. The entangled wisteria inside the walls, the white lilies in the pond, and the starry sky above the tiled roofs outside were all part of his dream.

He vaguely felt that the time for which he had waited so arduously had finally arrived.

Immediately he retreated from his recollections and returned to the present. He walked back to the mirror, where he scrutinized himself. The face in the mirror looked strange and unfamiliar; he had to reexamine himself. But the face in the mirror still looked strange. This excited him. This was the mirror's secret: it no longer reflected you. The interconnected folds and lines reflected in the mirror were not a reflection of the you standing before the mirror. The mirror did not serve to reflect something so superficial and ephemeral. For thousands of years now, people had misunderstood the function of a mirror.

12

Standing before the mirror, he no longer saw himself reflected there.

His concentration became ever more focused as he pondered the inconceivable depths in that layer of silvery brightness day and night. His sight was as sharp as a blade. In the mirror he chiseled out his own ideal contours like a sculptor chipping away unnecessary fragments of hard stone. He wanted to see the image in his mind appear in the depths of the mirror, as if it had burst out of stone. He seemed to have infinite confidence and patience to wait for the appearance of a brand-new reflection. With the immense power of his will, he forced himself into that dream.

He then decided to be reincarnated in the mirror.

He impregnated the self in his dream. For several years now, he'd had the feeling that the burden of his flesh would be transferred inside the mirror.

Day by day he spent more time standing in front of the mirror. In half a lifetime in the military, facing life and death, he had looked to the stars, amulets, and the lines in the palms of his own hands, but never had he felt as happy as when he looked at his mysterious fetal movements reflected in the mirror at that moment.

In this way he patiently awaited his own rebirth in that locked room in Taipei.

He could control his fate in the mirror just like in a dream. Who else could control the self in the mirror? Who else could destroy that life? He often found himself trapped in a dizzying vertigo when he tried to get inside himself with too much force. But it was only at such moments that he was able to see a different world, friendly and distant, flickering before his eyes. This would be followed by a sharp pain, after which he would gradually sink into a tide of indescribable joy.

He knew that this profound secret existed entirely within his powers of concentration. The slightest distraction would make the mirror blur and darken. He would be unable to see the land of his dreams, and he would fall back into his old self, returning to those ordinary days and nights.

Initially, this phenomenon occurred frequently, spoiling his mood. Therefore, each excitement was invariably accompanied by apprehensions. The moment he distrusted the mirror he would become unhappy. He would pace the small room, angry at himself. One day, he found himself on the verge of despair. The mirror was rebelling against him, betraying him. He ached all over, he was stiff, he had trouble turning his head, he could not move as he wished. He struggled alone in his room; each movement left him out of breath. The sudden change in the circulation of his blood made him feel dizzy. Within a matter of hours he fainted.

In that uncontrollable state his memories reappeared in his dream.

Though unconscious, a part of his conscious mind condemned the weakness of his willpower. He had no use for memories, for he had broken completely with his past. He had no desire to recall his former existence. His only wish was for the new image in the mirror. But he dreamed about his wife.

She had broken through the blockade and was running naked on the wild battlefield. She ran to Sun Chuanfang's side to rescue him. Her young body did not feel the bullets and the bayonets.

Waking up, he felt helpless. The dream had destroyed his magic strategy. Why did he have to dream such an absurd dream? He wasn't interrogating himself but rather scolding himself. Strangely, whenever he lost consciousness, the same dream always appeared. He forced himself to get up, mustering all his energies. As the days vanished, no, as they approached, he had to make a greater effort to force himself to stand before the mirror. But this time he was startled.

13

He never expected that the mirror would start to argue with him.

He stood before the mirror. The vaguely discernible human form with its blood vessels and skeleton was slowly losing blood and shrinking. The image that he had struggled to gestate was becoming increasingly unclear. He held his breath and concentrated, focusing the sum total of his mental energy in his gaze. But the mirror no longer obeyed him.

He grew restless and even ill at ease, unable to control himself. His eating and sleeping were disturbed and he had to stop his work. One day, he crushed a glass in his hand. Watching as the blood mixed with the ice water dripped to the ground, he came back to his senses.

Now the vaguely formed image returned to the mirror, but something had changed. Something shone behind what could be called a human shape. After a few days spent examining it closely, he finally realized that it was his old home; he understood that this was without a doubt the crucial point that the mirror had disputed with him.

From that day on, he ceased pushing away his memories.

For a time he had been presumptuous enough to think that he could erase his own past. No wonder he was exhausted physically and mentally. He never sensed that the image he struggled to create in the mirror was overshadowed by his wife and daughter, and his memories of his old home and mother.

With this sudden realization, he regained his physical strength and confidence day by day, until one day at dusk, the tropical sky with leopard spots painfully pierced his eyes. Nausea made him feel as if his body were splitting open from within. Self-control was again impossible. What was wrong with him? He had just recovered. How could he be on the verge of collapse again? He lay in bed knowing he was going to suffer from insomnia again. Although he was weak, his body actually exhibited a life force very unlike physical strength. Wide awake, he could watch its mysterious operation. Outside it was quiet at the moment, but he heard something like the wind blowing away the dust. He felt the approach of rain. At the end of his rope, he recalled the day he'd watched a solar eclipse on Mount Zhong.

14

That day he'd experienced the same feeling of exhaustion, because he had Zhang Fei executed before he went up the mountain.

He had overtaxed his mental and physical reserves. His eyes relaxed as the sun set, and he was unable to catch a glimpse of the vista. Stillness, silence, waiting, and then the sound seemed to come from all directions at once but from no place in particular. It sounded like a musical instrument, insects crying on a summer night, or hail falling from the sky. But if you listened closely, you heard nothing at all. The sun was about to be swallowed up by the Heavenly Hound. The people were uneasy, but the Taoist priest said it was better than being subject to the scorching sun for so long. The darkness filling the sky and covering the land was seen as ominous by the people, but in reconsidering the matter, he thought it might be able to relieve the anxiety that had so long been oppressing him. It really was like that good old saying: "Shiny like the mirrored sky, solemn as the abyss pried open."

The world was indeed thrown into terror by the eclipse. The sky was dim, the earth was ink dark, and a feeble color never seen before indicated that the earth's surface was cooling off, which made people feel uneasy, as if they were facing death. At that moment, he took a good look around him and saw that there was no sound or movement between heaven and earth. Everything was deprived of vitality. This state of affairs lasted for some time, until the crowing cocks and the barking dogs were heard later at the foot of the mountain. Silent space was suddenly changed to something else: the hubbub from a perpetual state of anxiety would deliver the human world back to original chaos.

The Taoist muttered incantations without stopping; at the same time he toyed with a bronze mirror that belonged to the host. You didn't want to miss a moment of the spectacular change during the eclipse. You sat upright and watched quietly and listened attentively; for a short while, your mind was empty of any distracting thoughts. Rather than watch the Taoist priest, you preferred to look at the distant mountaintops or the valley below. But a moment later you were distracted as the Taoist explained that he had collected the whole of Heaven in the bronze mirror. As he spoke, he showed the mirror to everyone in turn. Doubting, they examined the mirror in their hands, and had to admit that they saw a strange light emanating from the mirror at the moment of the eclipse.

The host at the mountain retreat had invited everyone to sit out on the balcony. He was determined to relish this extremely rare gathering. The guests, for their part, were content to make strained interpretations regarding his mirror. They watched as the Taoist raised the mirror in the air and then tapped it with his hand, producing a clear and plangent sound, which pierced the air like a lament and lingered for a long time. He held the mirror above his head and shook it till it roared like a wind blowing over the mountains and through the valley. The harsh sound was like an admonishment to one and all. A different sort of light, sound, and energy suddenly coalesced in the darkness between heaven and earth. One coming and another going, one appearing and another disappearing, they were linked into an endless cycle of different forms from one single source. Imprisoned by convention, the average person never notices this. It is only during rare occurrences such as a solar eclipse that a small mirror is able to reveal the truth that has not been delved into for ages. He left the mountain retreat on July seventeenth in the thirtieth year of the Republic. He was about to go to Chungking with seven of his trusted fellows to assume a new post. The host gave him the bronze mirror as a gift and wished him success in his new position as the General Secretary of the Executive Yuan.

15

The sound of movement outside the window was like that on the mountain during the eclipse. But this time a storm would be the omen for the coming end of the world.

The whirling wind gathered strength but could find no outlet. Confined to that limited space, it seemed to wail frequently.

The wind stopped blowing, and the dense red clouds enshrouded all, hanging low over the buildings.

This was only an intermission, but a deceptive one. For in the next moment, you heard the wind in the distance threatening again. It seemed far away, but actually it was quite near. If you listened closely, it seemed to be climbing the walls, scuttling away like a thousand geckos into cracks in the walls due to some unintentional movement on your part. Shortly thereafter, the clouds flew in chaos past the window. The lightning flashed, not in the sky but from the small locked room, and the dryness in the air did not find its source in the hot wind; rather, your own belly was stirring up trouble.

He forced himself, with the willpower of a soldier, to stand up. Walking to the window, as if by magic, he calmly judged it was midnight in early June. It was no different from previous nights except there was no sign of wind and rain and the stars shone brightly in the night sky. Once he was on his feet, he could see himself clearly. His judgment returned. As he lay there a moment ago, he felt the furniture shaking in the wind; now, observing all with cool detachment, he knew the window, door, desk, chairs, and walls were still all in their original positions.

He mustered the necessary courage, not to face his own lunacy, but to acknowledge that while it was indisputably a clear night, the storm he was witnessing was not illusory.

However, he had to admit that more than once over the last few days he'd suspected that his actions in his small room were reckless; his concentration on what was in the mirror to the exclusion of all else was just an illusion; and his fervent fabrications were just an obsession. His endless entanglements with his reflection, day and night, sometimes made the person in the mirror smile dubiously.

Was he mocking himself?

He knew he was sick, very sick. But he had no intention of seeking a cure. He had to lie down frequently, but strangely, whenever he did so, his mind changed and was not his own. It no longer seemed to follow his promptings and made mental journeys of its own free will. Could it be that standing provided a way to control one's mind? And was "human reason" nothing more than a by-product of standing? And dreams, which belonged to the spiritual realm, only approached when one laydown.

That was how he explained his experience of the storm. It was as if the whirlwind spun around enclosed in your skull and the whistling was the language you heard touching the pillow, the shrouding clouds were your tired eyelids, the clouds speeding past your window were your heavy breath, and the shaking of the building was the trembling of your own body. Only that flashing light was disputable; he knew that it was independent of thunder and lightning and wind and rain. It actually came from the mirror hanging in the hallway.

He had to admit that he intended to control the forces of nature, stirring up trouble in his body. For this reason, his illness didn't improve but grew worse, sometimes even delivering him to the point of death. At that moment, for example, he opened his eyes and saw a burst of intense heat ripping open his chest. There was a whistling in his ears. He closed his eyes and saw himself sinking into a bright bloody light. At the same time he was excited by the departure of his soul. His limbs slowly became paralyzed and prostrate; he collapsed. His whole body was racked with numbness; his physical faculties were exhausted. Darkness came before his conscious mind sank into sleep and engulfed him. Later, he discovered that he had fainted for a few seconds; he had been inexplicably happy just before blacking out.

He was not afraid, but even welcomed its coming. It was as if a silkworm had spun its last thread of life, sealing itself in a cocoon, where in the darkness it dreamed of future flight. The whole process of metamorphosing from a worm into a pupa was an emotional maneuver of divine apotheosis.

"Divine apotheosis" was not the metaphor as it was normally understood or spoken; rather, it was one's fulfillment in flesh and blood.

He was happy rather than distressed to see the progress of his illness. It was nearing completion. He knew that only in this way would the image become more formed and more possessed of a pulse.

"No one knows I'm sick."

One day he talked to himself; he was definitely a little lonely, and felt it was a pity that no one saw the image he had constructed in the mirror.

No one from outside had noticed his mysterious comings and goings of late, which filled him with regret. However, the next moment his regrets had vanished and he called himself to account and asked, "You actually hope to see the desperation with which you cut away your own flesh to feed that image?"

16

His old cook had added a red duck egg to his bowl of soup noodles. He realized he had entirely forgotten about his own birthday. The old servant's meticulous consideration gratified him. He ate the birthday noodles in his room, not to celebrate his own birthday but to celebrate the birth of the man in the mirror.

Retired life in Taipei slowly changed for him. As his mood improved, so did his health. A healthy glow returned to his cheeks, but he did suffer from heat rash here and there on his body. He didn't reject his memories the way he had done in the recent past. Now, the pursuit of memories and waiting had become important to him. He hadn't lost his courage to face the future. At night he still had dreams, but he harbored no doubts. When he woke up from a dream, he realized another new day had dawned.

Sometimes he laughed wildly, even hysterically as he dreamed, causing himself to wake up. Waking at night, he saw the auspicious light filling the room. He got out of bed, straightened up, and to wake himself, splashed cold water on his face. Almost immediately, he felt as high as the clouds and as calm as water. Now, waking from a short doze during the day, he could see the desk and chair and himself wrapped in smoky sunlight, as if the human world were light-years away.

He took the mad laughter in his dreams as a way of tempering himself. He just wanted to make a clear distinction between himself and others. Actually the new world on which he was standing was big enough. It continued to expand in the mirror's reflection, until he was no longer able to touch its edge. The incomparable emptiness, a dream, a chess game without a winner or loser, the mountain retreat, one unclear positioning of his troops, as well as the garden he cultivated in the backyard mentioned in his wife's letter all appeared at any time in the mirror.

Reality—the glory and the shame, victory and defeat, merit and demerit, even life itself—didn't influence him at all. He was startled when he recalled that he had consigned thirty years to killing as if it were a game of chess. Today, the ambitions of dynasties looked like nothing more than child's play. Now he was a bit shocked at having once played a part in the game. He was happy to lead a simple existence in his room. He had cast aside anything touching on bravery, and he was unmoved for any person or any matter. The fervor he'd known in the past made him feel downcast now, and all sickness and anger left him. The unremitting striving for victory seemed foreign to him. He could calmly watch as he walked steadily toward the end of his life. The only thing that made him feel the slightest bit uneasy was that the image of the person in the mirror seemed to exceed his expectations, appearing perfect. It seemed to belong to eternity, having nothing in common with him.

One night, the electricity suddenly went out. He blew out the candle they brought in for him. He quietly sat on the sofa without so much as a thought in his head. He felt himself right and favored. He realized that the superfluity of light would simply create misunderstandings. Such brightness was busy for nothing. Would people ever appreciate tranquility? However, with such a thought in the quiet darkness, the world would come and sit facing him.

He sat up calmly the whole night. He recalled again and again that although he had been of this world day and night, he had never met it face to face. This was the first time in his life. He experienced for what seemed like the first time a feeling of pleasant surprise, delight, and friendship, a desire to pour out his heart, even though he had nothing to say—language seemed to be an obstacle to silent and mutual understanding. In this way he faced the world, unable to bear parting until the dawn light appeared in the window. Several days later, when he was busy with something, he suddenly realized that the one he'd met face to face that night was the person in the mirror.

IV. Brightly Shine the Stars Tonight

Sacred arrow Please piece my heart
Divine gun Please penetrate my body
Thunder stone Smash me
Electric fire Burn me
—GOETHE

17

Before daybreak on June 18, he was awakened by a knock on his door.

He knew who had come to see him.

By the light of the desk lamp, he read the document that he had been handed.

Absolutely still, he displayed a soldier's caution and calmness. He paused, apparently to ponder something, and then resumed reading. The portions of the document regarding him seemed more to repeat the fate of another.

He returned the document.

"All right."

His simple words served to dismiss the person.

Taking the document, the person retreated from the room in a both humble and arrogant manner.

The day he had been waiting for had finally arrived.

He told the old cook to heat water for his bath.

Since being settled here, his only vanity in life was to make requests of the old cook, whom he had kept on. The cook had been with him since he was posted as a commander in the thirteenth year of the Republic, and looked upon him as if he were family. But the bathroom and the kitchen were downstairs. The cook prepared three meals a day for him, but it had been arranged for someone else to deliver them. He rarely saw the old cook anymore, but still he felt close to him because of the familiar dishes he prepared.

He didn't pay attention to his own body; only his head emerged from the water, resting against the rim of the tub. His muscles were still firm owing to long years of military campaigning and being perennially busy. His old servant was very careful about putting wine and calamus root—where it came from he had not the slightest idea—into the bathwater. He felt refreshed and comfortable in the water, its temperature just right, neither too hot nor too cold.

Outside it was not yet daybreak. There was still some time to go before the cock crowed.

In the darkness before dawn, he thought a bit about the matter of body and soul. Then he contemplated the light and shadow that had been completed in the mirror. This was followed by the heat of expectation, which, though not beckoned, flowed through his body. At the same time, he calmly looked at his four limbs at rest in the water. This was the final drill before departure. He knew that his labors in front of the mirror had not been futile.

The night air moved outside. The aerial roots of the lush green banyan tree hung like a beard, reaching almost into the pool filled with duckweed. If he looked up slightly, a few stars could be seen amid the branches and leaves. Soaking in the dark water, he quietly faced the window, and in the warm aromatic steam he saw the image of his wife before him.

He saw her still dressed in a blue silk unlined jacket and black skirt. She wore her hair coiled in the back like a magnolia flower. She looked the same as she had on the day she became a bride in the thirty-first year of the reign of the Guangxu Emperor. When he recalled the gongs, drums, and *suona* of that year, they changed into the present cries of summer insects in Taipei. The private feelings that he had always controlled floated in the warm water. He had never had the chance to declare that warm fire known as love; he had always kept it to himself.

18

He insisted that a soldier had no dreams. He had always roused himself from his own sweet dreams.

Nothing was of greater risk for a soldier than to indulge in private feelings; nothing was a sadder humiliation than to sink into a dream world.

A soldier was different from ordinary people: he voluntarily suspended his own life over a precipice, and rejected the comfortable life that most people desired. A soldier who was in love couldn't go to war; love, it went without saying, was the fast path to getting killed. "Just imagine a rope suspended high in the air and a dissolute soldier standing on the rope dreams of his lover," a Japanese officer admonished his students when he was in that officer training school.

However, it was different now; his mood was not the same as before, the circumstances had changed.

Now that he could do it, he wanted to be sentimentally attached to his beloved with all restraint scattered on the wind. *Why not get drunk?* he asked himself, soaking in the tub. Not a simple drink before a meal, he thought, but something to really liven things up.

He took himself back to that beautiful rear window of thirty years before. The spring snow in March had just fallen; his home and the whole city were especially bright. The days were getting longer; the warm afternoon sunlight radiated through the window. He vaguely heard the mirror peddler calling outside the wall, deep in the alley. In a flash her shadow went out the back door.

She stood under the peach tree in the backyard—that's how he saw her now—checking the flower buds. It looked as if she would stay there forever if it hadn't been for a warm breeze that sent the snowflakes falling from the treetop. (He recalled that the idea of turning the backyard into a garden had not yet entered her mind at that time.) In a flash, she was back inside the house—that's how he saw her now—brushing the snow and water from her neck.

She turned her head.

(The first time she mentioned turning the backyard into a garden was two years later in a letter.)

Noticing him behind her, she felt shy.

(How long had they been married at that time?)

Unexpectedly, she darted past him, smiling.

Soaking in the tub, he was hypnotized between his crazy memories and a cruel reality that was about to impinge upon him. His home seemed both near and far; he saw her heating wine and drinking with him. She always stood quietly at the window; the sunlight was on the floor, the house was bright and quiet. He forgot worldly affairs for a while, dropping his usual soldierly reserve. She could drink, but only did so when he was home. When he was away, she ran their home alone and made sure everything was in order, which he knew was not easy. She maintained a sense of justice and was conscientious in everything she did, even during the turmoil and chaos of war; she never gave in and admitted defeat. One time when she borrowed rice from someone, she was ill used. She merely said, "A woman must endure humiliation a man could never bear. You men are always so cruel, going off to war."

But always, the time for him to leave came again, and she would follow up by sending him clothes or other things. Leaving home, his sole concern was for matters of war; he had no time to think of her, save on the occasions he stared blankly at the hometown cancellation on the letters from home.

One time, like an unbridled horse, he perversely chose the wrong time to vent his long pent-up anger. He returned home after a long absence and, although he was already a middle-aged man, he acted like a young man engaged in a fierce battle. As soon as he stepped through the door, he made a dirty mess of everything, ruining everything she had so painstakingly readied for him.

Her fun was spoiled; she said a few words and withdrew silently.

He chanced to walk by the rear window, and his eyes brightened at the sight of the cultivated garden spread out in front of him. It was fantastic, as if he suddenly found himself in a world of unearthly beauty. He grew calm at once and realized his barging about was childish.

He didn't see her for some time.

He finally saw her in the bedroom.

She sat upright on the edge of the bed. Knowing he was there, she didn't glance up. Her calm and sedate manner told him he was forgiven.

He cursed himself in his heart, as if it were the first time he understood the beauty of a woman's mind. She, like other women, patiently wove the proper human appearance for their men. Even when they are wronged, they want to help them make their characters as beautiful as gardens.

The following day, under the eaves, he helped her wring water from the sheets as a gesture to make amends. He tried to please her by rolling up his pants and sleeves, playing up to her. He made an exaggerated show of strength, which merely elicited a smile from her. He asked her what was so funny, but she didn't answer. It was only later, at night when they were in bed, that she said to him, "I don't know how you fight a war, but wringing out the sheets that way, as if you encountered a mortal enemy, will ruin them." She hadn't said anything that day under the eaves. She'd simply let the water from the bedsheets drip on the green flagstones along the wall where the sun shone quietly.

He wanted to say something but couldn't. He was filled with the desire to turn over a new leaf. Pacing with measured steps, he, who often admonished the troops under his command, could not utter a confession to his wife. Walking to buy wine or small dishes in town or to visit the neighbors or relatives, he mumbled to himself, trying to find the proper words, but he couldn't until he happened to cross a stream where, seeing the water flowing under the noon sun, he finally uttered two lines from an ancient poem: "Do not talk about the empty matters of the world; Just pay attention to the present." Afterward he felt relieved.

He said to himself, *Time passes, never to return.* He knew he had acted recklessly and impulsively out of grief and indignation, and had been insufferably arrogant. *Well, let's look at ourselves now.* He seemed to go back to his student days. He changed into someone who was both obedient and ambitious. Even though he was now soaking in the tub, he recited the two lines of the poem aloud as he had once done for his wife.

Considering it carefully, he felt the poem very appropriate, and realized that the lines had been with him in recent days. Although he had never plucked them from his memory, they had informed his conduct for ages.

Happy at having encountered the lines at such a critical point, he found his train of thought interrupted by the sobbing of a man.

19

He couldn't help but turn to one side in the tub.

It seemed that every time he had a premonition in the heat of battle, a shadow would suddenly fall before him. Even though his feet were firmly planted on the ground, he would feel dizzy, as if he were floating on a rapid current. An ominous yet gorgeous light poured in all around him, presaging disaster.

Looking again, he saw that the Taipei sky was still dark with no sign of daybreak.

A short while ago in the backyard of his hometown, his wife was wondering why the water lilies in the cistern had produced so many leaves but no flower buds. Damselflies danced and darted, dimpling the water. Soaking in the tub, he blurted out, "Just listen now." His old servant, separated from him by a wall, wondered why he cried for no apparent reason.

He was angry.

He should have been angry at himself for still indulging in his mental journey to his old home at that moment. If he hadn't been interrupted by his old servant's cry, he had no idea how much longer he would have soaked there. He should have thanked him instead of being angry.

The old servant spoke from the other side of the wooden door. His voice was low but his spirit was upright and touching.

The person who cried was unable to control his emotions. His broken words mixed with sobs were unintelligible to him in the bathroom.

The old servant obviously spoke from his heart.

What was the matter? Was he deliberately trying to disturb his peace before he departed? That was the only reason he could find for being angry.

Keeping still in the water, he lowered his voice and asked what his servant wanted.

The old servant didn't answer. He grew more upset and while trying hard to hold back, kept speaking from the bottom of his heart.

In recent days, from his room, he had often heard his old servant. The sound of a spatula striking the iron wok or tongs knocking against the oven bothered him. At first he was angry at his peace being disturbed.

After listening for a while, he realized it was just his servant's thought-fulness. He made a sound once in a while so that he wouldn't feel lonely, so he would feel he had someone close by. That's why when he cooked, he deliberately made a lot of noise, or when he fanned the cooking fire, he made sure the smoke wafted to his window.

He savored the dishes, which the old servant had cooked for him over the long busy years, alone in his room—he would miss them and was grateful for them. It was like the continuous sobbing of the madman on the other side of the wall, which, upon reflection, he could understand.

That sound now opened a vast panorama for him. The urgent sobs of his old servant removed any doubts he had about his military career with a lifetime of setbacks, elation, and dejection. The old servant's tears illuminated deceptive dreams, mocked ravings and even the unfortunate madness. He saw a soldier who had never neglected his duties—he himself—soaking in an extra large bathtub enjoying his nearly unbridled intoxication.

20

He did not say good-bye to the self in the mirror.

He did not forget to put medicine on the heat rash on his body.

After dressing, he stepped out the door of his room.

The bodyguard, who was always polite and modest, still stood by the doorway.

He walked past the guard.

The guard bent forward slightly.

As he passed him, the guard turned and followed three steps behind him.

At the end of the second-floor hallway, he stopped. The guard behind him stopped too.

He started down the stairs.

His old cook's shadow quickly appeared and disappeared at the bottom of the stairway.

He had prepared a few words. Firmly and steadily he descended one step at a time.

After the battle of Bailingmiao, at his birthday party in the field camp when he was posted as the first division commander, he'd had a strong craving for a dish of hot pepper fried pork. Sitting on the ground with the rank and file soldiers horsing around, amid the steaming stir-fried cooking, he gradually felt homesick and couldn't help thinking of his wife. He had a favorable impression of the cook because he made the same dish his wife had cooked for him. From that point on, he kept the cook with him, and for half a lifetime he accompanied him, fighting in one place after another.

At the bottom of the stairway, he stopped.

He took out a pocket watch that he also had carried with him for half a lifetime. Then, approaching the old cook who was standing in the shadows at the foot of the stairs, he placed the watch in his trembling hands, and then said to him the words he had prepared earlier. Time was short. He had to keep things simple. He still talked as a superior, but his tone was apologetic and not commanding. Although there were dangers when they fought in one place after another, life had been easier then. But accompanying him in later years, it had been much harder on the cook.

The old cook didn't really take in all that he was saying. He had so much he wanted to say, but facing him now, he was upset because he couldn't find the words. "Commander, I will serve you in the next life." The words came like a cry torn from his heart to become a timely secret oath. His voice was muffled as if he couldn't get the words out. And he, as his superior, was no longer able to give his unequivocal consent.

He clasped the old cook's hand in which he held the gold watch.

He checked to make sure that everything that was happening was not a dream. He could feel the joints of the cook's hand.

He looked him up and down, examining the face of one who had cried all night without sleeping.

Just before leaving his room, he had stared at the mirror for a long time, and even had the desire to test his senses. For example, he could still smell the fragrance of the wood in the old wardrobe, and for the first time ascertained that it was raw wood. His senses, he knew, were perfect, and his body was still in the human world, which was very important at this moment.

Out of curiosity, he glanced at the map hanging on the wall just before he walked out of the room. It was a large map of China that had been on the wall when he first moved in and had long since yellowed. He reviewed the traces of his military career on the map, and felt calm.

Fully satisfied, he walked out of the room.

21

Leaving the old cook, he resumed his solemn and controlled pace.

Still, as before, the guard followed three steps behind.

Every step the guard took was in accord with the general in front of him.

As the general turned into the wide and straight hallway leading to the vestibule, the lights suddenly went on, illuminating everything. Immediately, the tightly spaced guards sprang into action from their immobile waiting positions. They were lined up like chess pieces all the way to the vestibule and from the vestibule through the front yard all the way to the front gate and beyond.

Each chess piece reminded itself to move following the general. They didn't talk, and orders were given with a glance of the eyes at most. However, the atmosphere became restless, the situation extremely tense, and a mysterious stalemate hung over the chessboard.

He stopped at the vestibule. Everyone around him, inside and out, also stopped.

He still felt strong and emotionally sufficient in his heart. He scanned the plants in the yard, distinguishable in the darkness, and told himself that today would be a day like no other. As a result, he felt nervously elated. He didn't pause for long. Descending the steps, he still did not look up but instead silently pronounced the characters written on the horizontal placard above the door: SPIRIT SWALLOWS DREAM CLOUDS.

Stepping into the car that was waiting outside the vestibule, he could hear the wheels of the iron gates rolling along their curved grooves on the other side of the cypress trees. The car started and moved slowly down the driveway. The sound of the tires rolling over the gravel seemed to hint distantly at transmigration, pressing one to dream.

There were more cars than usual along the road waiting to join the motorcade.

As the car he was in drove out of the main gate, all the other cars started. He didn't pay attention to the place of his car within the procession. From the car window, he saw how his car slipped smoothly into line.

The motorcade, like a snail feeling its way, silently entered the dark streets of Taipei from the Lizhi Society.

Again, the motorcade moved slowly forward like pieces on a chessboard.

What made it different this time was that it was still dark and the guards were fully armed.

Everything was perfectly composed, the way only two cool-headed, well-matched chess champions could stay so calm and silent.

22

Unreal city.

All was silent in the predawn darkness. The motorcade shuttled down the streets, turned, and moved on. Not a single soul was seen on the streets; not a single witness existed in the city. The residents in the houses on both sides of the streets slept peacefully behind closed doors. The time had been selected so that no one would observe the movement of the motorcade from start to finish.

Sitting in the back seat, he lifted his head and thrust out his chest a little.

He looked up, but not to look up at the sky, of course.

Through this movement that went unnoticed by the guard beside him, he wanted to release any remaining worries, as if he were opening a cage to release some birds. It wasn't that he wanted to get rid of the birds; he just didn't want to be bothered when the time came.

In the final moments before daybreak, still wrapped in thought, could he, a general who had braved untold dangers in battle (no, at that moment he preferred to imagine himself as the vigorous young artillery student in officer training school), with his eye for detail, miss any shadow in his consciousness that he had polished to a sheen so long ago?

The light color of the dawn appeared in the car's rearview mirror; it was like the mousy gray sky of his hometown.

He arose at this hour every time he left home to return to the troops. The last time he received a letter from his wife was right before he left mainland China. It read: "It's funny, but when I think of the days we were together, they amount to no more than three years. It's hard to say if we will see each other again." Then she mentioned an ancient story about Xu Deyan from the state of Chen, who walked to the capital after a war. Seeing someone selling a broken mirror in the street, he wanted to buy it but was told that he must have the other half of the broken mirror to buy this one. Xu Deyan then took out the other half of the mirror that he always kept with him. The two parts fit together perfectly, and he finally was able to locate his missing wife who had been forced to flee the chaos of the war. "I don't know what kind of token to use to locate you in the future."

She continued,

You and I are wandering like drifting clouds; it will be difficult to meet again. The news outside is pressing. Where are you? I have no way to know. Every letter I send goes many places before you receive it. A long time ago you said many times that you wanted a study. Do you still want it? The sun shines on the stream and mountains in our village. The best thing to do would be to close the door to the house with its black roof and white walls and study and farm. That's what you said. Do you remember? The study is being built for you, and the back wall is half done. The war has delayed the work, but work is being done every day. I'm sure the study you have dreamed about will be finished before you are demobilized and can return home.

Our hometown is a river town of peach flowers and willow catkins, the beauty of which even the flames of war cannot destroy. Now the days are long and the fields are short of men—only the women and children or the old and the weak are seen. The country is so large, so even if there are 101 things people don't like, there is no need for war and killing people. We must all share what there is to eat, what pleasure is there in anyone's death? However, I don't feel sad anymore when I think about it, because I am helpless. I'm also busy. It's a comfort that Wenying, our daughter, has grown up and can do housework.

It rained a while back. We took out your old clothes, those you wore so long ago, and hung them out to air under the eaves. Although the clothes are taken out once every year to air and beat, they have gradually faded. This year there were moths, and when I opened the box, a whole bunch flew out. When I checked, I found they had eaten many small holes in your clothes (it took Wenying and me a long time to patch them). Some of the clothes by the wall got very damp in this rainy season.

Brother Peng of Fourth Uncle's family came home to get married at the beginning of the year. I hadn't seen him for a long time. A bridegroom just getting married, and his hair was already gray. He stayed for just five days and had to hurry back to his military unit. He is a captain in the navy, and mentioned that they might be forming a marine corps like the Americans. He was very excited. His mother told him that taking care of himself was the only thing that mattered and that he should treat others respectfully and cautiously, regardless of what sort of outfit he found himself in, because when there is trouble, as you know, even an ineffective force has to work together. Dening, our cousin, was injured; I heard he is working as a ferryman in a small town in the south, and always mails money home for the new year. Changfeng, the third brother, who was teaching elementary school in Fujian, died of an illness a year ago.

The war is raging like wildfire; I have no place to flee, so I plan to stay put at home with Wenying, coping with the shifting events as I always have. It is hard to imagine the state of the country by the moonlight in the sky. War is a game played by men like you. I don't know where the heck you are. If you caught fire, I'd have no way to save you by dousing the flames. But do not take things too seriously when they come to a pass. In such troubled times, there is nothing to say and no justice to strive for; seek only a clear conscience, because a clear conscience laughs at false accusations. Man proposes and Heaven disposes. Therefore, take it easy.

The last words his wife wrote in the letter were: "In this time of chaos when nothing is certain, I feel sorry for all the good men who have suffered."

23

Color came to the dawn in Taipei. Smoke was seen rising from the kitchen chimneys of some of the houses along the streets. From the car he even faintly heard the sound of people getting up and opening doors.

Another day of life was about to start.

As people appeared on the streets, the motorcade had already left the downtown area and was coming to a wide-open, flat area by the river.

The cars stopped.

In a flash everything was silent and unmoving; even time seemed to stand still.

Foreboding floated in the air.

A shadowy figure approached with all haste.

A guard who had been waiting by the riverbank now rushed over to open the car door.

The guard sitting to his right got out of the car at once.

Then he slowly got out of the car. The cool breeze from the river cleared his mind.

The guard sitting to his left was the last to get out of the car.

Everybody was waiting for him.

He walked several steps and stopped, and, for a moment, looked beyond the shadowy figures to the other side of the river, then resumed walking.

The future had begun.

He heard the rhythmic beat of his heart, but there was no need to guess or ask why it was so.

However, he was still able to think calmly, and recalled the words of the Taoist at the mountain retreat: "Don't lock yourself in the prison of your body."

Everything came as a surprise to him, but he was unafraid. He coolly looked upon the people there as mortal enemies who had intentionally created such a grave atmosphere. All was silence save for the rustling of the people around him and the gentle breeze from the river.

He waved away two armed men who came to hold him.

They let him walk alone toward the empty space.

He heard the squad who were to carry out the execution loading their guns.

The setting wasn't all that strange to him; it had appeared in countless rehearsals. Dawn was near to breaking. The pale moon faded as the first gray light of morning appeared. The light had not yet colored the morning clouds and the opposite bank of the river was fresh green and clear.

The river was silvery smooth without a ripple. The breeze blew gently. His pace was steady and prudent; he had not relinquished his life in the slightest. His persistence was unprecedented. Now his dream had reached insane proportions.

"Is it a big dream?"

"It is a big dream."

He woke up in his nephew's bed that year. His nephew knew he had been dreaming, and the two of them started talking about it.

"However—"

"However, a soldier braves untold dangers, so a big dream will not alarm him."

At that time, separated by the river, they were engaged in a battle of wits with the enemy as they prepared for the decisive battle. On his side of the river, he sank into a vast and boundless dream, which created difficulties for his nephew. He realized later that he had been too direct. How could he at such a time ask someone to share his dream?

Perhaps this dream by the side of the Keelung River was so vague that it confused people; however, for him, it was entirely accurate and dependable.

The bullets sped toward him at an inconceivable velocity.

But still, he wanted to look back at his life for a moment.

Unexpectedly, what came to mind was the trip to the mountains to view the solar eclipse ten years earlier. The seven days he spent in the mountains, considered now, seemed like a dream from over a century ago. Now he walked forward to revisit the mist- and cloud-shrouded mountain retreat.

Outside his dream, he was once found guilty of advocating defection to the enemy and sentenced to death.

He had overestimated his nephew. No, he shouldn't have urged him to stop fighting. He didn't consider his nephew's situation. But old generals sobbed in the dark. Adopting such a son was no different from raising a tiger.

"It's one of the countless victories or defeats on the central plains; future generations will discuss its good or evil."

Yu Dingying, his old subordinate, who was going to be promoted to the post of minister of defense, came to the room where he was confined to visit him, the prisoner, and try to offer him advice. Yu Dingying suggested that he surely would be pardoned if he wrote a statement of repentance to the highest authorities.

He rejected the suggestion outright with a simple "Stop!" At the same time, he responded to his subordinate, who sought to comfort him with a poem.

"History will show that you are innocent."

"Stop, stop."

"But the poem by Lu Fangweng says . . ."

"Stop, stop."

He understood his subordinate's good intentions and his difficulties. But he had already made up his mind. He no longer took the disputes among men seriously; he was no longer as fond of life as he once had been. The chessboard that pitted enemies one against the other was waiting for nothing more than a move of a chess piece; the chess piece waited for nothing more than to be moved by the hand. The hand, for its part, waited for nothing more than a chance strategy that trumped human effort. The chess manuals handed down for thousands of years, regardless of their amazing insights, disclosed nothing more.

"Human history is not at all to be trusted / human dispute deserves no mention." He was, in fact, trying to enlighten his subordinate. "Lu Fangweng himself didn't clearly understand this point."

"But . . ."

"I frankly don't give a damn anymore about what is left of this game."

"But . . ."

"I have my own model."

He had situated himself in the world he had long been constructing. With one turn, he would find himself at the other end of time. What he once possessed, he no longer needed to possess. Insults or threats couldn't harm him in the least, for he was beyond holding or destroying.

Regardless of how the wind flipped the pages of the thick tome of history, all matters rested in utter darkness.

At the beginning, the officer in charge of the execution asked him if he had any last words.

"No," he uttered imposingly in his heavy hometown accent.

Everyone at the execution ground was disappointed. They were expecting a last violent protest of innocence from him, not unlike the voluble stand he'd made in court to defend himself.

He had nothing to say.

He just turned and walked steadily ahead. He stepped with dignity onto the sandy riverbank, drawing away from them, while walking step by step into the muzzles aimed at him.

And they were the ones whose souls were stirred.

Every move he made silenced them, made them hold their breaths, made them ill at ease.

He no longer cast a shadow, his eyes no longer needed to fix on anything, and the breeze passing his ears grew silent. The execution ground slowly vanished into the nothingness he had established.

Darkness had fallen. His favorite time was midnight. The dead of night was the only time his soul could wake. He no longer had to concern himself with probing the secrets of the dark. He was now walking in a dense wood, but being inside it, he couldn't make out the forest canopy, as if he were back in the dark mountain forest when light and dark merged during the eclipse. Everything became more real. All the genial things in the past, friends who had already passed away, conversations, expressions he liked, all came close and then departed. First it was a blur, then clear; whole, then broken; everything for one last union, rare and strange. He felt like he was again walking through the dense forest that led to the retreat, along the serpentine back of the world. The forest was no longer dark—even the finest leaf vein was clear in the density spreading around him.

He considered the abstruse meaning of his wife earnestly burying that mirror. Oh, what a crude, rash, and ridiculous man he had been, able only to consider the dangers of a strong wind, but without the slightest understanding of what a woman did in silence. When the mottled tree leaves fell under the horses' hoofs in the autumn forest, in the pale light of warmer scenes, everything became unclear, lacking in detail, withdrawing completely, to become the unconscious background. Only when walking on the dark forest path full of ferns did you long for the tiny bits of lamplight of the village houses; only by waking into the darkness did you see a woman's splendor.

He didn't really know that he—as the lead news story reported that day—was killed by three shots.

He only heard the report from behind.

He had painstakingly awaited the first bullet, and it became so warm and kindly, piercing his back and exiting his chest. He could feel the heat of being torn apart.

He was dazed. But he felt happy and carefree now that the wait was over—he sank into the state necessary before entering a world that he had long been weaving.

Points of light leaped before his eyes. The initial sluggishness turned light. Still he persisted.

The most surprising thing to them was the general's bearing.

He had been firm and calm from the moment he set foot on the execution ground till he fell to the ground before their eyes. He didn't overdo it or forget himself, even when the gunshots sounded.

He finished a drawn-out performance, lifting the veil on one of the body's secrets for them.

The heat of his body was dissipating; his collar felt too tight. However, the warmth in his chest made him think of the year his wife had given birth. He took leave to return home. By car and boat, impatient all the way, he finally made it. He hurried to the bedroom and took the baby girl from the bed. The little one peed all over him.

In that final moment, he felt that it had not all been a total waste.

Before he fell, amid the high-spirited cockcrow that he heard, he forced himself to take a deep breath. Then, just in time, a man invisible to all eyes stepped from his chest—it was the man in the mirror stepping out of the mirror.